What Happened to My Sister

Elizabeth Flock

What Happened to My Sister

A NOVEL

BALLANTINE BOOKS TRADE PAPERBACKS

NEW YORK

A Ballantine Books Trade Paperback Original

Copyright © 2012 by Elizabeth Flock
Random House reading group guide copyright © 2012 by Random House, Inc.

Published in the United States by Ballantine Books, an imprint of The Random House Publishing Group, a division of Random House, Inc., New York.

BALLANTINE and colophon are registered trademarks of Random House, Inc.
RANDOM HOUSE READER'S CIRCLE & Design is a registered trademark of Random House, Inc.

LIBRARY OF CONGRESS CATALOGING-IN-PUBLICATION DATA
Flock, Elizabeth.
What happened to my sister: a novel / Elizabeth Flock.
p.   cm.
ISBN 978-0-345-52443-0
eBook ISBN 978-0-345-52444-7
1. Sisters—Fiction. 2. Domestic fiction. I. Title.
PS3606.L58W43 2012
813'.6—dc23   2012004410

www.randomhousereaderscircle.com

Printed in the United States of America

2 4 6 8 9 7 5 3 1

Book design by Laurie Jewell

For Cathleen Carmody

Like a bolt out of the blue
Fate steps in and sees you through.

—JIMINY CRICKET
(Ned Washington, "When You Wish Upon a Star")

What Happened to My Sister

CHAPTER ONE

Carrie Parker

If you're reading this, I must be dead and maybe you're going through this notebook hunting for clues. It always bugs me when I'm looking real hard for something and after a long time it turns up right under my nose where it was the whole time, so I'm going to tell you right here in the beginning all I know for certain. It may or may not make sense right now but who knows, maybe it will later on.

The first certain thing I know is that Richard's not ever gonna hurt Momma again. The second thing is that I had a sister named Emma. Here's what else I know: we *were* moving to my grand-mother's house but now we're not. Momma says in the river of life I'm a brick in her pocket, and I'm not sure what that has to do with her changing her mind, but Momma is most assuredly not driving in the direction of Gammy's house. So until I figure it all out, the number one most important thing you need to know so you can tell ever-body is that I, Caroline Parker, am not crazy.

I don't care what anybody says—I'm not. I swear. People think

I cain't hear them say things when I'm in town like *shh, shh, shh— there goes that Parker girl bless her crazy little heart* but I'm not deaf, y'all. I'm just a kid. I'm not *peculiar* or *crazy as an outhouse rat.* And I'm gonna prove it once and for all. You wait and see. They'll be lining up to say *sorry* and they'll ask for a hug or something embarrassing like that but the best part'll be when ever-body finally admits they're wrong about me. I'm gonna do ever-thing right from now on. I'm gonna be like the other kids. I'm gonna be the best daughter in the whole wide universe—so good Momma's not going to believe it. Just you wait and see.

CHAPTER TWO

Carrie

Right now Momma and me are riding in our old beat-up station wagon with all we got to our names stuffed into Hefty sacks in the way-back. Momma has an old-fashioned square little bitty suitcase she calls her *travel case* locked up next to her in the front seat. I never saw it before in my life. Heck, I never knew it existed till we lit out of town. She must have thought I'd go breaking into it if I'd found it back at the house and truth to tell I probably would have because I love little bitty things of any kind. What I dearly love more than anything in the universe is little bitty animals. We don't have any pets but I'm hoping that'll change in our new life because I want a dog so bad and I'm thinking if I'm real good and I never say the name *Emma* and I do ever-thing Momma wants she'll give in and we'll get a puppy. I promised Momma she wouldn't have to do a dang thing because I'd take care of it but ever-time I bring it up she says I'd probably kill it along with ever-thing else. But I swear I wouldn't. I'd take perfect care of her. I'd name her Pip. Short for Pipsqueak.

Along with boring stuff like clothes, I own this notebook I like to draw and write in. My favorite thing is making lists. I can make a list out of anything really. You name it and I'll make a list out of it. It's *something else*. That's what Mr. Wilson our old neighbor says about my list-making abilities. *That's something else,* he said when I showed him how I was making a list of his guns and bullets and holsters. But that was before I used his gun to shoot Richard and now I ain't allowed to mention Mr. Wilson or guns anymore.

What I Own Personally

1. *Two pairs of shoes if you count flip-flops, which I do.*
2. *One polka-dot dress I hate because it's a polka-dot dress for goodness' sake and it's a dress and no one wears dresses to school if they can help it. I cain't recall when I ever wore it outside of church, back when we used to go to church.*
3. *A button-down shirt Momma calls a blouse that I've hardly ever worn on account of it being fancy and I haven't ever done anything even close to fancy because we're dirt-poor.*
4. *A book of words with the title* Vocabulary 101.
5. *Two pairs of shorts and one pair of blue jeans that don't fit no more.*
6. *Five old T-shirts from the Goodwill truck that used to come a couple times a year to sell things in the lot out back of Zebulon's.*

I just turned nine. One year from double digits. One more year till I'm a *young lady*—that's what my teacher in my old town, Toast, where we lived before moving to Hendersonville with Richard, used to call the older kids in school. The little ones—the single digits—she just called them *kids*. I wish I could be ten back in Toast just to hear Miss Ueland call me *young lady*.

My birthday must have slipped Momma's mind because the

first thing she said to me two days ago was "Go on get dressed I need you to run to the post office and get a change of address form."

I waited a second just in case she remembered what day it was but when she told me to *quit lollygagging and move my lazy behind* I knew it'd just be another regular day. I walked to town and when I was sure no car was coming in either direction I sang myself the Happy Birthday song real low. I doubled up and sang the "smell like a monkey" version too.

But our plans changed yesterday, after Momma went to use the pay phone in town. When she left the house the plan was to go stay with my momma's momma, Gammy, but when Momma came back home, all the sudden we weren't. Just like that. She said she *wouldn't go where she wasn't wanted.* Even though I didn't say so, I know just what she meant. That's how come I know the outside of our house better than the inside. With my eyes closed I could find the little hole behind the lichen and vines that grow over the mossy old tree stump out back in the holler. I know which rocks to step on if you want to cross the creek and which ones only *look* like they'll hold steady. I could draw from memory the dead tree trunk crossing the path between Mr. Wilson's and our house. To me it always looked like the thicket's taking that tree back to where it came from, with moss over most all of it, vines choking it to crumbling in parts, and a big opening where a gnome would live if gnomes were real and lived in piney woods. I liked it better outside anyway. I pretended little bitty forest creatures were watching, looking out for me and Emma. Whoops. I mean, looking out for *me.* I figured they liked for me to be there because they knew I'd never let anything hurt them, no sirree I wouldn't and that's a fact. Whenever I went back inside the house, when the screen door slammed and Momma looked up from whatever she was doing, she'd see it was me and the air would go out of her like a day-old birthday balloon. Then she'd say *oh, it's you* and turn back to her chores. I don't know who else she thought was gonna be coming through our door.

"Trouble," Emma would say. "Momma looks scared ever-time the door opens because she's used to Trouble coming through it."

I'd tell her, "But we come through it all the time and we ain't Trouble."

"You and me are small," Emma'd say, looking up from playing with the dirty old Barbie doll who lost her hair before we found her, "we're small but as far as Momma's concerned we're Trouble."

That's Emma for you—always knowing more than me about pretty much ever-thing that matters. If she were here I bet she'd probably even know where Momma and me are moving to. All I know for certain is it'll be a place we'll be wanted.

What with us fixing to leave town for good there just wasn't time for a birthday fuss anyway. I don't mind. Really I don't. *Emma* would have remembered, though. I know, I know—like Momma said, she ain't real. She was made-up, I'm supposed to say. But *if* she'd been real—*if* I'd really had a sister named Emma—I bet she'd have made me a real nice daisy-chain necklace with White Rain hair spray all over it so it'd last forever. Hair spray makes things last to infinity, just so you know. I'm not kidding.

We're *starting fresh*. That's what Momma says. To get ready for our drive Momma even cleaned out the crumbs, empty RC Cola cans, and chew-tobacco tins left over from Richard so the inside of the car would look *spiffy*. When she's in a good mood Momma says words like that. *Spiffy*. Or *Jeez Louise. Jiminy Cricket*. And when something surprises her, she says *well I'll be*. I helped her get the old car ready and when I opened the ashtray up front and asked what all I should do with the cigarette butts crammed in on top of one another she said *well I'll be, that sure is one full ashtray in need of emptying all right*. Once I even heard her say *jeepers*. That was when there was a long line of ants marching into our kitchen from outside. Momma's mostly been in a good mood getting ready to *start fresh*. That's also on account of her feeling loads better, I bet. Today Momma's neck bruise is about as wide as the rope Mr. Wilson tied his dog Brownie to the tree with. It's been fading pretty slow but at least it's thinner now. Last week it was wide as a hand, the exact shape of Richard's hand. In back, where his fingers dug in good and hard, it's red mixed with black but the blue is turning the same yellow ringing the mark on her left cheek. When a bruise gets yellow that's good news. It means your skin's trying to be normal again.

Momma hates it when I watch her closely. She says I been doing it all my life but I'm good at pretending I don't do it no more because I once overheard her telling Richard I study her like I was gonna be quizzed. She said to him *it makes my skin crawl, her looking at me like that.* So ever since I make myself think about other things when I'm around her so I won't make her *skin crawl*. That's where my vocabulary book comes in handy. I found that the best way to memorize a new word is to squeeze your eyes closed and picture it being spelled out on a chalkboard. Now, if Momma looks like I'm making her skin crawl I shut my eyes and pretend I'm working on vocabulary. It's worked real good so far because I usually end up leafing through the book (to make it look real) and landing on words I really truly *do* want to learn. *Peculiar. Plethora.* My mind wanders real easy, though, so before long I find myself wondering if Momma smiled much when she was a kid. *Penultimate.* I wonder if she knew how to dance. If she liked candy. *Palatial.* Did she love my real daddy when they got married? *Puny.* Did he carry her in through the front door after their wedding? Were they happy when they found out they were gonna have me? *Plebeian.* Does she know who killed my daddy? Why'd she have to go and marry Richard? I watch her close in case any of it comes out and if it does I write about it so I won't forget. You never know: she might do or say something that will be a clue about her life. I've gotten good at watching from the corner of my eye so it looks like I'm staring straight ahead but I'm really not. Like right now, for instance. Right now it's easy because Momma's got to keep her eyes fixed on the road to *starting fresh*.

But to start fresh we've first got to pass through Hendersonville to get to the interstate.

People I See on Our Way out of Town for Good

1. *Mr. Zebulon is standing with his arms crossed in front of the hardware store. I looked straight at him and he looked away.*
2. *Miss Lettie who cuts ladies' hair in her kitchen is about to get in her car when she sees us and freezes, still holding her key out, like the game Red Light, Green Light.*
3. *Mr. Willie Harding from the lumber mill watches our car closely then spits chew tobacco on the ground, showing off he can make a big gob of spit, I guess.*

Not a one of them waves goodbye. I guess it figures. Ever-one stopped smiling at me after I went and killed Richard and I cain't blame them no sirree—who smiles at a murderer? That's what they call me behind my back. *Murderer.* They whisper the word but it still reaches my hearing and part of me thinks they know it. *Psycho murderer.* Now, as we're driving down Main Street this one last time, they stand there blinking at us, watching our car move along like we're in a slow-motion movie.

I should've brushed my hair. Momma calls it a *rat's nest.* I close my eyes and make believe I have silky long pretty hair and we're in a parade like they have on Fourth of July and I'm in a dress that has a bow and sparkles and I'm sitting high up on a chair tied good and tight in the back of a shiny red pickup truck and there's tons of people from all over waving little flags, waiting to get a look at me and when our truck comes in sight ever-body cheers and claps because I just won a contest that makes me Miss Hendersonville, Queen of North Carolina.

So even though when I open my eyes and I see that I'm not in a parade, I got a rat's nest in my hair, and not a one person's cheering or clapping in real life, I smile and wave anyway. They'll remember me all right: to them I'll always be the child who shot her stepdaddy and smiled good and wide about it.

Momma says there's nothing but *cold stares* and *loose lips* in Hendersonville. I'm writing down what it's like there in case I read this when I'm in an old folks' home and I cain't remember anything about anything. Maybe my grandkids'll ask me about it and I don't want to be the kind of granny who cain't answer even easy questions like *What was Hendersonville like?* so I'm making a record of it.

In Hendersonville they don't honk at you but for waving. A little toot on the horn and your name's hollered out like you been lost to the world even if you just saw the person five minutes before. If a dog runs away in Hendersonville ever-one'll know where he belongs and how to get him there. When someone's sick, ladies bring food till the sick person's back on their feet. Ever-one talks ever-thing to death in Hendersonville. Trouble is, most times there isn't much to talk about so when Mrs. Ferson's hiccups didn't stop for three weeks it was big news.

Ever-body had an idea of how to get rid of them. She drank water backwards; she hopped ten times on her right foot, ten times on her left, then swallowed whiskey real quick; she even tried to stand on her head (Mr. Ferson *drew the line* at that which was too bad because we'd placed penny bets on whether a headstand would do the trick and plus who wouldn't want to see Mrs. Ferson standing on her head?). Nothing worked until out of nowhere Levon the knife sharpener knocked on her door one day and told her to drink quinine holding the glass in her left hand while her right arm was up like she was waving at someone a long ways away. Sure enough Mrs. Ferson's hiccups stopped right then and there. I wrote the whole thing down in case I ever got hiccups lasting three weeks.

Levon's Hiccup Remedy

1. *Get quinine*
2. *Pour it in a glass*
3. *Hold it in left hand*
4. *Put right arm up in the air*
5. *Drink*

Anyway, ever-one in town also knew about Mr. Zebulon's missing right pinkie and how the stump itched if it was going to rain. And ever-one—I'm not kidding—*ever-one* knew about Richard, my stepdaddy. Funny thing is, Richard was one of those people ever-one wishes they *didn't* know. So when he got killed last month the whole place near exploded like firecrackers in a dry barn. Then, when word spread that Sheriff had Momma and me in *for questioning,* it was almost like birds were flying stories about us from house to home same way they did in *Snow White* when they flew her clothes to her in their little beaks. The talk never stopped. Talk talk talk talk. Momma's beatin' marks were real bright, like someone used black and blue markers to paint her cheek and draw a ring around her neck.

After I shot Richard dead, Momma made me stop going to town for supplies. She said we had enough in the cupboard and icebox anyway. People drove real slow past the path leading from the blacktop to our front porch. With us not driving anywhere the grass started growing back in the two lines of dirt the tires used to make. One night two boys from the next county over burnt a cross on the dirt in front of our house because someone told them a white man'd been killed by a black woman. Momma called that the *final straw.* She couldn't take it anymore, said we had to leave. *I hope you're happy,* she said to me more than once after that but I don't know what I'm supposed to be happy about so I don't answer her but to say *yes, ma'am,* under my breath in case that's the answer she's looking for. We packed up sacks of what we were keeping but it was so boring and Momma was crabby the whole time saying things like *pitch it* and *don't even think of sneaking that into the keep pile,* so every once in a while I would sneak out the back door to the creek on the far edge of the holler. The creek is what made Emma real for me. I been real good about not saying her name too often so far. But I cain't not say it when I'm talking about our creek. The two are tied together in my mind like peas and carrots. Emma loved that creek more than anything and I do believe it loved her back. It's where I could always find her if she went missing. She'd set on the big smooth rock on the far side and poke at underwater things with a switch, her lips moving like she was telling secrets to the water. If you held a gun to my head right now on this very day I would still swear she was real. I'd be whupped bloody if Momma knew I thought that but dangit, this is my notebook and I need to write the truth. And that's the truth. Momma says that Emma was just an imaginary sister I made up after my real daddy died, but Emma was real, I could swear it. It got confusing on account of Mr. White at the drugstore back in Toast asking me *how's Emma doing?* And Miss Mary working the cash register always inviting Emma to *come and visit* with her even though Momma'd say she was sick of humoring me about Emma 'cause *Emma's something not very humorous.* Anyway, I take care not to mention Emma's name in front of Momma since Richard died, and even in my pretend world Emma mostly stays outside, out of Momma's sight line much as possible so they won't overlap in my brain. Like when we hauled out all our stuff for a yard sale on one of our last days.

I wanted to put up signs about the sale in town but Momma

said folks would find it without us having to say a word. She said the smell of us fixing to leave would reach them like how hot biscuits tell kids when to come in for supper. Sure enough, right when we put out the last of the chipped plates Gammy gave Momma and my *real* daddy when they got married, ever-body started up the dirt path like they'd been watching us the whole time which they probably were. I heard someone say they were gonna tear down our house after we left on account of no one wanting to live in a place where a man got murdered even if he did have it coming. We watched them pick through our stuff and somehow we knew no one wanted to buy a dang thing . . . they just wanted to look at us like we were zoo monkeys. They turned ever-thing inside out and upside down. Some tall string bean giant man I'd never seen before held up a glass pitcher and asked Momma how much she wanted for it and Momma said *best you got* and looked away. When she wiped her eye while she was fishing in her coin purse for change I couldn't right tell if she got something caught up in there or if she was crying. I never seen Momma cry ever—even when her shoulder got popped out of its socket the time Richard came home and dinner wasn't ready and he dragged her over to the stovetop to make sure she got it done. Momma always had dinner ready and waiting from then on.

"Look how he's holding the pitcher, Momma," I whispered.

I wanted him to get in trouble like me and Emma surely would have if we'd gone and held the pitcher that way. I wanted Momma to grab it back out of his hands. I wanted *him* to get skinned alive like *we* sure as hoot would've been. But she looked away.

We watched the Jolly Green Giant carry away the pitcher, dangling it from his fingers. She'd brought it out from the kitchen hugging it to her chest and for a split second I thought maybe she was gonna change her mind about sellin' it because she didn't put it on the table right away. She held it gentle to her chest, like it was a hurt dog or something. I pretended I hadn't seen her do that because something told me she'd want that un-seen. She never said so but I know Mr. White gave that pitcher to her and Daddy for their wedding. The three of them went to school together when they were kids growing up in Toast. Momma kept that pitcher high up on a shelf where no one could get at it. We never used it *ever*. It sparkled so clean and pretty like it just came from the store. The pitcher lasted longer than both Momma's marriages.

Momma never went into town because Richard used to say *a woman's place is in the home* so she didn't know half the people going through our things. I knew lots of them though. Mrs. Dilley was flipping through Daddy's old Johnny Mathis records in between staring holes in Momma's head. I guess Momma noticed it too 'cause she said *take a picture it lasts longer* under her breath on her way up the porch steps in the one dress she owned. When I asked her why she was in her Sunday best she told me *we might be the talk of the town but we got our dignity.* Momma's the most beautiful woman I ever saw, even with her black eye and cracked lips and a huge bear-claw-like mark on her arm. If you saw her all done up like she used to get for Daddy, you'd swear you'd seen her in the movies. Her skin is smooth without a single solitary freckle. Her mouth looks like an ad on the TV for lipstick. But it's really her eyes that make people stop and stare. They're big and blue (extra-blue when she's mad or been crying) and in school when we got to the chapter on Egypt it was like they'd gone and taken a picture of my momma even though it said Cleopatra was her name. Back in Toast, Mr. White used to say she'd been the *belle of the ball* in high school and I didn't want to hurt his feelings by telling him a bell isn't what anyone would rightly call beautiful so I just smiled and said *yes, sir.* Mr. White said *you be sure to take care of your momma, y'hear,* when I went to tell him Richard was moving us to Hendersonville. *You'll be fine out there,* he said that day, *but your mother needs someone looking out for her so you be sure to do that, understand?* I said yes but I didn't really understand. Momma had a *husband* looking out for her, didn't she? That's what I thought at the time. It didn't take long for me to see what Mr. White meant but by then it was nearly too late.

The people crowded at our things for sale like they were made of gold and found in a treasure chest. A man with a mustache curling up at the ends like a cartoon bad guy was at Momma to sell him the kitchen chairs with plastic seats for *a good price.* She waved him off and walked away but then he jingled change in his pocket and called to Momma that she drove *a hard bargain* like it was a compliment but she didn't look like she took it that way. After he loaded the third chair into the back of his truck and drove off, Momma called him a *cheap son of a bitch.* Thing is, he was dressed fancier than I ever saw in person—he had spit-shined black shoes without a speck of dirt on them and pants ironed so hard they had a line down the middle—and there he was jawing at Momma to lower the price from three dollars a chair to two. His truck looked good as new—no mud on the tires even. Momma said he probably didn't use it for work. It was *just for show.* If *I* had a car to drive for show it sure as heck wouldn't be a truck.

And then something real weird happened. It started when Mr. Wilson went and paid ten dollars for the three-legged table we had to prop up with a tree branch. Momma looked at him hard and I heard her say something about *charity case* but Mr. Wilson bought the table for ten dollars anyway, saying he'd be back later to pick it up. Momma watched him go and then looked over at me like I had something to do with it but before she could say why Mr. Wilson buying the kitchen table made her mouth go tight, Mr. Zebulon with no pinkie finger handed her a five-dollar bill for a beat-up cookbook that had Momma's loopy handwriting all through it, like "a TBS more of butter" and "set oven to 375 not 350." Mr. Zebulon walked away without taking any of the change Momma tried to hand back. Five dollars for one book! It made

Momma madder, though. I could tell by the way she shoved the five dollars into her money pocket—she crumpled it like she was going to throw it in the trash bin then jammed it in all while she was shaking her head. She clicked her tongue to the roof of her mouth to make the *tsk* sound she does when she don't like what's what. Then the men who played guitars at Zebulon's every Tuesday started coming up the hill, trudging along the dirt lines everyone's car tires made into a driveway again.

It was like the Civil War picture book Daddy'd kept by his bedside—they looked like those army men marching their bloody ripped-up selves home after the war. Mr. Harvey tipped his hat at Momma and put down two dollar bills for a Bic pen that was out on the table by mistake. Right behind him was Mr. Jim, who's colored black and who never once opened his mouth to sing or talk but played his guitar so good at Zebulon's the other men would stop and let him take long parts of songs, his hands flying up and down on the strings like they couldn't make up their mind where to be. He was the best player of all them—I could tell by the way ever-body watched him play. One time I saw Richard in town on a day I'd thought he'd be at work at the mill—I didn't yet know he went and got hisself laid off. He didn't see me because he was across the street going into the Fish-N-Fowl where you could find fish bait or a wallet or a head of lettuce—ever-thing got sold at Olson's Fish-N-Fowl. The sign out front said IF IT AIN'T HERE, IT AIN'T NEAR. I didn't want him to see me so I crunched myself small between parked cars and waited for him to come back out and get gone. That's how I came to see it clear as day: Richard punched the door open like he was a dang movie cowboy ready for a shoot-out. He was so mad he wasn't paying attention and walked head-on into Mr. Jim. I held my breath, knowing nothing good was gonna come from that, and sure enough, Richard looked up, pulled his head back like a rattlesnake before it bites, and I wanted so bad to yell out for Mr. Jim to run away but it was too late. Richard spit

right into Mr. Jim's face and said *get the f—— out of my way, n——,*
you know what's good for you boy so loud I could hear it from beside
Mrs. Cleary's station wagon where I was hiding. Richard used the
f-word right out where anyone could hear! Normally he just used
it hollering at Momma and me. Mr. Jim stepped aside for Richard
to pass and it wasn't till I was halfway to home when it occurred to
me Mr. Jim didn't hurry to wipe the spittle off his face like I
would've. But I guess Mr. Jim knew Richard right well by then and
expected about as much as Richard gave him. Mr. Jim must've
made a lot of money playing his guitar because there he was
standing in front of Momma at our yard sale putting a ten-dollar
bill on top of Mr. Harvey's ones. I bet Mr. Jim's the happiest of all
that Richard's dead.

Momma wouldn't say how much we made from the sale but I
figured when she wasn't looking I could count it. I knew she was
hiding it in a rolled-up pair of socks held tight by a rubber band I
used to flick at crickets. If I'd written the number down I'd remember but I didn't so all I can say is that it's so much money I
could only get the band around twice, not three times like I
wanted. While I was at it, I put the bills in order, all with presi-
dents facing right-side up. Ones, then fives, then tens, then the
one twenty-dollar bill we got. Momma'd call me crazy for doing
that. She'd say my neatness is another sign I'm *loony tunes* and
that I'll end up *talking in tongues and polishing the kitchen floor with*
a toothbrush at all hours. I say *no I won't* but if I did, well what's
wrong with that? Wouldn't you want polished floors? Not that I
would polish them with a toothbrush a'course but if I did, wouldn't
that be a *good* thing?

This morning, before leaving the house forever, Momma said:

"If there's anything you need to do before we go, you best go on
and do it."

She went inside for one last check that we got ever-thing worth
taking but I didn't. Out front by the old tire Momma planted little

daisies in is the rock I used to hide messages under when I pretend-played with Emma. It don't look like all the other rocks around here—*they're* all crummy brown, dusty and rough. In my head Emma called them *ordinary*. My favorite rock is smooth and when it's wiped clean it's almost snow-white with thin rivers of gray running all through it. It's about the size of the ball we played Spud with at recess. I have no earthly idea how it ended up here but it's plain to see it ain't from here, no way. We had a system, me and Emma. If I was outside and Emma was inside, she'd put a note saying "Good" if the coast was clear to come on inside. "Bad" meant stay away long as you can. Usually that meant until the beer put Richard to sleep still setting upright in his chair, or like when he gave whippings. He always whipped with the buckle end of his belt because it was his goal in life to get me to cry and I never would even though it hurt real bad. You never saw girls as stubborn as me and Emma.

From out by the rock I could hear Momma's steps on the wood flooring coming back down from checking upstairs so I knew my days as a Hendersonvillian were fading away. One last time I lifted up the message rock and it'd been a while since we'd used it so I jumped a little in my skin when a million bugs skittered off to other rocks, looking up at me ripping the roof off their house. If I spoke bug I'd tell them I didn't mean them no harm. After they ran for cover, I shook the dirt off the folded-up notepaper to find "Bad." I snuck it to my pocket for what I don't know and put the rock back exactly where it was but them bugs didn't know they could come on home and maybe they never will and maybe little bitty baby bugs got lost from their mommas and they'll crawl around forever, crying little bug tears, homesick for their old rock and the way it used to be, and then they'll die alone with no family or they'll be squished on account of them not having a rock-roof over their heads. I wished I could find them and shoo them back. I wanted to cry I got to feeling so bad. The screen door slammed behind Momma who hollered for me to *make haste.* She jingled the car keys and lowered her sunglasses from the top of her head.

Then a miracle of gar*gan*tuan, *ginormous* proportions happened. I'm listing it as *Miracle Number One.*

We're about to get in the car when Momma squints at me over the peeling paint car hood and says:

"Why you riding in back?"

"I always ride in back," I say.

Sometimes out of nowhere she likes to test me, see if I'll follow rules, and I didn't want to fail like I always do. Because I'm dumb. It's okay—ever-one knows I'm stupid. Once I heard Momma tell Gammy I wasn't *the sharpest tool in the shed.* So I thought Momma was tricking me to see if I'd follow the rule to always set in back.

"Best you get on up here with me," Momma says.

She says it like it isn't the first time I ever rode in front. She says it like it isn't my dream come true. I been wanting to ride up front forever. Soon as I come to my senses I say:

"*Really?*"

"Come on, now," Momma says. "Let's not make a federal case of it."

I hurry in case she decides to change her mind while she's lighting her cigarette.

Then, just before the tires push off the crunchy rocks onto the paved road, Momma turns in her seat to face me. She blows smoke out the side her mouth like Puff the Magic Dragon, points her cigarette in the V of her fingers at me, and *lays down the law:*

"From here on out, soon as we pull out of this no-good godforsaken town, I don't want to hear anything more about anything. I'm laying down the law. You understand me? I don't want to take any of that old shit with me. You listening? Look at me—I'm seri-

ous as a heart attack. You understand? We're leaving it all behind.
You hear me?"

"Yes, ma'am."

"And by the way, you haven't said it in a while," she says—
figuring rightly that I'd know what she was talking about.

"Emma was made-up," I say. I know the words by heart.

"Keep going . . ."

"I pretended I had a sister but I really didn't. I made her up.
Emma was made-up."

Like I said, I know the words by heart.

"I don't hear a lot of feeling behind those words—you're
sounding like a robot," she says.

"No, Momma, I know I made her up," I say, not wanting her
mood to go bad like it can do if you're not real careful.

"Promise?"

"Yes, ma'am, I promise," I say.

Her eyes went to slits like they do when she's making sure I'm
not *being smart with her,* so I knew *yes, ma'am,* was definitely the
answer she needed to hear. But I'm still not a hundred percent
sure if *anything about anything* also means the murder. If that's
what she was talking about she would've said *that* instead of *anything about anything,* right? I'm trying to think up a list of what she
wouldn't want to take along with us but other than Richard (who's
dead anyway so he couldn't come with us even if she wanted him
to) and Emma, I got nothing to write down. So it's not really a list,
it's more like two names taking up space in my notebook.

Momma turns back to the steering wheel, puts the car in Drive,
and says, "We're turning the page, Caroline Parker."

And then *Miracle Number Two* comes along and near to blows
my head clean off my neck.

Completely out of nowhere and for the first time in the history
of the world, Momma pats my knee. First she lets me sit in the

front seat. Then she pats my knee. Momma doesn't *ever* touch softly so I figure it's best not to call attention to it in case it scares her from ever doing it again. I hold real still. I try to breathe through my nose so my body doesn't move but you got to have a big nose to get enough air in and my nose is little. It's a kid's nose. I hope when it grows it'll end up looking like Momma's. I cain't recall what Daddy's nose looked like but I bet it wasn't all that bad because people used to say he was *a real catch*. After a second or two, the pat on the knee ended even though I stayed as frozen as ice in Alaska.

When she checked left-right-left to see if it was safe to pull out of our dirt driveway I looked over at her real quick and I swear on a stack of Bibles I caught her smiling big—showing her teeth even. Momma hasn't smiled since . . . well, I cain't remember the last time I saw Momma smile.

"Here we go," she said. And there it was again, Momma smiling bright as day right out in the open.

That's most certainly *Miracle Number Three*.

CHAPTER THREE

Carrie

Coming down from the mountains where it's shady cool to the flat land is real exciting even if it *is* 102 degrees down here like the radio man just said. I never been off the mountain before so my head's a windshield wiper turning right-then-left-then-right trying to take it all in. All this time we had a big ole front yard—miles and miles of it—and I didn't even know it. No one ever told me. After a spell, I look back at where we came down from, across the farmland to the hills, and to me it looks as if a giant swept rocks and trees into piles of mountains and just let the flat land in the middle do what it was going to do anyway—stay flat. The air carries this grit you cain't see till after it's got itself all over you and ever-thing around you. Even in your mouth—you crunch it. You can taste the dust.

 ."How you doing over there?" Momma hollers over the radio playing some singer she says she used to have records of. Sounds like old-fogy music to me, if you want to know the truth.

 "Fine," I holler back.

I decide not to mention the dust because Momma would call me a complainer. Momma *can't abide* complainers. She says *the only thing to complain about is a complainer.*

"Put that window all the way down," Momma says. "Let's get a better crosswind going."

This is a great idea. I figure the crosswind'll keep the dust from settling on us. Our car doesn't have air-conditioning on account of it being as old as Moses. That's why we have to open windows. The window on my side is hard because the crank handle's long gone. What you have to do if you want it down is use these pinchers from Richard's toolbox, stick them real careful in the hole where the handle used to be, like in the game Operation, and turn hard until the glass decides to start moving. My hands are so sweaty I wipe them on the front of my favorite T-shirt, the one with a unicorn that has a flowing white mane and a sparkly pink body. But I'm so dumb I forgot about the dang dust so I got smears of red on the unicorn's neck and now it looks like she's bleeding to death. The pinchers keep slipping and it takes me a while— *please dear Lord in Heaven please open this window soon so Momma doesn't get mad. The day is going so good but this is just the kind of thing that'd ruin it Lord so please . . .*

Phee-you, my window's finally down, the wind thumps against my eardrums. It's so loud I cain't hear the radio no more but I don't care. The whipping sound of the wind makes it feel like the car is a rocket ship about to take off into outer space. We drive for hours this way and I figure I could ride shotgun with Momma and the wind and the radio and even the gritty red dust forever.

We pass barns with huge pancakes or waffles or hamburgers or fried chicken painted on their roofs. So many of them I stopped counting an hour ago. It's got to where if I see a barn my mouth starts watering even before the roof picture comes to view. Not all of them have painted food. Some are blank and I start to feel sorry for those ones—they look buck naked. Downright embarrassed they don't have pictures. We pass cows. More cows. Cotton fields. Tobacco fields. Pine trees. More cows. Stores selling quilts. Gas stops with *Fireworks Galore!* and *Cigarettes Real Cheap—No Tax!* The more we drive the more it feels like the Flintstones when Fred runs but keeps passing the same things again and again.

I flap my arm up and down out the window and pretend it's a bird wing. My hand karate-chops the wind. I discover that, if you let it, the wind'll flap your arm just like a bird flaps its wings without you having to do a dang thing. Hey wait a second! Maybe the birds know it. Maybe they fly for hours and don't get tired, the wind being what's moving their wings so they don't have to lift a feather. I bet that's what they talk about. Old birds chirping to young ones *Psst! It only looks like we're doing the flying! It's the wind, kids! It's the wind! Pass it on.* I put this on the list of things I need to check when I finally get the *Encyclopaedia Britannica* set I been dreaming about forever and a day—ever since Orla Mae Bickett showed me her daddy's. Each letter gets its own book, gold lettering on the front. You really don't need anything but the *Encyclopaedia Britannica* 'cause it has ever-thing in the universe all right there in one place. If you ask me, you don't even need schooling if you have the *Encyclopaedia Britannica.* I copied down how to spell it so I'd know what to wish for when I blow out birthday candles from now on.

Things to Check On in the Encyclopaedia
Britannica When I Get It

1. *Why do streams and rivers go to the ocean instead of the other way around?*
2. *Is Frankenstein good or bad? (He gave the girl a flower = good; he's a scary monster = bad.)*
3. *Do snakes have bones? If they do then how come they can bend ever which way without breaking?*

4. *What happens to girls whose second toes are taller than their big toes? Do they die when they get to thirty? (Orla Mae Bickett said so in homeroom.)*

5. *Do birds really fly or do they just stretch out their wings nice and flat so the wind can do the flying for them?*

My arm goes up and down like an ocean wave and it's cool for a minute. I'm staring out the window, thinking nothing in particular, and right when we pass a Waffle House with a missing *o* on the sign, right that very second, this flash picture pops into my brain. I get them sometimes. *Visions.* For as long as I can remember, every once in a while if I'm setting real still and nothing's taking up space in my head, a picture of something that doesn't make any sense at the time will pop in front of my eyes. Like how, when you stare at a lightbulb for a long time then look away and close your eyes a picture of the lightbulb is burned on the inside of your eyelids. This one summer me and Emma were taking turns balancing on the log fence when into my head came a picture of a little moss-colored glass ball rolling up to another one the same size but the color of the sky just before a storm. I could have sworn I even heard the click of the two balls hitting each other. I didn't say anything about it and pretty soon I forgot the balls altogether. A few months later Mr. White from the drugstore gave me and Emma a set of glass marbles for Christmas but I'd already forgotten about the picture flash. Then, after we moved away, Richard caught me and Em playing with the marbles when we were supposed to be helping Momma in the kitchen and his boot came down on the pouch that held them and the crunch of the breaking glass made me cry something awful. With Richard hollering *boo fucking hoo* after us, Emma and me ran to the creek and settled on a rock at the edge. She said she wanted to show me something she had in her pocket and when she opened her fist I *finally* remembered the picture flash because there in the palm of her little hand were two glass marbles: one moss green, the other stormy-sky gray.

So anyway, I look out at the Waffle House missing an *o* and *pow!* I have myself a vision of a milk white pudgy baby arm reaching out, wriggling its teensy fingers. It's gone as fast as it got here. I'm trying to decide whether to tell Momma about it when a loud clanking gives the both of us a start. The hood's huffing and puffing like an old mule carrying a load of coal. Momma hears it too and slows down, saying *please dear Lord don't take her now,* and for a second I think she means me but when the car starts choking and coughing I see she's praying for *it* not me. The wind's gone on account of us going real slow now. It's spooky quiet and I hear Momma say to herself *if the car dies we're done for* and now I'm officially scared because Momma never says things like *we're done for* so I'm gonna pray. Even though her first husband, my real daddy, got shot dead right in front of her back at our old house in Toast, even though her second husband had the same thing done to him but by her own flesh and blood, and even though we're *broker than spit at a swap meet,* Momma's never said *we're done for.* So I'll pray harder than ever even though God don't pay attention to little kids' prayers. Emma and me, we done experiments over it and it's true. But just in case things have changed since the prayer experiments, I promise God that if He lets the car live I'll pray ever-day and I'll never get on Momma's last nerve again. I think those exact words over and over—ten times. Probably more—and I really and truly mean every one of them. *I swear, God, if You let the car live I'll pray ever-day and I'll never get on Momma's last nerve again, I swear.* I say it in my head but I move my lips so He'll know I'm for real.

A car honks at us and Momma says *Jesus H. Christmas can't you see I'm trying to get out of the way,* and like a magic trick, smoke starts slithering out from under the hood and Momma starts pumping at the gas pedal hard, even though it makes no difference. And now I know it's a fact: God don't pay mind to little kids' prayers. He's busy on more important things than dying cars carrying families driving on burning hot two-lane interstates. Momma's hunched over hugging the steering wheel with her head to the side listening real careful like the motor's whispering its last dying words. She pumps the gas pedal—"come on, come on, come on"—and the way it keeps crawling, the station wagon looks like it's sorry it's letting us down. We inch to the gravelly side of the road and the motor hisses itself out for good. It's so quiet now I cain't hardly believe it's the same day as it was just a little while ago with the wind and the radio and the painted barn rooftops. The metal siding creaks and I'm betting it's the old car saying goodbye. It really did the best it could because it happened to cough to death right under a shade tree. Like a final act of kindness. Like it knew we weren't the ones kicking it and hitting things with it all those years, it was Richard. I believe maybe this car had a soul and maybe that soul went up to Heaven and maybe up in Heaven it's shiny new and Daddy's behind the wheel, tooting hey to us from Up Above.

I don't think I'll bring that up with Momma now though. Out of the side of my eye, without even moving an inch, I watch Momma because it occurs to me that what happens next depends on whether she hangs her head down like it's the end or tilts it back to the headrest like the car dying is just a stumbling block and she's not worried. Like she's just figuring out our next move and we'll be under way in the shake of a lamb's tail, as Miss Mary at the old drugstore used to say. I breathe in and out four times before Momma drops her forehead to the steering wheel that has little dips for where your fingers go. Uh-oh. Momma doesn't have a next move.

After a short while, she sits up and stares out ahead like the car's still moving.

"Maybe it just needs a rest, Momma," I say. Why this has not occurred to me till now I don't right know but don't that sound like a possibility? "Maybe it wants to cool down or something. It wasn't this hot up back in the hills—it's probably not used to the heat."

I sounded too schoolteachery. Too know-it-all. Momma hates know-it-alls. I guess I'm wrong because Momma doesn't say anything back. I look over to find she's in one of her trances again. If you saw her like this you'd swear on a stack of preachers' Bibles a magician swung a pocket watch in front of her, saying *you're getting veeery sleepy . . . veeery sleepy . . .*

This time I'm not so worried because Momma cain't stay in a tired old car forever like she near done in her bedroom after Daddy died. Back then, Momma took to her bed and that trance took infinity and a day to wear off enough for her to come back out. A minister came by once or twice to check on her and so did Mr. White and Miss Mary but I didn't know them real good yet. On his way out Mr. White patted me on the head and said, "She'll come around. She's a survivor, that one." Once I heard Mr. White say a part of Momma died when Daddy did. He told Miss Mary that Momma *went into her room one person and came out an altogether different one.*

So I know the best thing I can do right now is stay still. Wait for Momma to come around again. I doodle little hearts in my notebook. New ones coming up out of the dips in the tops of old ones so you cain't tell where they start from. Mrs. Ferson once said me drawing hearts means I got a whole lotta love packed inside me just dying to get out, making it sound like I might barf love if I got sick. So I think of Mrs. Ferson every time I doodle. I been working on covering a whole page in hearts and I'm almost to the bottom when Momma lifts her head and says:

"Well all right. Let's get out to where someone can see us."

Then she tells me to *hop to* and get the stuff out of the back. I kinda hoped we'd sleep curled up on them Hefty sacks like little kittens if we had to camp out in the car tonight. I guess not.

Momma only has to bang her door twice this time to get it open and if you ask me, that's almost a miracle right there. It usually takes five or six shoulder hits before the door'll let you out. I climb over the seat and open the way-back door like normal since now we don't need to mind the silver duct tape that'd been keeping it attached to the rest of the car.

Jiminy Cricket! The road's hotter than I thought it'd be, that's for sure. I jump out and in two seconds I'm hopping up and down from bare foot to bare foot.

"My flip-flops, my flip-flops! Momma Momma ow!"

"Get your own damn flip-flops," Momma says from under the hood she's jimmied up like a car mechanic. "I got bigger bears to skin."

We're in bad moods. Even me and I'm not ever in a bad mood. Not even when I stepped on a yellow jacket wasp with a bare foot when I was in first grade. My arm's all the way almost to the bottom of the clothes sack feeling around for flip-flops. Emma used to call them *flippy-floppys*. Mine have rainbows on the bottoms so the person walking behind can have something cheery to look at.

"They're here somewhere." I say this to myself, honest. I sure didn't mean for Momma to hear when I made the groan sound she calls the *woe-is-me*. If I got the *woe-is-me* in my voice she'll ask if she should call the *whaaa-mbulance*, making it sound like the crying a baby makes.

"Oh hush up," she says from right behind me. I jump at her being close all the sudden. "Momma this, Momma that. Like I don't have anything to do but wait on you hand and foot. Move aside and hold your water."

This makes my bad mood a little better because *hold your water* is what Miss Juni Moon used to say ever-time someone tried to hurry her up. Miss Juni Moon used to come watch us back in Toast if Momma and Daddy stayed out for too long. Miss Juni had this angry-looking scar on her forehead the shape of a sliver of the moon and she was born in June 1960, the only baby born during the month of the worst flood the town ever had so, thanks to two strokes of bad luck, she was Juni Moon and that was that. Pretty soon no one could remember her real name.

After fishing out my flip-flops Momma stands under the tree that's so spindly she's got to stand sideways for shade. She lights her cigarette with one thumb flick of the lighter wheel. Momma can light a cigarette on a windy day with one hand tied behind her back. I bet she could light one in a snowstorm. Also, she can smoke with no hands if she needs to—she rarely does because she says *it's not ladylike.* But here on the side of the empty road to no-where she lets the cigarette dangle from the side of her mouth like a gunslinger in a shoot-'em-up even though she ain't doing anything with her hands.

Since we got nothing better to do, I pull out my notebook. *Today is Tuesday,* I write—even though I don't know what differ-ence that makes, marking days of the week like that. But I figure the small stuff might could come in handy one day, who knows. So I write:

The car just died. I'm wearing my green shorts the ones with a peace sign on the right. My now-dirty unicorn T-shirt I got from the Goodwill dollar bin a long time ago . . .

"What in the Sam Hill you think you're doing?"

I jump in my skin for the second time in the day. I hadn't heard her coming—she's real good at surprising me that way. Momma's cigarette bounces up and down between her lips like it's dancing to the words. The ash at the end clings on and I worry it'll fall right into Momma's clothes and light her afire. Then I realize she's got that look that tells me, even though her voice is quiet, she's madder than a wet hen.

"Must be nice to set and draw pictures all day while I'm here *trying to figure out how to save our hides,*" she says. "Here I am, dealing with shit we got on us once again and you're over here all comfy scribbling Lord knows what kind of craziness in that— Gimme that goddamn thing. . . ."

I scramble to close it, shoving it under my fanny so she cain't work it from me, and I pray she hadn't set her mind to taking it 'cause if that's the case then I might as well kiss my notebook goodbye now and make it easy on both of us.

"I'll snatch your arm out of its socket and beat you with the bloody stump if I find your crazy talk in there, y'hear me?" She tries to get a pinch hold on it but I bear down to make myself heavier until she finally gives up.

"Oh, fine." She waves it off, pretending she never really wanted it in the first place. "You can keep your precious little book, but the first sign of you losing your marbles again and it's gone, you understand me? *I don't want to hear anything about anything,* y'hear me?"

She goes off to fuss with the glove box and I try to calm down my heart that's going so fast it likely could bust up. I believe that's the first time I ever stood up to Momma and won. I need to remember this so I can write it down later, when she's not looking.

The road must've been freshly tarred, it being near as soft underfoot as mossy forest floors. The sun soaked all the way through it and I do believe my flip-flops could melt. Momma must've read my mind because she says:

"Go on and fish out your real shoes," she says. "Those won't survive the trip."

"Trip to where?" I ask her while I hop back up to the trunk gate to fish out my only other shoes. "Where we going?"

She either didn't hear or she's too busy shading her eyes and scanning the distance for signs of life in the flat farmland. Or she don't want to answer because she don't know.

"What trip, Momma?"

"Oh for Christ's sake just hurry up," Momma says, stamping out her cigarette in the gravel. "I want to get to where we'll end up before nightfall."

My real shoes hurt even on a cold day so I know there'll be problems in this heat with my sweaty feet but there ain't much I can do about it so I bend my toes at the tips to make for more room and cross my fingers it goes okay. Momma says we got to *get cracking* so I hurry to pull out the other Hefty sack. Emma would be too weak to carry anything. She's seven. She *was* seven I mean. She was strong if she needed to punch on a boy at school but not strong enough to carry heavy loads. Momma's getting a grip on the *odds and ends* sack while she tries to get her pocketbook strap to stay on her right shoulder by shrugging it. In her other hand she's holding tight to the travel case she won't let me near. She leans to one side then the other like someone invisible is tickling her. Holding on to the sack with our clothes in it is harder than I thought it'd be on account of my arms being too short to reach all the way round and sweat's making me and the bag caught-fish wet.

We walk and walk, resting every now and then to give our arms a break. It's hard to keep up with Momma—for every one of her steps I have to take two, sometimes three. For a long time, not a single word is said out loud. And since all the cars seemed to disappear once ours died, this road might as well be a graveyard, it's so quiet. And then I have to go open my mouth.

"Momma, I got a blister on my heel and it's bleeding."

She slows down but she don't look back at me. You could park two cars between us—that's how far ahead she is.

"I'm sorry Momma. It's bleeding though."

"I hate to break it to you but I don't have a first aid kit handy at the moment," she finally says, over her shoulder.

"It's hard to walk with it," I say, hoping this don't count as complaining.

She quiet-curses. I hear it on account of there being no cars, no wind, nothing making sound anywhere. Two steps later she puts down her bags, reaches into her shirt, and pulls an old kerchief out of her bra to mop the sweat from the back of her neck. Momma keeps lots of things in her bra. Things she might need handy. A dollar bill. Or a scrap of paper with something written on it. A recipe. You never know what's gonna come out when she reaches into her shirt. It's like hocus-pocus tricks.

I said *sweat* and that reminds me of Miss Ueland who made us call it *perspiration*. She said the word *sweat* ain't proper. Tally Washington always forgot how to say the new word—she called it *per-sip-a-don* or something. Tally Washington said her people came over on the first boat to America. She said Washington was her name because of George Washington. But Tally Washington's a liar and that's a fact. Anyway, Miss Ueland gave us a list of twenty words we weren't ever to say and the boys made it their number one mission to make up sentences using as many of them as they could fit. Billy Bud Moore made it to fourteen words but Miss Ueland turned the corner right when he got to *sweaty stupid-ass fart face*. He was sent home with a note from the principal which I thought would be the worst thing that could ever happen to you in your entire life, but Billy Bud Moore just shrugged his shoulders and grinned like a mule eating briars.

"We hardly got a spoon to cook with much less a *Band-Aid*," Momma says. She takes the edge of the kerchief in her teeth to start a rip she finishes with just her hands. And guess what: no scissors and it's still straight as an arrow. You cain't question Momma too much and anyway she always makes sense in the end so I'm waiting on that to happen. For her to make sense.

"Here," she says, holding out the smaller half of the kerchief for me. "Well? Get over here and take it. We ain't got all day."

Momma said *ain't* and she hates that word more than life itself. More than pork rinds even. Momma says *ain't* is *low class,* something only *hillbillies* say.

I limp over but don't want her calling me a *drama queen* like usual so I stand straight thinking it will help me walk normal. It don't though. She's standing there shaking the piece at me and when I take it from her I figure she'll tell me what it's for. I squeeze it in my fist waiting to find out what all I'm supposed to do with half a wet kerchief ripped by teeth and hands.

"We *haven't* got all day. Get going, little Miss Drama Queen," she says. Dang it all she called me a *drama queen* after all. She rubs the bottom of her back and bends down to pick up the bags again, hiking the first bag over to her hip like a mother with a baby.

"What're you waiting on?" she says. Then she starts walking, but slow, saying stuff to me even though she ain't looking my way.

"You've driven me crazy since the day you were born into this godforsaken world, you know that? I tell you what," she says, more to herself than me. Then she's talking more than I heard her talk in my whole life.

"Cried all the time, like a cicada with food, and why're you always underfoot like you are? And then the *other* thing—don't you dare say anything—you know what I'm talking about without me having to say the words I never want to hear again. For the life of me I don't know why I didn't leave you back there with your guns and your Mr. Whatever-his-name-is. I should have my head examined. You're not worth the gunpowder it'd take to blow you away."

"Wilson. His name's Mr. Wilson," I say. Me, I'd want to know the right name. Who wouldn't? I didn't count on it coming out sounding like it did.

"Listen to her," she says like there's someone else to talk to.

"*His name's Mr. Wilson,* she says. Well I got some news for you: I don't care if his name is *Jesus H. Christmas,* he's got *some nerve* wrecking my life like he did. I should've left you with him, see how you like that. *His name's Mr. Wilson.*"

I don't sound like she's making me out to sound with her voice up high, but it doesn't hurt my feelings. I used to think Momma was serious when she said stuff about throwing me out with the trash or about putting her out of her misery by me getting gone forever but I know she don't mean it. It's just how Momma is. It's her nature. What I'm really wondering about is how come I never knew Jesus's whole name is Jesus H. Christmas? Sheesh. I wish I could add that to the list of things to check in the *Encyclopaedia Britannica,* but Momma's back to picking up the pace and I'm still standing in the same spot holding her rag.

"Fold that into a square and put it between your heel and shoe, keep them from rubbing up against each other," she hollers over her shoulder on account of her being so far ahead by now.

Then all the sudden Momma drops the bags real quick like they're on fire, whips around, and hollers so loud I cain't hardly understand her. She's louder than I ever heard her fight with Richard even.

"No. You know what?" she yells. "I'll tell you what. *That goddamn Wilson ruined me,* you know that? You think he gave any thought to *me* when he showed you how to shoot that goddamn gun? Huh? If he thought Richard was so rotten and if he couldn't keep his nose out of our *family* business he should've straightened Richard out himself, man to man. But noooo. He goes and teaches a crazy half-wit girl how to shoot a gun. That's his big solution. And what about *food*? He think we have money coming out our ears, me with no job? He think we can afford to eat goddamn *steak* every night?

"How we gonna *live*? Tell me that. Tell me how you figure we're gonna *live,* huh? I'd like to hear it. Are you a *magician*? You

Houdini come back from the dead? *Answer me!* How're we gonna *eat*? I bet you didn't think of *that* when you pulled the trigger, did you? Huh? Answer me, you goddamn crazy murderer!"

"I ain't crazy, Momma, I swear!"

Stupid me. Now she's charging at me. I drop the bag without meaning to—my arms got scared. *Be brave. Be brave.* I tell myself this over and over because I used to get so fearful of her I'd wet my panties. But that was when I was little and I'm brave now. *Be brave.*

"Sorry, Momma. Momma, I'm sorry, I'm sorry, Momma," forgetting altogether that Momma hates it when I say it fast just to get out of a whipping. She says I sound like a whiny baby.

Normally her fingernails would hurt my arm but they're short today so it's not too bad this time. When they're long that's another story. Plus the good news is this time I stay standing up when she shakes me. I used to flop to the ground like a rag doll some kid don't want to play with anymore.

"You with your crazy brain." Shake. "It probably didn't even cross your crazy-ass mind that killing Richard was a nail in our coffin too. Did you think of that, you half-wit piece of *shit*?" Shake.

"No, ma'am."

"I can't hear you! Did you even think of me and what I'd do without that man?" Shake.

"No, ma'am."

What I really want to say is: *That's all I was thinking of, Momma. He nearly beat you dead. He was about to kill us. I wanted to protect you, Momma.* That's what I want to say but that ain't what Momma wants to hear, I know that even though I'm nine years old.

So I say "No, ma'am," instead.

"No you didn't. That's exactly right. You *didn't* think about how we're gonna have to pick through trash for supper from here on out. You learn how to pull a trigger all right but you didn't near think of me being flat broke. You know what I did at the truck stop back there? When I went to the washroom? I stole a stack of paper towels, is what I did."

She lets go of my arm and I make sure not to rub it even though I really and truly want to. She gets so her face is right up in mine and she spit-says:

"You know what those paper towels are gonna be for, smarty? Little Miss Smarty Pants. Huh? They're for *that time of the month*. I've got to use what little money we have to put a roof over our heads so I don't have the *luxury* of lady products anymore. Did your Mr. Wilson think about any of all this? *Did* he?"

"No, ma'am," I say.

It's best not to look at her when she's mad like this. You have to stay scarecrow-still or she'll say something like *you better clamp shut that fast-talking, excuse-making, tear-jerking jaw of yours right this very minute or I'll do it for you.* And you do not want her to do it for you. My jaw hurt for days after she walloped me in the mouth when I was five.

But like I said, Momma don't mean anything by it. She might get mad a lot but she keeps me around. Mothers who don't want to be mothers give their kids away. She has a short fuse is all. And it's been stored up 'cause she couldn't exactly cut loose when Richard was alive. I figure she's just getting it all out from years of being quiet as a feather on a cloud.

Here on the *road to nowhere* she stops hollering mostly on account of her being out of breath. A big ole crow caws from the high wire. Momma straightens herself up and smooths her dress but it don't do much good—she still looks like a week-old birthday balloon. A pretty one, though.

I shove the half a hankie down in my shoe and we start walking again and I pretend like Momma and me are the only people on the whole planet. Like ever-body got a secret note telling them to hide real good but they forgot to pass the note to us. Or like the movies where someone says *it's too quiet* right before something scary happens. Or maybe a spaceship landed and we're the only ones who escaped them kidnapping us like they did all the people in the world. Ever-one knows aliens kidnap humans onto their spaceships. Aliens with huge heads on top of stick bodies. Some people don't think they're real but Emma and me always believed they are.

Let's pick up the pace is pretty much all Momma says for the rest of the day. She don't even say *ow* when she trips and skins her knee on the gravel right after a huge truck goes by us, whipping up wind that feels real good but almost sucks me into the road. We've had three trucks, four cars, and an old pickup pass us since we started. Two of the trucks honked the loudest horns I ever heard but they still kept on going. Momma said cusswords to their tail-lights.

It takes a million hours for someone to pull over to give us a ride. In the dark it's hard to see his face. All I know is his name is Eldin. *Eldin Fisk, at your service,* he said when we climbed in. I never been so happy to get in a car as I am to get into Eldin Fisk's. My legs had started turning into concrete blocks. Momma sets in the backseat with me which is weird but good and Eldin didn't seem to care where we were setting, so long as we *let the quiet keep going.* He said that a few minutes into the ride. *I hope y'all let the quiet keep going.* When Momma asks if he'd mind if she smoked he said *yes.* I never did meet someone who said *yes* to that question. Somewhere after a sign pointing to a place called Hockabee I must've fallen asleep 'cause the next thing I know Momma's shaking me awake.

"Where we at?" I ask her.

"Shhh," she says. "Carry that one. No the other one—it's lighter."

It feels like we're in a hurry and I'm trying to get my eyes to stay wide awake but they're fighting me on it. All I hear are bits and pieces of words between Momma and Eldin Fisk. *Thank you so much.* And *All righty then.* And *Oh you're so kind to lift that out of the trunk. Please don't trouble yourself, we're just fine.* Momma's talking in the voice she uses with grown-ups. It's fake but they don't know any better.

"Caroline, say thank you to the nice man," she says.

That's the other thing: when grown-ups are around Momma uses her phony voice *and* she calls me *Caroline. Caroline* sounds more proper. I don't like it, though. I wish I had any name in the world *other* than Caroline.

"Thank you, sir," I say.

"Pleasure," says Eldin Fisk.

He slides back into his car and we watch him until his tail-lights are two teensy dots.

"Where are we, Momma?"

"We're on the outskirts of town," she says, staring at something in the distance. I turn to see what she's looking at—bright lights all clumped together way up ahead.

"What town?"

"What is this, Twenty Questions?" she says. "Grab hold of your sack and let's get this show on the road. Here, hike it up like this . . ."

Miracle Number Four:

Momma's helping me with stuff she never used to help me with. And she's being sweet as honey on a pretty girl's finger. Miss Mary back in Toast used to say that about me. That I was *sweet as honey on a pretty girl's finger.* She said it to Emma too. She was always real good that way, never wanting Emma to feel left out.

We stand where Eldin Fisk left us, at a corner with street signs making a **V** on a light post so thick I couldn't hug it all the way around if I wanted to. I never saw a light this big and tall. Pasted up on it is a peeling sign for a *weight loss program guaranteed to melt the pounds off or your money back.* The only sign I saw up like that was in Hendersonville and it was for a missing cat named Otis who was *probably hungry.* The sign stayed up awhile, until Ally Bell (who got to skip gym on account of her curvy spine and back brace), until Ally Bell's daddy came and ripped it off saying it was *high time* we stopped *littering our town.* Ever-one said he was just doing it because he didn't have any say-so at home on account of his being *henpecked.* Thing is I knew for a fact Ally Bell's family didn't have hens. Not a one.

Momma and me look out at all the lights up ahead and then, at the exact same second, we look at each other. Right before she blinks, just for a teensy tiny second, she looks like a little girl. Like she's my age. It's like Momma and me both wish someone would come along and say *ever-thing will be okay, just you wait and see.*

Even *I* can tell we're about to do something big and important. And scary. I feel like saying *Momma, I don't want to turn the page anymore. Momma, I'm scared.* I wish Emma were here. She wouldn't have a lick of scared in her. She'd probably be the one to say *ever-thing will be okay just you wait and see* and we'd all know she was lying but hearing the words said out loud sure would be nice right about now.

"Momma?"

We're both still looking up ahead.

"What?"

"Momma, um, I'm . . ."

Right when I'm about to tell her I'm too scared to move, Momma says:

"You can talk and walk at the same time, can't you? Let's go."

"But . . ."

"Your *butt* is what's gonna get whipped if you don't get in gear," she says.

"Momma, what if it's bad up there?"

She waits a second like she's really thinking on an answer for my question and then Momma says, "If it's bad at least it'll be a different kind than we're used to and anyway we've already been through the worst. I got a feeling our luck's about to change."

Miracle Number Five:

Momma smiles. Again.

CHAPTER FOUR

Honor Chaplin Ford

My mother never met a conversation she didn't like. Nor does she miss an opportunity to act strange. Which she has been doing all morning in spades. It's not even noon and she's asked me three times how I'm feeling—as if I had just come down with scarlet fever or something. And now, assured that I am perfectly fine thank you very much, she is having a little too much fun at my expense.

"You've been quiet so long it must be some kind of miracle," I say.

Look at her. Ruth Chaplin. Smiling like the cat that ate the canary, arms crossed, waiting on me to admit she's right, which she is. But if I say so she will gloat from here to high heaven so I'm trying not to look at her, which is a difficult undertaking since she takes up the whole doorway to the kitchen.

"Well?" Mother says, trying to force the smile off her face.

"You know, *most* mothers would be happy their daughters

wanted to keep them alive and safe," I say. "But you? I guess you want me to ignore you and let you starve to death when . . ."

Uh-oh. I slipped up.

"When what?" She pounces on it.

"When, um . . . I mean when . . ."

She lets the smile stretch back across her face, turns and waddles into the kitchen.

"Just say it: you're talking about the Armageddon thing again," she says, reaching into the icebox with some effort, bringing out a Styrofoam container—one of many packed in so tight it's a real trick to pull something out without everything tumbling onto the kitchen floor.

"How long does chicken salad keep?" she asks, her nose crinkling up. "This smells funny but didn't I just make it three days ago? You going south on me already, chicken salad? Come smell this and tell me what you think."

"First of all, it's not *the Armageddon thing,* just so you know," I say. "It's called *Armageddon*—just the one word, for one thing. And I don't think I've ever even used it in conversation. What you may be referring to, however, is my Emergency Preparedness Plan . . ."

"In case of the Armageddon thing," she says, holding out a forkful of chicken salad for me to taste. "You think it's still good? Try it."

"I'll pass, thank you, and you should too if it smells weird," I say. "Why do people do that? Who would want to taste something that's already been declared borderline rotten with a gross smell? Are you listening, Mother? And by the way—"

"Here it is! I knew I had cream cheese in here somewhere," she says, her arm reappearing with a blob of tinfoil I know used to be rectangular but is now wrapped around what's left of the Philadelphia cream cheese that's been in there God knows how long.

"Ha. Lookee here," she says, holding it up like it's a trophy. "Were you hiding from me, cream cheese?"

There are two truths in my world, such as it is. One: my mother has a freakish habit of talking to inanimate objects as if they're people, and two: evidently I must now worry about her poisoning herself. Tonight I'll clean out the icebox. I don't care what she'll say.

"Hey by the way, you never told me what the man from City Hall said." I change the subject. "I had to get Cricket over to her father's after ballet class and by the time I got back you were asleep and then it totally slipped my mind. You went to bed awful early last night, come to think of it. You feeling okay?"

"Hand me the paper towels, will you? No, they're right by the sink. There you go. Thanks," Mother says.

"Mom, I'm trying to talk to you here," I say. It is so dang frustrating when she gets all scattered like she is right now. "Did they have any news about the appeal? City Hall, I mean? Can you just slow down a sec? I'll do that later, Mom. I'll clean it out. Just leave it and come sit down for a minute before I have to go."

She appears to be deeply concerned with the shelves in the fridge.

"I take it the news wasn't good," I say. "About the National Register I mean."

She is rubbing the glass shelf so hard I can hear the paper towel squeak with Windex oversaturation. In between wipes she answers me in a mumble like the kind you do in the shower when you're rehearsing an answer to something troublesome. Fragments come first.

". . . short memory . . . ," then " . . . after all this family's done . . . ," followed by " . . . heartless . . ."

"Tell me," I say.

"He says we lost the appeal," she says, sighing. I watch her enormous back jiggle with even the smallest arm movement. "He says we fought the good fight and I should be proud about how far I got. Something like that."

"You should be proud about how far you got?" I say.

Now her whole body is rippling from the strength of her vigorous cleaning.

"That's what he said. He said most people would not have reached the courts but because our family is important to the city of Hartsville—that's exactly what he said, *important to the city of Hartsville*—and because we have been a tourist destination, they agreed to hear the case."

She pauses in her cleaning long enough to reveal what's really been gnawing at her.

"The thing I don't understand," she says, "is why, if we're so dang important, they can't just go on and list this house in the National Register and be done with it. He said Uncle Charles was an icon—an icon!—but he was not *an American of historical significance.* Can you believe the nerve? The *audacity*? He said such hateful things, you can't imagine. And that's just the tip of the iceberg compared to what else he said. I wanted to reach across the table and strangle him. I wanted to ask him if he liked going to the movies. I wanted him to say yes and then I would have told him he had Mr. Charles Chaplin to thank for enabling him to be entertained by moving pictures all these years. He probably wouldn't know *The Kid* from *Star Wars,* though, so I guess it's just as well I sipped my tea and kept my mouth shut. Chaplins take the high road, you know. I'm just glad your father wasn't here to witness it, God rest his soul. Your father— Oh my Lord, your father would have spread him on a cracker and had him for lunch. Your daddy wasn't a Chaplin by blood but he was by marriage and he took as much pride in it as I did. Heck, I used to think he was more proud of it than me, the way he'd go on and on. Why else would he let me keep my maiden name like I did? That kind of thing wasn't done back then, you know. Now, a'course, it's all you see: hyphen this, hyphen that, kids not having the same last names as both their parents is common now but back then no Southern man worth his salt would've seen fit to have a wife who kept her family name. We were trendsetters and we didn't even know it! But there he was, that horrid man from City Hall, just sitting there on the living room couch helping himself to a *second* piece of almond pound cake, telling me there wasn't anything more I could do to get the house listed in the Register. Boy, did I have to bite my tongue. Because Chaplins always take the high road."

"I know, Mom, I know. *Chaplins always take the high road.* I've heard it all my life," I say with a sigh. "I'm sorry, Mom. I know how much that meant to you."

"It meant more than you know, I'll tell you that much."

"What's that supposed to mean?" I spot the clock on the microwave. "Oh good Lord, it's eleven forty-five? But my watch says— Oh, great. Just perfect. My watch is officially past the point of no return. It says it's ten oh five. I've got to leave to pick up Cricket from school in ten minutes. Listen, Mom? I'm putting the knapsack back downstairs in the basement by the laundry table where it used to be, okay? I've updated it and added some new things so now it's all set."

"Windex, you are running me ragged," she says, turning back to her scrubbing. Somehow she's managed to fit her whole head between the milk carton and a Tupperware containing yet another mystery substance. "Honey, can you get the 409 out from under the sink and hand it to me before you go? Windex, you're letting me down, honey, so I've got to go to the big guns!"

I still haven't gotten used to the smell snaking out from under the sink. I hold my breath when I open the cabinet door but the smell above the sink is nothing compared to the wallop down below. It's so sickening I swear I can taste it.

"Mom, we have *got* to do something about this smell—it's getting worse by the minute. Holy shit!"

"Language," she says, her voice hollow from inside cold storage.

"Good Lord, it's a mess down here. I thought the plumber was coming on Monday? We called about this leak weeks ago," I say. I come up for air, then go back down for another look. "Oh my God, the cabinets are rotted out they're so wet. Here's the 409. The mold's spread across the entire space. You can die from black mold, Mom, you know that? We're going to have to rip that whole cabinet out. I bet that's what's got to happen."

"Y'all have only been living back here a few weeks and already you're renovating a house that's been just fine and dandy through *three generations* of Chaplins thank you very much. Four, if you count Cricket. How on *earth* has it survived without you, I wonder?"

"Mom, first of all, I'd hardly call replacing a cabinet a *renovation*. And anyway, what's the alternative, waiting until we all have hacking coughs from black lung or whatever it is you get from that disgusting *fungus* inching across all the walls into our beds?"

"Are you finished, Bette Davis? You really are a Chaplin with all the dramatics you have swirling around in your head," she says.

"If Eddie weren't, I mean if Eddie and I were, well, *you* know what I'm trying to say. I'd have him come over and take a look at it but I can't so let's get the plumber in here."

"Oh, fine."

"You know, if you just did a little planning these things wouldn't happen."

Now *that* got her attention but what the hell was I thinking?

"Since we're on the subject of things that need fixing," she says.

"Forget it, Mom, it's nothing," I say. Too late.

She emerges from the refrigerator. Dang it all. Now she's going to go off on me about my thing. Again. For the millionth time. She's wiping off her hands, closing the icebox, making her way to the Big Chair for yet another lecture. I've never known what else to call this habit of mine. It's not an obsession or OCD or whatever they call it. It's just . . . it's just that I hate surprises. Lots of people hate surprises—I'm not the only one. I am, however, the only *smart* one, because when life throws you curveballs—*and we all know it does*—I will be prepared. I like to say that with careful planning I've taken the *un* out of *unexpected.* Which basically means I've wiped out any chance for a surprise to catch me off guard. It's not easy, you know. And hardly anyone appreciates the tremendous effort that goes into it.

I've always been a "doer." That's what my daddy called me. "You're a real doer, Honor," he'd say with a wink. According to Daddy, there are two types of people: diners and doers. Doers go out and get the job done while diners sit and eat supper, figuring they'll get to work the next day. I never did get the comparison—don't doers have to eat too?—but I did learn that *doing* something was the better way to go in Daddy's eyes. And in mine too. I've always liked projects of any kind but I wouldn't say my *thing* started that far back. If I had to pinpoint when it started taking up my focus, I'd have to say it was high school.

Back then Patty Werther was in charge of the senior prom but I did all the work, which meant the dance was surprise-free and therefore a flawless success in my humble opinion—*one of the greatest in the school's history,* Mr. Kipper, the principal, said. He said those exact words: *the greatest in the school's history.* He gave the thank-you flowers to Patty Werther, mind you, but I didn't care. All I cared about was getting through the night with no calamities.

At community college I went to every single class, I took copious notes, and I didn't even mind photocopying them for whomever missed class, just so long as they signed my petition to ban touch football on the quad (you know how much it hurts when you get hit by an errant football? A lot, trust me. It hurts like H-e—double hockey sticks).

After college I worked as a secretary at the local television station, and Larry Diesel, the weatherman, once told me it was common knowledge that *if anyone needed something done well and fast they should give it to Honor.*

And frankly, I don't think it's a crime to sleep with a notepad and ballpoint pen by your bed. I don't know about anybody else, but for me it's not uncommon to wake up halfway through the night with a scenario that would require a set of skills or equipment I haven't yet considered. So in the morning when I see a word or two scribbled down in that middle-of-the-night handwriting, I remember what I have to do. For example: one time I wrote "frying pan" and I knew that meant I had to get a new one because the Teflon was peeling off my old one something awful and what if a houseguest requests pancakes? Another time I wrote "red ribbon" to remind myself I needed to pick up more at the dollar store in case mine runs out on Christmas Eve after all the stores are closed. Okay, so maybe it was July when that happened, but you can't put a time line on preparedness. Mother will run out of red ribbon and guess who will have the last laugh. That's right. Little ole *prepared* me.

Our older daughter's diagnosis came on a Tuesday afternoon. By Thursday I had the three-ring binder color-coded and collated, and I firmly believe the decision of which chemo to do was made easier because we had all the information right there at our fingertips. Plan A tab = red, Plan B tab = blue. Plan C (the clinical trial) = yellow. Later, by the time the search for a bone marrow donor was under way, I'd turned our dining room table into a grid of neat piles of research I could easily cross-reference. We had no way of knowing how it would all turn out, but we did the best we could under the circumstances and anyway no amount of preparedness can help you when you go through what we did. Cricket was nine when her older sister died, almost exactly three years ago. An anniversary I've come to dread so much I very nearly block it out.

On September 11, 2001, before the second tower fell, when the TV people started saying things like *act of terrorism*, I didn't panic or run to the store for supplies. I felt terrible about the whole thing, mind you—just horrible. But I knew I had emergency backpacks under the bed, and because I have an inventory list I know they're each packed with two flares, an army green canteen, a Swiss Army knife, three bottles of water, four packs of matches and a lighter, a jar of peanut butter, MREs, iodine tablets for water purification, a large bag of raisins, a ball of twine, a map of the United States, a compass, two hundred dollars in twenties with the Andrew Jacksons all facing out, and, at the very top, gas masks I got at the Army-Navy store some years back. So even biological warfare won't catch me off guard. Last night I finally finished updating an identical backpack for my mother, and today I let her know it's back where it's supposed to be if she ever—God forbid—needs to use it, and you'd think I'd tried to ax-murder her, the way she's acting right now.

"Honor, honey, listen to me for a minute," Mother says. "Don't make that face, just listen. Now, I'm your mother and I can say what other people who shall remain nameless can't. You've gone a little too far with this *being prepared* thing. You can't plan life, honey! Things happen. *Life* happens. You know that. No one knows that better than you and Eddie. You need to show Cricket life throws punches but you get back up and you go on with your life. You don't—"

"I refuse to see how an emergency backpack filled with flares, bottled water, a little cash—"

"Cash?" Now it's her turn to interrupt. "Now, what's *that* for?"

"It's for when the ATMs go down, but that's not the point."

"Then what *is* the point? And when, by the way, do ATMs go down? I've never heard of that happening."

"As a matter of fact, on nine-eleven the ATMs all ran out of money," I say.

"But they didn't *go down*," she says.

"No, I guess if you're going to split hairs they didn't *go down*, but they might as well have because everybody ran to get cash in case the terrorists invaded and there was none and safety experts said afterward that it was a good idea to keep some money on hand, just in case."

"Just in case what? Just in case the terrorists need to buy something at the Gap?"

"Ha ha, very funny. I've got to go pick up Cricket in about two minutes, just so you know."

"Honey, this is too much," Mother says, her face serious now. "It's gone too far. Cricket's finally doing better. She'll start making some new friends soon, I'm sure. And you're, well, you're getting up every day. That's a start. You're trying—I see you trying, honey, and I'm so proud of you for it. I'm fine. Your brother— well . . . he's about as good as he'll ever be, God help him. Everything's getting somewhat settled finally, and you're convinced the world's about to end. Can't you see there's something wrong with that, honey?"

"I don't think *the world's about to end*," I tell her. "I like being prepared for emergencies is all."

"You really need a comb in a Tupperware container? What kind of emergency would require a comb?"

"I've got my reasons." I say this with little conviction because, now that the kidding has stopped and she's focusing, Mother's going to tick off all the things she calls crazy and there won't be a word I can get in edgewise.

"Okay, so, what's the reason for the comb?" She calls my bluff.

The chair creaks as she settles back into it. The Big Chair. That's what Eddie and I secretly call it because that's what it is: *Big* with a capital *B*. Mother was always on the heavy side, but when my father died, ten years ago, she started eating and never stopped. I'd find candy wrappers everywhere—jammed into the glove box, stuffed under the couch cushions, under her bed. Literally, everywhere. At first we thought it was a phase, that she would even out or taper off when the grief subsided. I tried talking to her about it gently, telling her we just worried about her eating habits for health reasons, but she got really defensive and teary and over time began cutting me off with a raised hand and "don't even start" any time I broached the subject.

When it became clear Mom's fat was here to stay, I had Eddie remove the arms of one of the kitchen chairs and reinforce the legs with thick pine spindles interspersed between the delicate existing ones. The whole thing looks like a chair version of Frankenstein's monster. But it will hold Mom's weight, so at least I don't have to worry about her crashing onto the floor.

"All right, fine." I give up. "What if Cricket comes home from school with lice? *Some*one's going to have to comb through her hair and all the other kids' hair to check if they've spread and they'll need a comb to do it and guess who'll be there, ready and waiting."

"Honor, honey—"

"You know how many kids are in this neighborhood?" I ask her. "There are eight on this block alone, and that's not even counting the missionary kids, who, if you ask me, are the exact ones who'll probably get lice. Where are they now? Nicaragua or something? Shoot, I've got to hustle if I'm going to get Cricket on time. Can we talk about this later, when I get back?"

"Oh well fine," she says. "Go on and go. By the way, they're in Guatemala not Nicaragua, and that's mean to say about a family out there doing God's work . . ."

We both know she agrees with me on the do-gooder neighbors but feels she has to pay them lip service.

"I love you so much," Mother says. She reaches out, and I can tell she wants to push some hair behind my ears—she hates it when my hair gets in my face—but because of her size she can't get close enough, so I lean forward so she can mother me because that's what she loves to do. She loves to mother me. And her granddaughter, Cricket.

"I worry about you is all," she says. "You're the best thing I ever did with my life, you know that? You are, don't roll your eyes. I don't know what I'd do without you."

"Well, you won't have to find out," I say. "I love you too, Mom. Look, I've got to go. Call me on my cell if you need me to pick up anything on my way home."

"Help me up before you go, will you?"

Mom holds the edge of the table while I get behind her to help her out of the chair. She rocks back and forth to get some momentum going.

"Hold on now. Hooold on—okay, I'm ready. Chair, be good to me, y'hear? One two three . . ."

And she's up to standing. Every single time it's a triumph.

And then she catches my arm, looks meaningfully at me, and, for the fourth time today, she asks, "You *sure* you're doing okay, sugar?"

Like I said, she is one strange woman. I love her to death, but boy oh boy is she strange.

CHAPTER FIVE

Honor

Last year was not my best year.

Every December I go for my annual checkup with my psychic, Misty Rae, and every year, even though I tell her not to give me any bad news even if she sees it heading my way, she still always ends up telling me about some horrible calamity that will befall me and my family in the coming year. I spell it out clear as the Carolina sky—in fact, I *beg* her not to tell me—but it comes tumbling out anyway, and then it's burned on my brain just the same as if I was cattle-branded. What can I do? You've got to take the bad with the good, I guess.

Last year on December 30, just like always, Eddie helped me get ready for the trip to see Misty Rae. Even though we're estranged, he fusses over me, and I don't let on as much but deep down I don't mind it. So there he was in his driveway wearing that crummy old Cabela's ball cap, lecturing me to turn off my cell phone but leave it on the passenger seat in arm's reach, wear my seat belt, keep the radio down low. It comes with the territory I guess. Eddie's a police officer at Precinct 140 across Hartsville, over in what I call the *sad section,* though most people think of it as the *bad section.* Eddie comes from a long line of law enforcement—his daddy, his granddaddy, even his *great*-granddaddy were all on the force, and his brother is a firefighter, not that that's law enforcement but still. Anyway, last year, just like always, Eddie came by, got my car all washed up and filled with regular unleaded (on the radio they said there is *no discernible difference* between super unleaded and regular unleaded so why spend that extra money), and put a note in the glove compartment: "for later," it said on the front. Turns out he had Cricket write me instead of his usual "good luck and don't let the bastards get you down" note I always secretly hated (because it made no sense! For one thing, I'm only going to see one person, one *singular* person not plural, and the second thing is—just because Misty Rae sees into the future, she is not a bastard. And plus, I'm not so sure women can be bastards. I've always thought of the word as being masculine).

Cricket's letter was just precious, with the handwriting she will never be able to overcome because poor penmanship runs in the family, telling me how next year will be filled with *rainbows* and *balloons* and *wonderful things we'll all have together,* and then she said *we have an angel up in Heaven watching over us now so no matter what Misty Rae says, our angel will keep us safe.* I went and had that letter laminated at the Kinko's downtown. A few months later and she's nearly a teenager, she's gotten so sassy. She's still my baby, but she isn't even thirteen yet and I'm already losing sight of the little girl who loved rainbows and balloons.

In our session last year Misty Rae said Mother would get cancer though she couldn't say what kind, and would need to have chemo which would make all her hair fall out. Of course that's bad news for anyone, but in Mother's case? Let me explain it this way: Mother's hair is her best and favorite feature, still shiny dark brown, almost black, and without one single gray hair, I kid you not. So beautiful. She takes real care to keep it that way—once a week she mashes up an avocado and has her hairdresser, Krystal, use it in place of shampoo and yes it's disgusting but Mother's hair is thick and healthy and never been dyed so who am I to judge? It would kill her if her hair fell out. Especially now that she has the weight issue. Her hair is the one thing she feels good about when it comes to her appearance.

Misty Rae said that it would grow back *but*—and she made a big deal out of this part, made me write it down even—she said that if Mother used a brush on her hair while it was trying to grow back "it will fall out all over again and she'll stay bald the rest of her days." Those were Misty Rae's exact words. She said we were to use a comb when Mother's hair was "coming in," as if it was the ocean tide.

"Go on and get yourself a comb," she said, "and keep it clean and where you'll remember it. Your momma will thank you for it later on."

So just now, when Mom brought up the comb I keep in a Tupperware container, I had to do some fancy footwork to concoct a plausible reason I had it. There is no way on God's green earth I would tell her about cancer and chemo. She's got enough to worry about without *that* pushing its way into her mind.

Misty Rae saying Mother would have cancer was just one of many awful Misty Rae predictions—several of which have proved correct, I'll have you know. Not that I'm glad that Cricket broke her leg in three places and had to stay immobilized for almost five weeks last summer. Or that I lost my job as a secretary at the law firm of Marlowe & Hayes due to the unforeseen recession. Of course I wasn't glad Misty Rae was right about all that. It did confirm to me, though, that Misty Rae is a psychic of the highest level so me paying her money I hardly have is justified, because, of the predictions that *didn't* come true, I'm certain at least half were prevented because I knew about them in advance. I will say some made no sense whatsoever. What was all that about a box that gives an electric shock to the person who opens it? I asked Misty Rae if she meant a fuse box or some electrical outlet and she shook her head with her eyes squeezed shut and described what she was picturing: sawdust, a dark room, a box the size that could hold a pair of ladies' shoes, and a hand slowly reaching to open it and whipping away after the shock.

Then there was a three-legged brown dog kicked by a child's foot. She was dead certain it was a little girl's foot, but my girls would no sooner have hurt an animal than they would have driven a railroad tie into their own feet. There were a few more crazy visions like these but they made no sense so I paid them no mind. You can't be one hundred percent right one hundred percent of the time and Misty Rae's only human after all.

The past year was bad for many reasons, but the thing I thought was the worst of all has turned into a blessing, if you ask me. Cricket and I had to move back in with my mother, and honest to goodness I think we've all needed one another in ways that would have stayed invisible had I not lost my job, my marriage, and all my money. The big surprise of it all is that it turns out Cricket needed the move more than anybody. She needs someone who doesn't inexplicably break into tears one minute to the next. She needs to be with people who aren't thinking about her dead sister around the clock. I've tried so hard to pull it together for her, but I know she sees it's a real struggle for me. Hell, just getting out of bed has been a struggle, I won't lie. Mother is perfect for Cricket right now. She focuses on her the way girls need a grown-up to focus on them. The two of them can roll their eyes at me together, and maybe that makes Cricket feel normal. I tried to tell her people mean well when they become solemn, cock their heads to the side, and ask how she's *really* doing, but I myself know that it wears you down, always being associated with sadness in other people's minds. I see Cricket watching friends greet one another in front of school, smiles breaking out (and what's with the hugging? The girls hug each other in greeting now, as if they hadn't seen one another in school just the day before). I ache watching their smiles melt into looks of concern when Cricket walks up. Many times—more times than not, actually—she is ignored completely, as if grief is contagious. It kills me in a million different ways, knowing this is what Cricket faces on a daily basis.

Oh good Lord, there's Evelyn Owens clickety-clacking up to the school door in her high heels and pearls in the middle of the day. And I had to pick today to wear this old pair of JCPenney shorts that make me look fat. I forgot I need to get out of the car—for summer school pickups they make you come inside to personally fetch your child, which is silly and wastes time but those are the rules and I'm not about to do anything to jeopardize Cricket getting the extra help. I believe she got accepted to the program on account of the Chaplin name and because of Eddie. He gives the "stranger danger" talks to the young kids and talks about self-defense to the older ones. They all love Eddie over at the school, so when the insurance company said Cricket's ADHD medication was no longer covered I had Eddie do some sweet-talking to get our girl into the extra-help summer program everybody says is the best in the state for kids with attention issues. Gives kids ways to calm down and focus so they can sit still and do their homework without their minds racing too much. Plus, Eddie and my separation's been real hard on Cricket and I thought some structure this summer might be just the ticket. The death of a sibling plus ADHD plus separated parents equals one sad child. Take my word for it.

Of course, Misty Rae failed to predict our firstborn would die of a horrible illness. She failed to predict I'd be so full of rage and grief that I damn near attacked Mrs. Childers from down the street when she said it was God's will.

No, Misty Rae didn't tell me about any of that. Or about the silence that would descend on our home after the funeral. Which I found ironic because all we wanted to do was scream. She didn't tell me how people would cross the street to keep from bumping into us—for lack of what to say, I know, but still, it stung. Misty Rae neglected to mention how hurt I'd feel when Eddie completely shut down, then decided to cut short his bereavement leave to go back to work. How it'd tear my heart in two, watching him from bed as he'd get ready to go in each day as if none of it had ever happened. As if he was *relieved*.

So why do I keep going to see Misty Rae?

It's simple: when the worst happens to one child, you'll do anything in your power to keep anything bad from happening to the other one.

The other one, who, when I got laid off and lost my marbles again crying, sidled up to me on the couch and said:

"It's okay, Mom. Everything's going to be okay. You know why? Because we're Chaplins. And Chaplins . . ."

"Always take the high road!" we finished the sentence together.

CHAPTER SIX

Honor

"Hey, candy lamb, how was it today? Here, give me that backpack. Honestly, they should make a law against schools loading y'all down with these heavy books. And it's summer! You hungry? We'll stop by Wendy's on the way home."

I reach out to rub Cricket's head and notice that her hair is a rat's nest. I have to get Mom to cut her hair. Thank God she inherited Mother's thick hair, though she got the blond from Daddy's side. It's the shade women pay a lot of money for at the salon. A gorgeous spun gold that turns baby blond in the summertime. She has no appreciation for it—in fact, she shows no interest in anything girlie at all. She's a tomboy, start to finish. Ed used to say she's the son he never had. Her sister had the market cornered on femininity, so Cricket went the other direction early on. Her slight frame doesn't much lend itself to sports, though God knows that doesn't stop her from trying out for teams. Volleyball. Soccer. Basketball. Bless her heart, she isn't any good at any of them, getting tripped up on her gangly limbs. *She'll grow into them,* Dr. Cutler, her pediatrician, said a couple of years ago. When she does, God help us all—she's such a bundle of energy, that one.

"Yeah, I'm starving. Wait, Mom, can we stop by the library on the way back please can we please cuz today I finished *L* and someone might check out the *M* and I can't go out of order so please can we go please? I'll run in you won't even have to get out of the car pleeeease . . ."

"Maybe tomorrow we can swing by the library," I tell her, "but I've got a lot to get done this afternoon and *you* didn't straighten your room like you promised you would last night, ahem, so you've got a lot to get done too, missy."

"Aw, Mom, please? It'll be gone if we don't pick it up today."

"Honey, I've got news for you: the *M* will be there tomorrow. No one is going to check out the *M* volume of the *Encyclopaedia Britannica* tonight, I can pretty much guarantee you that."

"How do you know? Maybe someone will have to do a report on something starting with *M* like, like . . ."

I can see her struggling to keep her argument from going south.

"Like—Madonna?" I smile into the rearview mirror.

"No, Mom," she says, sighing and rolling her eyes. "They can get stuff on Madonna anywhere. Duh."

"Oh, oh wait I know: Malta," I say. "Or wait: mold! Speaking of which, I have *got* to call the plumber—"

"Or Mary, baby Jesus's mother," Cricket says. "Or mitts, like baseball! Wait, what's Malta?"

"It's an island off the coast of somewhere I don't know. Meer-kats!"

"Molecules!"

"How do you know about molecules?" I ask. "Have you already covered that in science?"

"Um, yeah, like eons ago, *duh*," she says.

"*Excuse* me?"

"Sorry. Mom, please please please can we stop at the library please please please please please . . ."

She is like this, my Cricket, she chirps and chirps and chirps until it gets so bad you think you might have gone and lost your mind. It's how she got her nickname in the first place. She doesn't do it to be rude or mean. She is just a loaded pistol, that one, full of curiosity about every tiny little thing you can imagine. Which is why she's checking out the *Encyclopaedia Britannica* one letter at a time and trying to memorize it. She has complete and total recall of anything she makes a point to remember. You've never seen anything like it. She could go on the *Today* show with it. Dr. Cutler says he's never known a child with ADHD and a photographic memory at the same time, but that's our Cricket. One rare bird.

"Hush for a second, Cricket," I say. Traffic's a bear today—no one's slowing to let us out from the school back onto Ferndale Road, and the line of cars is so long we could be here all night for heaven's sake.

"Look to the left and tell me when there's more room between cars, will you?"

"Can we please get the *M* today, Mom? Please?"

"While I think about it why don't you tell me— Oooo, they're letting me in! Thanks, sir! Wave to thank the man, honey. Thank you!"

I wave to the man in the Jetta and we are in business.

"I can see you picking on your nails from the rearview mirror, Cricket—stop that. Now tell me about school today."

The pause is what I notice first. When you're talking to my Cricket, there are no pauses. Ever. She's staring out the window, but I look in the same direction and don't see what could be so riveting unless you consider a big office supply store riveting.

"Honey? You okay?"

"If I tell you something, you promise you won't get mad?" she asks, catching my eye in the mirror.

What parent has ever heard that and not felt a little twist of nerves in their gut for what they're about to hear?

"Do I promise I won't get mad? Well, did you break the law?"

"No, ma'am."

"Did you hurt another human being or creature?"

"No, ma'am."

"Then I promise I won't get mad," I say. "What is it, honey?"

"Um, well . . ."

"Stop picking."

"Okay so I didn't know it and I don't think anybody did but today was dissecting day in lab because the frogs came yesterday and Mr. Taylor didn't want to wait until the dissecting chapter because he can't wait to rip open frogs and I told you I wasn't going to do it and you said I didn't have to, remember? You said I didn't have to dissect a frog, you said that and so I told Mr. Taylor that you gave me permission to leave the room but he didn't believe me so I waited but when I smelled the formaldehyde the frogs had been soaking in I told him I was sick at my stomach and needed to go to the bathroom and could I please have a hall pass and he gave me one and I left the room and it's a good thing I did because I knew I was gonna hurl and if I'd done it in front of everybody I'd never be able to show my face in school ever again ever ever ever. It's bad enough as it is."

"All right now, honey," I say. "Remember what the doctor said about taking a breath in between every other sentence. It helps with the concentration."

She is so damn cute. I see her take a breath and blow it out like she was holding a bubble wand. God, I miss those days. I've said it before and I'll say it again: I just can't figure out how she got to be almost thirteen so fast.

"Okay good. That's real good. Now go on."

"I made it to the girls' room just in time and no one was there so I threw up and no one saw me. When I went back in the hall I couldn't figure out where I could go to hide until the bell for the next class and that's how I came to be following the ninth graders to the auditorium, where they were having some assembly I didn't know about which is weird because I always read the bulletin board but I never saw anything put up about a ninth-grade assembly so I wanted to know what all they were going to see because everybody knows ninth graders get to watch movies like all the time pretty much every day. No one even noticed me or if they did they ignored me so it was easy to hide in the back row of seats because they were empty because Mr. Learson said for everybody to gather up front—he didn't want any lollygaggers he said. Lollygaggers. Lolly-lolly-lollygaggers . . . you know where we got that word? In the encyclopedia it says—"

"Stay on the story, Cricket. Focus."

"Mom! You totally just ran that red light."

"It was yellow. Go on."

"Okay so then he talked into a microphone he really didn't need because there weren't many people there to not hear his voice it was just the ninth grade. He told them that because they had agreed to attended the assembly—"

"*Attend* the assembly, not *attended.* Go ahead."

"Because they had agreed to *attend* the assembly, and only if they signed in *and* out, they could have a half day on Friday and they all clapped and one kid even whistled and Mr. Learson had to say *people, people, come on now, people!* Then they showed a movie and Mama you would not have believed it—it was so gross I thought I might throw up all over again! With pictures of babies in bellies, killed little bitty babies on bloody hospital floors and sad-looking pregnant girls who looked real young to be having babies and Mama I was *so embarrassed* because they looked like Cousin Janey's age and that means they did the nasty and do you think Janey's done it, Mama? I don't but do you? Has Janey gone all the way?"

When I try to swallow, my tongue sticks to the roof of my mouth and I realize my mouth's been hanging open. If I let on how shocked I am, though, she might flitter on to another something and it will be like marching in quicksand getting her back to this. I know how it goes. There's a time limit. So you've got to get the information you need real quick before it slips through your fingers forever.

"No, honey, Janey has not *gone all the way* I can tell you that. Shoot, the drive-thru's closed. We're going to have to go in. Keep talking. The movie had dead babies?"

"Yeah! It was so disgusting and awful. So then the lights came back on and this man this guest speaker everyone had to clap for he came out and with a lispy loud voice said *don't let this be you* and made everyone turn to the person on their right, shake their hand and say *I promise I will abstain from having sexual relations before marriage* only it was so funny because the boys messed with the words saying *I promise* to have *sexual relations before marriage* and more stuff I shouldn't repeat and Mr. Learson kept hollering *settle down now* and *let's give our visitor our undivided attention* and *we're ambassadors of Hartsville today* so let's make Hartsville proud but by the end he was yelling *that's it I'm taking names* and two kids I don't know got sent out. Can you believe it, Mama? Dead babies all over the place. It was so gross."

"I'm going to pause you there for just a second," I say, once we're inside. I take a place in line and read the menu board even though I get the same thing every time. "Do you know what you want? Cricket, look at the menu and tell me what you want. Hi, I'd like the salad bar and a large Diet Coke. And my daughter here will have . . . Cricket?"

"Um, chicken sandwich with nothing on it."

"Please?"

"Please."

She rolls her eyes at me, but honestly, how else is she going to learn? Her father turns to mush where she's concerned—God forbid he insist on anything but a hug and kiss from her.

"Honey, go get us a table over by the salad bar, will you?"

While I wait on her chicken sandwich, I watch Cricket sitting by herself. Looking around hopefully to see if there's anybody she can talk to. There's the rub: this child is so friendly she could start up a conversation with a rock, but as endearing as that gregariousness is to adults, it's kryptonite to kids her age. It's *uncool*. So there she sits. The loneliest girl in the world.

CHAPTER SEVEN

Carrie

The first thing we get to on our walk into our new lives is the Love-less Hotel and Motor Lodge of Hartsville, North Carolina, and even though the name ain't so great, Momma's getting us a room. We never stayed in a hotel or motel or anything like it ever and if I weren't so dang tired I'd be real excited but right now even tooth-picks would have a hard time keeping my eyelids apart. The front office looked real warm and friendly when we were limping toward it from the blacktop. It had a yellow glow that for some reason made me think inside it would smell like biscuits just out of the oven. Instead it smells like cat pee and barbecue and Clorox bleach mixed together on purpose to dare my stomach to stay calm. Momma's talking to a scary-looking old man behind the counter who's so skinny he looks like a skeleton with a thin sheet of skin barely covering his bones. I'm leaning against the glass window when he looks over his half eyeglasses pinching the tip of his nose and says to me:

"You holding the window in place for me over there?"

He says it serious-like but when I say "Sir?" he breaks into a smile and says, "Just busting on you, girlie. The missus says I need to get some new material. Says I need to keep my day job because my humor ain't the humorous kind and I guess she's right. How old're you?"

"Oh, don't mind her—she won't be any bother," Momma says, waving her hand in my direction like she's shooing a fly. "Hey! Stand up straight when someone's talking to you."

The way his right eyebrow shoots up I can tell he's a man who's been lied to all his life. Or had lots of crank phone calls.

"You gonna be a bother, girlie?" he asks me direct. He's smiling, which doesn't make much sense since he's asking about me bothering him.

"No, sir."

"I promise you won't hear a peep from us," Momma says.

The smile he'd given me fades when he turns back to Momma. He sizes us both up.

"Y'all look like you could use a decent night's sleep. Let's see now. Looks like the only rooms available now are the de-luxe," he says, running his finger down a list in a big old Santa Claus ledger book. He looks at me and Momma like he's judging a pageant, sighs, looks over his shoulder to make sure no one snuck up on him, and in a low voice he says, "Tell you what I can do. You put down the deposit on the key and the first week's rent and I'll put you in the de-luxe room at the regular room rate minus twenty percent. It's late and anyway there ain't much difference between regular and de-luxe 'cept the de-luxe has a mini fridge and a hot plate. And basic cable of course. The AC's free. Local calls too, but you got to use a phone card for anything outside of Hartsville even if it's the same area code."

"Thank you so much, sir," Momma says. "We sure can use a break."

"You tell Mrs. Burdock I gave you a cut rate and I'll deny it, y'all hear me?" he says. "And you're to look after yourselves. This here's a fine establishment. But every once in a while we get some rotten apples and I can't be responsible for anything—anything *squirrelly* happening. The missus, now, she don't want to take kids—we can't make it a policy so to speak, course that'd be against the law for discrimination of some kind. We like to say we *prefer* adults only. We make some exceptions here and there. But in general, families bring heaps of trouble and I don't want to send Mrs. Burdock tossing and turning all night, you read me? She got the anxiety gene in her so it don't take much for her to go batshit—pardon my French—with worry. You understand?"

"Yes, sir," Momma and me say at the same time.

"Y'all are on your own."

"Yes, sir."

"Oh, and write down your car's tag number alongside your name we don't up and call the tow truck on you. The bus stop's a stone's throw away and we get commuters trying to park here for free all day," he says, sliding a piece of paper to Momma.

"Oh, we don't have a car," Momma says. I want to correct her and say *yes we do—it's broke but it's still ours,* but I bite my tongue. Momma don't like to be corrected. Mr. Burdock's sizing her up over the rims of his eyeglasses, like us not having a car might change his mind.

"How'd y'all get here?" he asks.

"Our car broke down back on the interstate," Momma says, "but it was a heap of junk no one could breathe life back into so we set off on foot and finally caught a ride that got us pretty close by."

"Well, all right then," he says, straightening up, puffing out his skinny chest and flinging his arms wide like *ta-da*. "Welcome to the Loveless. Stairs are just across the driveway. Vending machines are on both the first and second floors. Ice machines too, though the one on the second floor's been giving me problems. If it ain't working let me know. Maid service is *sporadic*—our girl up and quit on us and Mrs. Burdock's liking the money it saves us so don't count on us hiring anyone new anytime soon. Rent's due by end of business on Fridays."

I didn't know I'd been holding my breath but when he hands Momma the block of wood attached to the key I finally let the air whoosh out.

She takes it but when she sees the number 217 printed on it her face falls from fake-smiling and she loses all her coloring.

"Something wrong?" he asks.

Momma looks up at him then at the number then back at him.

"Oh, ah," Momma says, "no, sir. This is just fine."

I can tell it's not *fine* but I cain't imagine what Momma's got against the wood or the number 217.

"Well, all right then. Name's Hap Burdock," he says, smiling and reaching over the counter to offer his hand to be shaken. "Pleased to meetcha."

"My name's Libby Parker and this is my daughter, Caroline," Momma says in a fake-nice voice through her smile. "Honey, come on over and shake nice Mr. Burdock's hand."

He winks at me and says, "You mind telling me why you keep a penny behind your ear?"

"Sir?"

He reaches out—at first I think he's going to hit me so I back up. He gets a sad look then says, "It's all right, I ain't gonna bite you. Just pulling that penny out from where it's hiding," and sure enough his fingers touch my hair at my right ear and he holds up a penny for me and Momma to see.

I feel behind both my ears but I think I'd remember putting money up there. Especially since I never do it.

"Hey. How'd you do that?" I ask him.

He winks at me again and hands me the coin for keeps.

"It's *magic*," he says, fanning his hands in front of his face.

I ain't never seen a person like him back home, that's for sure.

The Loveless is an almost-square with all the doors and windows on both floors facing all the parking spots in the open middle of the square. I figure ever-one can keep an eye on their cars better that way. The rooms on the second floor are along one long outside balcony with a black railing making sure you don't trip and fall into the parking lot.

"You heard the man," she says real low. Momma's voice goes back to normal when we're outside on the way up the stairs to the second-floor room. "You better keep quiet or I'll do more than throw you out on your behind, you can count on that."

"Yes, ma'am," I say, rubbing my arm where she pinched me.

"We're lucky to get a place for the money we got," she says, "no telling where we'd end up if we lose a room here. Things are always more expensive the closer you get to the center of a town."

I don't know how Momma knows all about prices and centers of towns considering we never been in a place with stoplights even but then there's a whole lot I don't know about Momma. She don't talk much about her growing up.

"All right then," she says.

It's dark and the light over the parking lot isn't real bright so Momma has to squint and get close to the doors to read the numbers. "Two eleven. Two thirteen. Two fifteen. Here it is."

She turns the key, pushes the door open, and flicks a light switch just inside.

It's the best room in the whole entire world. Two beds! A TV on a chest of drawers across from them! And it's near twice the size of the old half-broke black-and-white one we once had.

"Whoa! Lookee, Momma! The TV's huge!"

I rush in and rub the tired out of my eyes so I can get a better look at ever-thing.

"We each got our own bed, Momma, look! And there's new soap in a wrapper, and two cups. This is great! There's a shower over the tub so's you can take one or both, Momma! Come see."

Momma hasn't set foot in the room yet.

"It's real nice, right, Momma?" I ask her. I take the soap over to her. "Smell it—it's piney, like home."

"Just hush up, will you," she says, stepping in dainty-like. As if the room might swallow her up whole.

Momma hates lots of things. Pickles. Blue jeans. Cats. Fast drivers. Hillbilly talk. Hendersonville. Kids. Emma. And from the way it's looking, I guess you could add the Loveless Hotel and Motor Lodge of Hartsville, North Carolina, to the list.

I check all the drawers for anything left behind and sure enough in the table between the two beds I hit pay dirt.

"Hey, Momma, look! Someone left a book in here."

She doesn't look.

"Leave it be," she says, taking full measure of the room. "That's no book—that's a Gideon Bible. Put it back. No soul's ever been saved in this family as far as I can tell. Besides, if the devil wants to find you he will—no Bible's going to keep him from doing his job."

It's brand spanking new with a man's name in fancy gold lettering on front. Wouldn't you think if Mr. Gideon went to all the trouble to get his name in gold letters on his own Bible he'd remember to take it with him when he left? That's a mystery I'll have to solve or it'll drive me crazy. I get out my black-and-white notebook and write *ask Mr. Burdock if there's anyone come by asking for the Bible he left behind.* If no one has I aim to ask if I can hold on to it. Finders keepers.

"This'll be great, Momma," I say as she sets herself down on the very edge of the end of the bed, hugging her purse up tight to her chest like a robber's trying to pry it from her. I watch in the cracked mirror over the sink. She slumps a little then goes hunting through her pocketbook. She's been real good about waiting till we got here to have her whiskey.

"Momma?"

"Hmmm?" She's fingering the bedspread, tracing the stitching. She takes a second pull from the bottle.

"You want me to go fetch some ice from that machine we passed on the way up, Momma?"

I know it doesn't suit her, drinking from the bottle like she is. The sound of clinking ice cubes might make us both feel more at home.

"That'd be fine," she says, coming as close to *yes please* as she ever does.

I want so bad to run over and hug her. Not that I would. I want to, though.

"It's really and truly gonna be great," I say on my way out the door.

And for the first time, I believe my own self. This'll be great. I got a feeling it really will be.

CHAPTER EIGHT

Carrie

Momma's reaching over her shoulders holding the two sides of her dress together at the back.

"Get over here and pull up this zipper," she says. "I can't get it to save my life."

Momma's said more lately than she ever said to me. Ever.

I inch the zipper up slow because the middle part of her back's got an angry scar from Richard's beer bottle and even though it healed a while back I always think it must hurt her still. She'd never say, though, and I'd never ask.

"Momma, please can I come? I'll stay real quiet," I tell her. "You won't even know I'm there, hand to God."

"No you most certainly cannot. Last thing I need is them seeing a kid waiting on me," she says under her breath while she's fussing with her hair again in the cracked mirror.

I love watching her get ready for job interviews. Zipping up. Fixing her hair. Lipstick. Most of all her talking. I never heard her say so many sentences at one time in my life as when she gets ready to look for work. I know it's on account of her being nervous but sometimes I pretend she and me are getting fixed up for a dance we're gonna go to with Daddy.

"What're they gonna think?" she's saying. "They'll think I'll be wanting time off to care for my kid. They don't want to think their people have anything more important than work to worry about. And right about now there is nothing more important than work if we want to eat. Where's my lipstick?"

She puts it on and starts talking again, to her own face in the mirror. I try to keep from smiling at her using the word *we*. She never says *we*.

"When I was your age my momma told me I'd never amount to anything more than a waste of oxygen." She squinches her eyes while she sprays a halo of White Rain. The mist will turn the counter sticky and I know I'll wipe it off after she leaves. I'm real good about keeping the room *spick-and-span*.

"Even though they called me Miss America back in school," she says, eyeing herself from different angles. "Bet you didn't know that. I was voted best-looking in the whole school. My momma never knew that and I didn't tell her because she would have thought I was uppity. But I was pretty. I was pretty and I didn't give it a second thought, that's how stupid I was. I figured I'd always be pretty. Damnation will you look at that—I got makeup on my dress. Well, don't just stand there—get over here and help for Christ's sake!"

She wets one of the thin rough washcloths and I hold my hand under the fabric of her dress while she presses against it trying to dab the smudge away. Luckily it's her flowered Sunday dress so you cain't see the thumb-size smear of pink but it makes her mad all the same. Her neck bruise's nearly faded away and what's still there is covered by the makeup she got at the dollar store. But when she gets angry the mark does too. No makeup can hide that.

We don't talk about her bruises or marks, though. We never have. Not hers or mine. It's probably better that way anyhow.

The smudge comes out pretty good and I can see that eases her mind so I figure I can ask her something that's been weighing on me, since she's so talkative and all. Momma's usually not so good with *thoughts* and *feelings* and all that.

"Momma, you ever get pictures flashing into your head like from a movie?"

She's standing on the chair out at the spot in the middle of the room where you can see your whole self in the mirror.

"What do you mean, pictures flashing into your head?" she asks me while she turns to get a look at the backside of her dress.

"Pictures of things that make no sense but you sorta feel like they should. Like when something's on the tip of your tongue but you cain't quite recall it?"

She steps off the chair and next thing I know she's pinching my jaw between her finger and thumb.

"You mark my words right here and now," she hisses at me, "if you get crazy again—don't you dare try to pull away from me when I'm talking to you, I'm serious as a heart attack—if you get all crazy, loony tunes again I will dump you by the side of the road and never look back, you hear me? Hell, I'd love an excuse to do just that so don't go giving me one if you know what's good for you."

Through pinched fish lips I say, "Yes, ma'am."

"I will not put up with it again," she says. "You understand what I'm telling you?"

"Yes, ma'am."

She lets go of my face and turns back to getting herself ready to go.

"It's bad enough they all treat me like I'm a damn hillbilly. Like I never worn shoes before. Like I don't know their language"— she's back to muttering to the mirror—"them talking real slow and loud like I'm a foreigner. These people here thinking they're better than me when I probably got more Carolina blood in my veins than the whole lot of them put together. It's like I've got the word *stranger* stamped on my forehead. Like *I'm* the one with the accent. They see I've got a loony tunes girl clinging to my skirt that'll be the final nail in the coffin, I'll tell you what."

She closes her lipsticked lips around a tissue. *Blotting* them, she calls it. I got to remember to fish that tissue out of the trash bin. I'd love to have Momma's lips in my notebook. I finally got enough hairs from her brush to make up a lock of hair that I taped into the book yesterday.

"Well," she says, stepping back to get a better view of herself in the mirror, "this is about as good as it gets, though I don't know why I bother. I ain't—I'm *not* qualified to do much of anything anyone'd see fit to pay money for. But I'm no charity case so that puts me square between a rock and a hard place."

With the makeup covering the scar on her cheek and with her hair long enough to pouf up over the spots where it never grew back after Richard's fists took clumps of it, she's pretty for the first time since Richard came into our lives. What's left of that neck mark of hers is the last hold Richard's got on her. When it disappears—even though he's been six foot under awhile now—Richard will disappear from our life. Forever. That's why I keep track of how it's healing in my notebook.

"I get a good enough job I can get the hell out of Dodge and get back on track to where I should have been long time ago," she says.

"Where should you have been a long time ago, Momma?"

She don't answer. She probably didn't hear me.

"Now remember: you stay put. Don't be giving them any reason to kick us out, y'hear me?"

"But Momma . . ."

I don't tell her I hate being alone in this room with the walls so thin I can hear everything on all sides of us. The whole place shakes every time someone slams their door which happens every five seconds and once a man with a deep voice banged on our door over and over calling out for someone named Melanie and I almost wet myself I was so scared but then he must've realized he had the wrong room and he went away. I don't tell her I've already hunted through all her stuff, looking for that travel case she guarded with her life on the drive out of Hendersonville. I don't tell her I been sneaking out after she leaves and no one's caught me yet.

"Momma I just want to come with you please? I won't be any bother. I'll disappear when you go in places. You won't even know I'm there. Please, Momma. Take me with you."

She's back hunched over at the mirror turning her head right and left but it's hard to get a handle on how you look in a mirror with only the bottom half not spiderweb cracked.

"Get over here and open this cup for me. I'm so damn thirsty. My head's about to split open with this damn headache."

On Wednesday, Mr. Burdock gave us two new plastic cups wrapped tight in plastic and Momma doesn't want to ruin her nails. Her fingertips look so good, you cain't hardly tell it's Magic Marker.

"And turn that goddamn TV down. I don't understand why you set your sights on bugging me every goddamn minute. TV turned on night and day, day and night. Loud as hell, like in old folks' homes."

"It won't go down. I tried. It's broken or something. You have to unplug it to get it off and on and the sound buttons don't work."

Momma's fixing her eyes on me and I back up just in case. Best to get out of her way when she's going to find work. Or just in general.

"What do you mean it's broken? When did *that* happen? We better not be getting charged for the damage, I'll tell you that much."

She slips her feet into her shoes like Cinderella with her glass slippers only Cinderella made it look easy and Momma winces on account of her feet being rubbed raw from wearing the same shoes ever-day. We used the black Magic Marker to draw in the parts that had faded from all the walking and they look like new, hand to God.

"I don't know," I say. "It just started happening."

She limps over and fiddles with the knob on the front of the old TV then feels around the back of it.

"Perfect," she says, sighing. Only I don't see what makes a broken TV perfect.

"See I told you," I say.

"You being smart with me?"

Now I've gone and done it. She ain't mad at the TV any longer. It's me she's mad at and I'd feel a lot better if the bathroom door had a lock on it. The other night she pushed her way in and got me even though I had all my weight up against the door. But that wasn't her fault. The liquor store man gave her the whiskey but didn't give her the job, so it was his fault she was feeling blue. In this room there ain't nowhere to go when it turns her mean at night.

"You're lucky I've got to go," she says, smoothing her dress then hitching her purse onto her shoulder. "Keep the door locked. We might have nothing to our name but what we've got we need to hold on to."

"Yes, ma'am."

She squints at me hard and I know she's trying to figure out if I'm sassing her but I'm not and in a second she gives up and leaves.

I say goodbye but I don't think she heard me through the door.

I got to stop giving her reasons to get rid of me. I thought she'd gone and figured out a way to do it back before we left Hendersonville, after I shot Richard. That was a real close call.

The days right after Richard died are sort of blurry in my head but I remember Momma going to see if she could leave me with some lady who works for North Carolina. Now *that's* a whole other mystery: How does someone work for a *state*? The state is her boss? They say I'm the one who's crazy but *that's* what's crazy. The lady came and talked to me like I was a baby, asking me did I know my own name and what is it and without looking in the mirror what is my hair color (like I'd need a mirror for the answer). She asked me all kinds of stupid questions and went out to *have a word* with Momma, who was outside the house pacing back and forth and smoking one cigarette lit from the last. Finally the lady got in her shiny car and drove away and Momma came in looking like a storm was brewing behind her eyes. She didn't say as much, but I could tell she was hoping the lady would take me off her hands. She told me I was going to stay with her after all but *things were going to change.* The deal was I had to go with the lady every day to an office the next town over. It had a little room with toys and small chairs and finger paintings taped to the walls. The lady and me sat cross-legged on a hard carpet that left bumpy marks on my legs for hours after I left. But it was great on account of the peanut butter and jelly sandwiches and potato chips. I got those free and the only thing I had to do was answer her questions and watch her scribble things down on a pad she held up against her chest like I was wanting to steal it. She told me I should think of her like a friend and that I could tell her anything at all but I don't know any kid who's best friends with a grown-up. Also, for all the time she talked to Momma you'd think she already knew the answers to the questions like:

"What was your daddy's name?"

"Do you have a grandma? Where does she live, do you know?"

"Do you have any brothers or sisters?"

That last one was where the trick of it was. Like I said, those days and weeks right after Richard died were real blurry to me. I tried real hard to *concentrate* like the lady said but my brain felt all mushy and loose. I remember feeling tired all the time but even with all that I knew she was up to something. I knew she was trying to get me to talk about my sister. She wanted me to say *Yes, ma'am, I have a sister.* That's what she wanted to hear. I knew it even then. What's more, I may have been eight but I knew if I talked about Emma I'd never see Momma or Mr. Wilson or Hendersonville again. I knew something bad would happen if I told the lady yes but I didn't know what to do at first. Because the fact is, yes I believe I had a sister but something happened—she disappeared and I wasn't supposed to talk about her ever again.

When Emma was a baby Momma talked about her. Her and Daddy both. No matter what Momma said when I was eight, no matter how close the state lady watched me when she asked if I had a sister, even when I was telling her *no, ma'am,* in my head I could hear Momma and Daddy talking about the baby. I can *still* hear it. What's funny is that it was the state lady who reminded me of it when she asked if I ever heard anyone *else* saying I had a baby sister. *Whammo!* It came back to my ears like we were talking to each other with two tin cans and string, me on one end, Momma and Daddy on the other. When she was a baby I remember I lifted Emma up out of the drawer they used for a bassinet and took her over like she was a play doll. Momma didn't mind. If Emma got hungry or needed changing I'd bring her over to Momma, who'd tell me to go somewhere to *get out from underfoot.* She hated people being *underfoot* so I'd have to leave baby Emma with her and get out of the way. But Momma knew how much I loved Emma so when I came back in she'd have already put her in my room on the middle of the bed where she couldn't get into any trouble. That was back when Emma couldn't even turn over, she was so little. Nothing better than going into a room where there's a baby's happy to see you. I loved it when Emma was itty bitty. I can say she *never existed* till I'm blue in the face but I swear I remember her.

When she got older I kept taking care of her—because at some point Momma stopped talking about her or doing anything for her at all. Momma had a lot on her mind back then, even before Daddy died. He wasn't home all that much, my daddy. Which I guess is why Momma was sad all the time. So Emma and me, we were all we had. We stuck up for each other.

Then, years later, after Richard died and the state lady came, Sheriff and Momma and her all watched me real close when they said the name Emma. They asked if I knew an Emma, like did I know if she even existed. Momma said *no she never did*. The lady hushed Momma and asked me if I thought there'd been an Emma. They seemed happy when I slowly shook my head no but because I was staring at Momma when I answered, the state lady had to ask Momma to *give us some time to visit, just Caroline and me alone*. The more she asked if I was sure there was no such person as Emma and the more I said *no, ma'am*, the happier the state lady got so I guess you could say I passed the test. Then something super-incredibly weird started to happen. I started to forget what Emma looked like. The harder I tried to remember, the worse it got. I knew her hair was near-white blond only because mine is the opposite, a dark mousy brown that matches my eyes. But her face was fading in my memory. Then it was her voice that left me. I wanted so bad to hear her in my head but it was like someone was turning a knob on a radio real low, where you know there's music playing but you cain't make out what the song is. I remember feeling terrible. Like I was betraying my sister. Leaving her to die or something.

After a few more times like that where the state lady asked if the name Emma *rang any bells* and who did I play with when I was growing up, they said I didn't have to go to see her no more. Momma said she was *this close* to putting me in the loony bin for good and back then I didn't know what a loony bin was so Momma drew circle in the air by her ear and told me it's where they lock up crazy people. She said they have loony bins for kids and that I'd fit in perfect there. I haven't had a peanut butter and jelly sandwich since I stopped meeting with the state lady, but at least I don't have to go to the loony bin.

I count to a hundred with *Mississippi* in between just to make sure Momma's good and gone across town to find a job, but I don't need to—she never doubles back. Once she's gone, she's gone. It's brighter outside than I thought it'd be and I have to blink a few times to get my eyes used to the sunlight. I take care to keep as far from the edge of the road as I can and I will myself invisible just in case someone from the Loveless happens to see me. I'm hungrier than a sow full of babies. Momma only brought the whiskey home last night but it was okay because I still had four ketchups I saved aside thinking she might forget food again.

Ketchup's free at this place down the road called Wendy's. I couldn't believe my eyes when I first went in there the other day. They got hundreds of packets of ketchup plus millions of paper napkins, which come in handy for toilet paper when we run out— Mrs. Burdock won't give out more than *our fair share*. And Wendy's has food just out there for anybody to take. Bowls of all kinds of vegetables and lettuce and stuff.

Any day of the week you'll find at least ten ketchup packets in my pockets, thirty if it's a good day. It's not like I'm stealing or anything but I do try to hurry about it when the businesspeople dressed real nice line up for lunch. Or when the moms come in for early supper with their strollers, hand-holding little ones. It's always so busy no one notices me taking fistfuls of ketchups and plus I'm small because I haven't yet had my *growth spurts,* which if you ask me sound like something that'd come out of water guns. Some kids have the spurts all in one summer so when they come back to school it's like they're strangers. Candy Currington had bosoms when she came back for fifth grade. Ever-one knew she got her period that year too because Mason Brawders—who was named after a mason jar because when they filled in his birth certificate his momma looked up at his daddy drinking sweet tea from a mason jar, and that was that. Ever-one called him Jarhead. Anyway, Mason Brawders found *evidence* of Candy's *menstration* in the purse Candy hugged close to her chest. I never knew whether she slumped that way because of the bosoms or the period *evidence*. I won't walk that way when I get bosoms or my period, which I hope I never do.

Today I'm gonna grab even more packets than yesterday. I'm trying to get through thirty-five ketchups in four minutes which I bet is some world record or at least I pretend it is. Most I've done so far is thirty-one. I have to cup my hands around my eyes to be able to see clearly through the glass and near as I can tell it's good and busy right now so I might could get a handful of olives this time. Maybe even some of those crunchy little bread cubes. But the ketchup's what makes paper taste like it could be real food so it's got to be the *first order of business*. Like my daddy used to say when he'd come in from being away from home. He'd walk in the door and, before Momma even, he'd hug me and say "getting a kiss from my little princess is my *first order of business*."

The Burdocks get loads of free catalogs in the mail and what they do is they leave the ones they've already gone through on the front desk. That way, if you happen to want anything from Plus Size Woman or Gander Mountain or Johnny T-shirt, all you've got to do is stop by the front desk and the catalog's yours for the taking.

"Now what on God's green earth would *you* want with Orvis?" Mr. Burdock says when I ask him if I can have it.

"I like the pictures" is all I can come up with.

"Have at it," he says, laughing at a joke I guess I'm too young to understand.

It's true, I do like the pictures. But not the way he thinks. Here's what I do. I take the catalog to the room and when Momma's in her whiskey sleep, I cut out pictures with scissors I borrow from Mr. Burdock. Then I swish them around with my finger in a cup of water, until the paper gets to where it almost tears. Then I eat each picture. One by one. It sounds weird I guess but it fills up an empty belly as good as anything else I've tried. When I cut enough pictures out, I mean. With the Orvis catalog I start with the fish. I pretend each picture is a real fish, cooked in a cast-iron skillet like Momma used to fry up catfish. I pick it out of the water gently and flatten it and cut it into tiny pieces, like I'm cutting bites for a baby. That way I can fool my brain into thinking it's a real plate of food. The trick is to chew real slow. Last week I squeezed ketchup on every bite I could and I swear it tasted so good. I try not to do that every time, though, because I don't want to get to where I *need* the ketchup for the paper to taste good. I've decided that adding ketchup will be a special treat. Like going out to a restaurant like I will someday I bet.

There are plenty of Burdock catalogs that don't have pictures of things I'd like to eat so lately I been having a problem training my brain to pretend I'm *not* eating a Plus Size Woman. Or Needlework. Paper is paper, I tell myself. Today I noticed the only catalog on the front desk is something called ExpressURWay, so I better get extra ketchup in case the pictures are super-gross. And this time I remembered to bring the plastic bag I fished from the trash so I can load it up with olives and fried bread cubes. If no one's looking.

CHAPTER NINE

Honor

"Cricket, go on and get a table, I'll bring the tray over when the food's ready," I say.

Wendy's is ridiculously busy today. With all this time in line you'd think everybody'd know what they wanted to order by the time they reach the front, but they stand there deciding at the last minute, like it's all a big surprise.

"Here you go"—I put the tray down in front of Cricket—"I'll be right back. You want me to get you anything from the salad bar? I can put it on the side."

"No, thanks," she says, popping a French fry in her mouth.

By the time I get up there, most of the people making salads have finished so it's just me and a red-haired woman in a pantsuit hogging the tongs to pick through the mixed greens for the iceberg lettuce. I'm waiting on her to move along and that's when I see it: across the sneeze guard is a little girl elbow-deep in the croutons. Taking fistfuls of them, for goodness' sake.

"Oh, my word." I tap the red-haired woman. "Excuse me, but I think your daughter might be needing a bowl."

She looks up and across the plastic at the girl, who's now taking as many cherry tomatoes as she can grab and shoving them into a dirty plastic grocery sack she has looped over her arm.

"Oh, that's not my daughter," the woman says, shaking her head and shrugging as she spoons sunflower seeds into her bowl. "I saw her here the other day doing the same thing. I think she's here on her own. Disgusting . . ."

Well, that is just not acceptable. The girl hasn't seen me watching her because she's too busy checking over her shoulder, so I make my move easily. I cross around and catch her in the act, holding her at the wrist right over the croutons.

"Excuse me, young lady, but you're old enough to know better than to use your hands. Who are you here with? Where's your mother?"

"Please, ma'am," she says, trying to wriggle out of my grip.

When she looks up at me all full of worry, I am thunderstruck. I am face-to-face with a ghost. The resemblance is uncanny.

"Please, I'm sorry—I'll go now—please," she says in a thick accent I can't quite place.

I try to hold myself together. Cricket's right over there—I've got to hold it together. Maybe I'm just seeing things. Maybe I'm losing my mind. I look again at this child, with her chocolate-colored hair and deep brown eyes—maybe I'm imagining it.

"Let's step over here for a minute," I say.

"I'm real sorry," she says again. She's given up trying to wrestle her arm free and lets it go limp in defeat. When we're out of the way, she starts crying.

I'm looking around for an adult who might be looking like they lost sight of her, but it seems everyone's accounted for. There's Cricket using her eyes to will me to come back so she can start eating—we have a strict rule about waiting until everyone's seated to begin. And believe you me, it's like swimming upstream trying to teach kids manners these days. In a futile attempt to find a friend for Cricket, Mother invited the daughter of a neighbor over for supper the other day and half of that girl's meal was finished by the time I sat down.

"Honey, what's your name?" I ask the little girl whose wrist I'm still holding.

I squat down to help dab her tears and to see her eye to eye. It takes my breath away—the resemblance is spooky. I choke on words, and I'm aware that she's watching me carefully.

"Are you here with anybody?" I manage to squeak out.

The little girl shakes her head and sniffs but the crying continues.

"Are you in trouble, honey? I'm sorry, I didn't mean to hold on to you so tight. Oh, sweetheart, it's okay. Did you get separated from your family? Don't cry, sugar, it'll be okay. Are you lost?"

Hold it together, Honor. Seriously. You've got to hold it together. You're a grown woman with a daughter yards away and a crisis staring you in the face. God only gives us as much as we can bear. I honestly don't know what to do here, so I start asking anybody walking past.

"Excuse me, does she belong to you?" I ask a woman struggling to keep her toddler in his stroller. She shakes her head no.

"I better call nine-one-one," I say. "Hon, I'm going to make a quick phone call so we can get to the bottom of this and get you back to where you need to be."

Her sobbing stops as abruptly as it started, and her eyes get pie-wide when I stand up to stop an employee.

"Sir? Are you the manager?" I ask a man in a Wendy's visor and shirt. As the words are leaving my mouth I catch sight of the little girl, who looks both betrayed and stricken, probably thinking I'm turning her in for using her hands at the salad bar. She's frozen, paralyzed with fear apparently.

"No, but I can get him," the Wendy's man says.

I see her looking up at me with eyes too old to be a child's, and something weird happens. It sounds crazy and maybe I'll regret saying this, but in that moment we recognize one another. I've decided to trust my mother's intuition on this one. Turning her over to a Wendy's employee isn't going to do this child any good. All right, God. I get the message. I'll take it from here.

"Actually, ah, no, thank you," I tell the Wendy's employee. "I've got it covered. Sorry to bother you."

He looks relieved not to have to exert the energy and goes back to jamming more napkins into the dispenser, and I look back down at this dirty little girl in clothes a size too small. My Lord, I think I may be looking at a runaway. I just saw something on runaways the other night on cable. On MSNBC I think.

"Why don't you come on over here and have a bite to eat with my daughter and me," I say, signaling with my head to where we're sitting. "We'd be happy to have you join us. What'd you say your name was, honey?"

Here comes Cricket. Oh God, should I stop her from getting a look at the girl? It'll give her such a start. But maybe I'm reading too much into this. What if I'm not, though? Cricket will be so . . . Too late . . .

"Mom, I'm *starving*," Cricket says, standing with her hands on her hips. "Seriously, can I start—you're taking, like, for*ever*. The food's getting cold."

Then Cricket looks at the girl and her mouth drops open. Her hands fall involuntarily from her hips to dangling by her sides. Her skin drains of all color, like a reverse Polaroid.

"Oh my *God*, Mom."

"This is," I say, pausing, hoping the little girl will fill in the blank. "This is my new friend . . . Honey, what's your name?"

I put my arm around Cricket to steady her.

"So it's not just me," I say to Cricket, both of us staring at the little girl. "You see it too."

Cricket says what I've been thinking. She murmurs it, actually. Without taking her eyes off the girl, Cricket says, "It's Caroline."

It's not like we don't say her name—we do. I made sure of it from the beginning. The day we buried Caroline I told Eddie and Cricket and my mother that I didn't want to be one of those families that tiptoed around her name. I thought—I still think—it keeps a person alive to talk about them. And I want Cricket to always remember who her older sister was. So the name isn't a bombshell of any kind. Still, *nothing* could have prepared us for what happened next.

"How'd y'all know my name?" the little girl asks.

If we were stunned before it was hardly noticeable compared to our shock now.

"Wait, what?" Cricket reacts first, her head cartoonishly whipping from the little girl's face to mine then back again. "Are you saying your name is *Caroline*? C-A-R-O-L-I-N-E?"

"You can call me Carrie, though, if you want," the girl, nodding, says to Cricket. "Lots of people call me Carrie."

"Honey, I'm sorry we're both being so rude staring at you like this," I say, trying to get back on course. "It's just that you remind us of someone . . . of . . ."

"You look just like my big sister," Cricket says. "Like, if y'all were standing next to each other we would barely know the difference. Except for the height. And you're younger."

"Oh, really?" The girl looks mildly interested, but of course how could she understand the impact she is having on both of us.

"You're like her *spitting image*," Cricket says. "It's like someone made a clone of her or something, Mom, right? It's freaky, right?"

"I can't say it's not bizarre," I say, "but poor thing—you look like you've had just about enough of these crazy people staring at you, talking about someone you don't know. Let's go over and sit ourselves down for a minute, can we? I need to catch my breath here."

Without coordinating it, Cricket and I step aside to let little Caroline walk ahead of us, mainly because I think we both want to take her in. She is breakably thin with spindly legs and arms, the kind you'd draw on a stick figure. Our Caroline got real thin like that from the chemo. Then they put her on prednisone and she bloated into a person we barely recognized.

"Caroline," I say, "we need to fatten you up, honey."

She's a flight risk, this one, I can just tell. Still behind her, Cricket and I exchange looks and I try to pantomime to her that we should act cool about this little girl. Casual.

"Mom. Seriously. Can I start or what? It's been like an *hour* practically," Cricket says, picking up on my silent directive.

"Oh, it most certainly has not been an hour, Cricket, for goodness' sake. Oh my—we forgot to introduce ourselves. Carrie, what must you think of us! My name is Mrs. Ford. And that's Cricket, as you now know. Cricket Chaplin Ford. Come sit down with us, honey. It's okay."

Without taking her eyes off Cricket, Caroline—Carrie—lowers herself into a seat at our table.

"Ugh! It's practically frozen it's been sitting here so long," Cricket whines as she takes a huge bite of her chicken sandwich. She sizes Caroline up as she chews. "Hey, Caroline. I mean, Carrie. You want a French fry?"

"Cricket! Good Lord, don't talk with your mouth full," I say. I find it as tempting to use the name Caroline as Cricket clearly does. "Carrie, where's your mama, honey? She's not here, I know that much."

The French fries are spilling over onto the plastic tray, which Cricket pushes toward Carrie.

"Seriously, have some," Cricket says. "I'm not going to eat all of them."

"No, ma'am, she's not here," Carrie says, tearing her eyes off Cricket only to look down in wonder at the French fries. I can see she is practically salivating.

"Can I give her a call maybe? Go on and help yourself to the fries, honey."

"Are you sure?" Carrie asks, looking from me to Cricket then back down at the fries. Her arm shoots out when I nod to say *it's okay, go ahead.* Cricket catches my eye, looking just as worried as I am when Carrie's eating. It becomes clear as day to me that Carrie is coming home with us while I try to figure out what to do.

"Why don't I call your mother and let her know where you are so she knows you're okay?" I say.

"Oh, wow. What happened to your arm?" Cricket asks Carrie, using a voice I seldom hear. She's acting, by golly. My daughter has figured out the perfect way to deal with this emergency—act like everything's completely normal so Carrie will feel more comfortable opening up. Less scrutinized. Well played, I blink across to Cricket. Good girl.

"Oh my word, Cricket, do you wait until you have food in your mouth to talk? Because that's sure what it seems like," I say, clearing my throat to let her know it's mock reproach. "Carrie, don't mind my daughter here with her *lumberjack manners.* Please wait to talk until you've finished your bite, young lady. Evidently I've raised a wolf."

Then I see the marks on Carrie's arm Cricket is asking about.

"Oh, my goodness." Without thinking, I reach out to feel the marks but she flinches and pulls at her sleeve to try to cover them so I take my hand back. "What happened there, honey?"

On the underside of her forearm are a number of scars, all perfect circles but not in any particular design or formation. I have a sickening thought: they're the size and shape of cigarette burns.

"Nothing," she says, still tugging at her sleeve. She stands up, clutching to her chest the plastic grocery sack filled with stolen food. I've scared her off. "Well, I better go now. Thank you so much for the French fries. That was real nice of y'all."

"Oh, honey, wait just a second," I hurry to say. *Casual. Stay casual,* I tell myself. "I mean, why don't you keep us company a little while longer and I can take you home. I can drop you wherever you need to go. How about that?"

I can tell she's reluctant to leave Cricket and the French fries— but I also see she's on more of a hair trigger than I realized.

"I'm sure Cricket would love to talk with you some more, wouldn't you, honey?"

The fake cough I threw in at the end may have been over the top but there is no way I am letting this child slip through my fingers. It's like God has sent Caroline back to us in another form, and I simply won't blow this chance to spend time with her.

"Yeah, stay," Cricket says to Carrie. Casual comes easy to her. She throws in a shrug for good measure, and Carrie tentatively lowers herself back into the chair. "So how old are you?"

"Nine," Carrie says.

"You're *nine years old*?"

She looks seven. Then again, a seven-year-old wouldn't be at Wendy's all by herself, so that couldn't have been right. Well, a nine-year-old alone at Wendy's isn't much better. This is getting worse by the minute.

"Do y'all live nearby, Carrie?" I ask.

"Um, well," she says, "kind of. I mean, we're new. Here in Hartsville, I mean. So we're just, um, staying up the road, at the . . ."

"Don't worry, it's not a quiz," Cricket says to her. "My mom likes to ask a lot of questions so it feels like it sometimes, *doesn't it, Mother?*"

"Well, excuse me," I say, relishing our little act, Cricket's and mine, even as my worry escalates. "But I'd like to get to the bottom of this, thank you very much. Carrie, where are your people from—I can't place the accent."

"Hendersonville? In the mountains?" Her voice is soft, her accent thick. "It's a real small place. I never even saw a traffic light before we came here. We never had one in Hendersonville. Or in Toast. That's where I was born—Toast, North Carolina. My daddy— I mean, um, we had to move to Hendersonville, but then we had to leave and . . . here we are."

"Who's *we*?" Cricket asks. Thank goodness for Cricket.

"Um, *we*? Um." Carrie seems to struggle with an answer. "*We* is me and my momma. It's just her and me. Just the two of us. No sister or anything."

"Where's your mom right now?" Cricket asks.

"Um, I don't know." Carrie looks increasingly uncomfortable with the questions but answers them because Cricket's doing the asking. "She's job interviewing somewhere she took a bus to get to. I like your shirt."

Cricket and I both look at Cricket's shirt, a V-neck T-shirt from Abercrombie. Nothing special about it at all except that it's on Cricket. From the look of it, Cricket could be wearing a burka and little Carrie would fawn over it.

"Thanks," Cricket says. "I see you like flip-flops like me—I wear them all summer till they're so paper-thin it's pretty much like being barefoot."

"She's not kidding," I say. "They are vile by Labor Day—I think even the trash men wish they could steer clear of them."

"Ha ha, very funny," Cricket says. She pops the last bite of her sandwich into her mouth and slurps the dregs of her Coke.

"Oh my," I say, looking at my watch, "we've got to get going. Listen, Carrie? Honey, I noticed you didn't get a whole lot to eat, so let's get you something to have on the road—I'm giving you a ride. What'll it be?"

Maybe she's developmentally challenged. She waits a little too long before responding. Cricket must sense it too, because she gives it a try:

"Do you like hamburgers or chicken sandwiches?"

"Um, oh, either one is more than fine, thank you," she says, barely tearing her attention from Cricket. "I might could pay y'all back later, but I don't have any money right now."

"Oh, don't be silly, it's on me," I tell her. Poor thing.

By the time I come back with a hamburger sacked up, they have become thick as thieves, Cricket and Carrie. Cricket and Caroline—Lord, give me strength. Just thinking about those two names coupled together gives me a start.

"Now girls, how about we keep this conversation going in the car?" *Casual. Stay casual.* "I've got about a million things I need to get done."

They're not hearing a word I'm saying, which is just as well.

"Let's move it, girls."

"Back home? In the mountains? Up there we stay barefoot from June to September." Carrie is chattering away to Cricket and squeezing in close to fit through the doorway, reluctant to part ways even for a moment of single-file exiting. "By the time the cold comes our feet are so hard with them callousness or whatever they're called, they're tougher than any shoe you could put on. Plus, it's better being out of flip-flops if you want to balance on something. Like a fence. Or if you want to bounce on the moss floors in the holler. It's cool in the holler, even on the hottest days."

"I like the way you talk," Cricket says. "The words sound better coming from you than from any of us. What else? Say what else it's like."

"The doors are unlocked, girls, come on," I say. "Hop in."

Carrie pauses and peers into the minivan before stepping up onto the running board and into the backseat, as if she's looking for signs of stranger danger.

"You're right to be careful, Carrie honey," I tell her. "Your mother and daddy taught you right. I promise you, though, it's okay to come in with us."

"Ma'am?" she says, climbing into the back. "Oh, no. It's just that I never saw a car like this before. Those doors open like that? On their own and all? How'd they do that?"

"Ugh, it's such a mess back there. Cricket, throw that empty box into the way-back, honey, will you? It's a button I push here on my key chain, Carrie, see? They open and close, depending on which button I push. Now buckle up back there. Cricket, help Carrie with her seat belt, will you? It's okay, Carrie, she's just strapping you in. Great. Okay, girls, we're off!"

I turn the radio on loud enough to where it won't seem like I'm eavesdropping but low enough so I can. Cricket asks her what she usually does in the summer, and I roll my eyes—I swear that daughter of mine has got to stop finding ways to complain about summer school.

"I don't know. There's always something to do in the mountains in summertime. We were sure-footed about ever-where we went. Up on the log fence, like I said, the fence that marked where our land stopped and Mr. Wilson's started. He was our neighbor, Mr. Wilson. We probably spent more time on his side anyway, what with him learning us to shoot and whatnot. He had a three-legged dog named Brownie. He even made it a wooden peg leg."

Shooting guns, running around barefoot, log fences—it's right out of central casting for hillbillies. I know the general area she's talking about and no one, I mean *no one*, has more than two dimes to rub together up there.

"You're *so lucky*," Cricket says, interrupting. "Summer here sucks."

"Cricket Chaplin Ford, we don't use that word—you know better than that." I catch her eye in the rearview mirror.

"What! It's *so* not a cussword, but whatever. My mom's like *obsessed* with not using words that even remotely sound like cusswords. Anyway, it's *so* boring here in the summer. Time dies a little more every afternoon and it gets so hot it's like the whole city's holding its breath till the sun goes down. It's *suffocating*. Seriously. I might even die from the heat."

"That's a little dramatic, don't you think?" I say. "Oh my. Carrie, honey, you might want to slow down a little—maybe try chewing a little more in between bites—oh, well look at that. You're finished. I guess I've never seen someone eat a hamburger so quick."

"There's this one girl?" Cricket is telling Carrie, "I think she's on the track team or something. Anyway, she *almost died* from the heat—everyone knows it, Mom, what? It's true! The coach made her do like twenty million push-ups and she started crying and he still made her do them. She was in the hospital and everything. Wait, how'd the dog lose its leg? That three-legged dog you just mentioned. What's its name again? Blackie? I want a dog so bad but—"

"Me too!" Carrie says, becoming quite animated. "I want one too! I keep telling Momma I'll take care of it but she says no way."

"So does my mom. I want one of those little weensy dogs."

"That's the kind I want too! You could carry it around with you all day like a baby, and dress it up in cute little doll outfits."

"Exactly!" Cricket's saying. Both girls are excited to bursting. "Wait, did you ever watch that show—what's the name of it? *Sister Love* or something? You know what show I'm talking about—what's it called . . ."

"Our TV broke and then we didn't have one so . . ." Carrie

trails off, then says, "Um, ma'am? Mrs. Ford? Um, how do you get the window to go down?"

"Not *Sister Sister,*" Cricket's saying, "but kinda like that. Wait, *you didn't have a TV*?"

"Oh, I know. It's so hot out, isn't it?" I say. "The air-conditioning will cool you off in two seconds, I promise. If we put the windows down it'll never get cool in here. You okay back there?"

"Um, I don't feel so good," Carrie says. She's got her forehead against the window glass.

"Oh boy," I say, holding back the curse I want to yell at the driver behind me laying on his horn. "Okay, honey, I'm pulling over, just hang on now," I say. It's trickier than I thought, moving from the far left lane to the shoulder on this stretch of road.

"Mom, Carrie didn't have a TV! I'd kill myself. Seriously. I'd totally kill myself if I didn't have a TV."

"Can the window go down?" Carrie asks. Her voice is drained now, her skin the color of Kleenex.

"Wait, why are we stopping?" Cricket finally catches on.

"Carrie, honey, it's okay, let me just . . . pull . . . a . . . little . . . more . . . onto . . . the . . . shoulder . . ."

Too late. She throws up on the floor mat.

"Aw, *rank*!" Cricket says, waving away the smell. "Sorry, Carrie, but it smells so bad. Mom—open the windows! The safety lock's on the windows, I can't open—"

"I'm so sorry," Carrie is saying, still bent in half, her voice muffled, "I'm so sorry, I'm so sorry—I'm so sorry I didn't mean to do it in the car, I tried to . . ."

"Oh-Em-Gee, your hamburger came out almost whole!" Cricket says, her voice nasal because she's pinching her nose shut against the admittedly horrible smell.

"All right, all right, everybody calm down . . . The windows are unlocked now."

"I'm really really sorry," Carrie says. Cricket reaches across to put Carrie's window down for her.

"Honey, Carrie, honey, it's okay, sweetheart. Of course you didn't mean to. It happens to everyone from time to time," I say. "Cricket, hand me those napkins or paper towels or whatever's there in the pocket on the back of the seat. Stay in the car, both of you. I'm coming around to your side, Carrie."

I do the best I can, getting as much vomit scooped out as possible. Just good enough for us to make it home, where I can clean it up right. There's no way I can just drop this child off to an empty home, feeling sick the way she is. I probably should call Eddie. Or maybe I should've called 9-1-1. But what good would that have really done? And now if I call they'll wonder why I didn't call right away so it'll make it look like I'm trying to kidnap her. With my track record, that's exactly what they'll think. I don't even know what her home situation truly is—I just know what she's told me, and that's not much. Mother will know what to do. I'll just bring her in, clean her up, then Mother and I will figure out who to call. First, though, I'll swing by their place and double-check to see what the deal is.

"Okay, girls. We're good to go," I say, sliding back behind the wheel.

After a few minutes blasting the AC with the windows open for a good airing out (sorry, environment!), the smell doesn't seem so bad and the girls are chatting away as if nothing happened.

"Carrie? Honey, where'd you say y'all live?"

"Um, the Loveless Hotel and Motor Lodge?" she says. These kids have the habit of talking in "upspeak" so even statements sound like questions.

"That pink place up the road on the right?" I ask her. Please, dear Lord in Heaven, don't let her be staying there.

"Yes, ma'am," she says.

She turns back to Cricket and whatever tangent Cricket's off on.

". . . and I change things in my mind," Carrie is saying, "and after a spell I cain't tell the difference between what happened and what I only *wished* had happened."

"Oh-Em-Gee, me too!" Cricket says. She lowers her voice and I have to strain over Pure Prairie League's "Amie" so I can hear. "Like when I got blood drawn for my sister? Don't go telling anybody I said this but I imagined the nurses in back saying stuff like 'I've never seen blood so rich and strong—whose blood is this?' and someone else will go 'Why, it's Cricket Ford's,' and the first one will be all, 'I should've known: that girl does everything perfectly. What a lovely child,' then the other one will go, 'I wish my daughter could be more like her. She's a credit to her family,' and the first one will say, 'She's a credit to the whole city, having blood so strong and healthy.'

"You know, stuff like that," Cricket says. "Wait, I think my mom's listening. Mom? Can you hear me when I talk at this level?"

Of course I pretend not to hear. Who wouldn't?

"Oh, phew," Cricket says. "I totally thought she was eavesdropping. . . . Wait, you know how to shoot? Like, a *gun*? I wish I knew how to shoot. My daddy's a police officer and he's got a gun on him like twenty-four-seven and *still* he won't let me learn it's so ridiculous whatever I don't even care . . ."

"Okeydokey, girls," I say, putting the car in park outside the dumpy registration office at the Loveless a few minutes later.

"Wait, Mom? Can't Carrie just come over for a little bit? If her mom says she can I mean? Please?"

I would have thought Carrie would've been the one to beg to stay, but Cricket looks to be on the verge of tears.

"Please, Mom?"

With deliberate movements heavy with sadness at having to part but resigned to the fact that she will have to separate from her new BFF, as Cricket would say, Carrie climbs out.

"Thank you so much for the ride, Mrs. Ford, and I'm sorry I threw up," she says, eyes downcast, toeing the gravel.

"Carrie, we're totally gonna hang out soon." Cricket is frantic to unclick her seat belt. I've never seen her this determined to hold on to someone but then we've never been faced with a mirror image of my dead daughter. "You should come over and see my grandma's house where we're living now. It's so freaky. Mom, please can't she come over, like, *now*? Why do we have to leave her?"

"All right, simmer down," I say.

I want to tell them that I don't want Carrie out of my sight any more than Cricket does, but I think it might freak Cricket out more to see me just as googly-eyed as she is over this spectacular find.

"Carrie, honey, how about we try to find your mom to see if you can come over to our house for a bit? I can call her cell. What's her phone number?"

The smile across this little child's face is so big you'd never believe her face was glum only seconds before.

"Oh, no, ma'am, no need to call," she says, putting her tiny self between me and the front office. "Like I said, Momma's looking for a job? She'll not be back for a long time. I can come over, it's okay. She'd say it's okay, I mean. She's always telling me to go out and make friends and whatnot. It's fine."

"Well, let me just pop into the office here and get the lay of the land," I say. "Why don't you wait in the car with Cricket?"

"Yay! Come on!" Cricket pats the empty seat next to her.

The smell of air freshener hits like a punch in the gut before I'm even half in the door to the office. When someone's got that much fake smell, you've got to wonder what they're trying to cover up. I learned that on *Law & Order*. Detectives notice things like that when they're looking for dead bodies. I've always thought I'd make a good detective. Not that I'd ever say that to Eddie, who's been trying to make detective ever since he joined the force. Unfortunately for him, Hartsville isn't exactly a hotbed of criminal activity. Detective openings are few and far between.

"Hel-lo?" I call out in a singsong voice. "Anybody here?"

I hear a newspaper rustling, the groan of someone reluctant to get up off a couch, footsteps, then a door opens from the manager's living quarters. I am face-to-face with a strange-looking man so rail thin you could break him in half with a flick of your fingers. He is so emaciated his eyelids don't seem to be able to cover enough of his eyeballs, leaving him looking bewildered or scared.

"Hi, there. I'm a . . . I'm a friend of Caroline . . . oh, dear, it appears I can't recall her last name. Carrie? A little girl from out of town," I say. "I'm sure you know who I mean. She's got dark hair and eyes. Real thin. Nine years old. Anyway, I just stopped by to ask, well, I guess I'm here because I'm wondering about her mother."

"I know who you're talking about. That's Carrie Parker. She all right? What about her mother?" He squints at me and chews on a toothpick sticking out of the corner of his mouth. "She in trouble? I knew the minute I laid eyes on her, that woman spells trouble. Like that Travis Tritt song—you know the one?"

"Carrie's fine," I say.

He looks relieved, then starts humming and bobbing his head to music playing in his head.

"You know the song," he says.

"No, can't say I'm familiar with that one," I say. "But why do you say that about the mother?"

"He spells it out. Travis Tritt does. You know. Like T-R-O-U-B-L-E," he says. He looks at me hoping to see recognition, but I keep shaking my head, and finally he shrugs and with his tongue moves the toothpick to the other corner of his mouth. "You'd know it if you heard it," he sighs.

"You were saying? About Carrie and her mother?"

"Can't put my finger on it," he says, "I just knew I'd be hearing something bad about them at some point. She came in here not long ago looking like the losing end of a prizefight. Bruised all up and down, dried blood in places. I told her I didn't want any trouble. I said those exact words as a matter of fact. *I don't want any trouble here, lady,* I said. The way she looked I just knew there'd be an angry husband on her tail. That what happened? Her husband finally catch up with her?"

"No, I don't think so," I say. "I mean, I think she's fine. Do you see much of her? Do you know where I can find her? Her daughter says she's looking for work."

"I see her nearly ever-day," he says, "going off to do who knows what. I ain't no parole officer or babysitter—I got no idea where she hies off to. But I tell you what, she's got an attitude, that one. Ever-day she's walking out to the bus, her purse real high on her shoulder like she's sure someone's gonna mug her. Constantly looking over her shoulder. I guess you get mixed up with bad folks you pretty much assume they're always gonna be with you. That's her manner, see? When she's sober, I mean. Not that she's sober much. Boy, that one can drink. She's got that little girl a'hers run ragged between here and the package store. And that's not counting the bottle she brown-bags home at the end of the day, pulling on it like she's dying of thirst in the desert. Meantime, that kid . . ."

"Carrie?"

"Yeah, that's her name," he says, giving it thought then shaking his head. "My wife's after me about that little girl day and night."

"Why?"

"Oh, who knows," he says, waving off his wife's invisible words. "She winds herself up about lawsuits and liabilities and whatnot. I tell her look, if the girl gets hurt climbing in and out of dumpsters and sneaking over fences to the empty pool and all, well, it's their word against ours and ain't no judge in the land gonna believe hillbillies over good upstanding business persons such as ourselves. No sense making trouble where there ain't none."

"I'm afraid I don't understand," I say. "She climbs in and out of *dumpsters*?"

"You don't understand because you've probably never gone hungry," he says. "I seen all kinds of things here, believe you me. All kinds of things. And what I learned is folks'll do just about anything to feed themselves. The Parkers ain't no different—well, except that kid's a sweetheart. She's real careful and polite. Plus, she's clever beyond her years. She finds some pretty funny ways to put food in her belly, that one does. Reminds me of myself when I was little, if you want to know the truth. That's why I tell my wife to lay off her. Let her be. All she's trying to do is keep her hunger at bay, and let's face it, her momma ain't exactly doing much on that front."

He tips an invisible bottle to his lips and winks at what he doesn't need to say.

"When does Mrs. Parker usually come back?" I ask.

"Last I checked I don't have eyes in the back of my head," he says, "but best as I can tell she ain't never back before dark. Not that I ever seen. You ask a lotta questions—you a cop? I don't care one way or the other, mind you, but the missus'll have a fit she hears the police been asking around about them two."

"I'm not a cop," I say. "I do appreciate your time, Mr. . . . ?"

"Burdock," he says, stretching his face into a painful but genuine-looking smile. "Hap Burdock."

"I appreciate you taking the time to talk, Mr. Burdock."

"It's Hap," he says, tipping his head, "and it's my pleasure to make your acquaintance."

See, now there's another example of me jumping to conclusions and judging harshly. It's not his fault he's got no meat on his bones. He seems like a real nice man. I've got to work on that. The world doesn't need another conclusion jumper, that's for sure.

"You're a good man, Mr. Burdock. I mean, Hap. I can tell," I say, figuring I'll make him an ally whether he likes it or not. If he feels invested in Carrie, he'll watch out over her. "I guess I don't need to tell you I'm worried about that little girl, and maybe I'm off on this but you seem to be concerned as well—no no, don't worry, your secret's safe with me, ha ha! You men—always so careful not to let on you're all softies underneath. But I want you to know I really appreciate you looking out for that child. You shake your head like you don't know what I'm talking about, but we both know you do. Anyway, I better get going. I just want to thank you for watching over her."

"Whoa, Nellie! I'll tell you what I told them," he says, holding up his hand to stop me from talking. "I ain't no babysitter. I don't want to get involved with any of that. I'm just telling you what I know, is all. Hey, I got it! It's been eating at me the whole time you're standing in front of me. I'm thinking, gee, she sure looks familiar but I can't put my finger on where I know you from . . ."

"I've got to skedaddle," I say, backing toward the door. "I'm glad to meet you, Hap."

"I seen you in the papers," he says, pointing a eureka finger in the air. "That's it! You're the one who was in all them papers a while back . . ."

I ignore it like I do all the other times.

"Bye, nice talking with you!"

I'm careful to use my knuckles to push the glass door open—it's so grimy there's no telling what kinds of germs are plastered all over the metal bar. I use the palms of my hands, I get those germs on the steering wheel. Whoops! There I go again. Judging.

This door might be cleaner than my whole minivan, for all I know.

"I ain't no babysitter!" I hear him calling after me. I know he's just saving face, so I don't pay it any mind. If he didn't give a hoot, he wouldn't know all their comings and goings like he does.

"Okay, girls, we're homeward bound," I say, closing the car door behind me.

"Yay!" they say in unison. Carrie is aping everything Cricket says and does.

Before putting the car in drive, I turn back to Carrie. "You sure you're fine coming over for a little bit, Carrie honey? You feeling a little better now?"

"Yes, ma'am, thank you so much," she says. Her eyes are real wide, like getting to come to our house is winning the lottery.

"Well, all right then. You need to buckle your seat belt back up and we're off."

"What's with everybody telling everybody what they *need* to do," I hear Cricket say to Carrie once we get under way. "Like *what you need to do is get a needle to get that splinter out* . . ."

Carrie laughs as Cricket assumes different voices:

"What you need to do is take your second left," she says, her voice as man-deep as she can make it.

"I'll tell you what you need," she says, now in a high-pitched voice, *"you need to read up on the French Revolution if you think you're going to pass that test next week."*

More laughter from Carrie. I can't remember the last time Cricket's held court like this. Then Carrie chimes in:

"Or, wait wait, I got one! *What you need is a good slap—that'll wake you up!*"

The only one laughing now is Carrie.

"What in the . . ." I see it clear as I'm pulling into the drive-way.

"What's that thing on the front door of Grandma's house, Mom? Why's there yellow tape up?"

Cricket bounds out of the car and up the front steps and is reading it aloud before I even have the keys out of the ignition.

"Slow down, Cricket, and wait for your guest! Sorry, Carrie, she's fast like this all the time. Oh, don't worry—I'll clean that up honey, just leave it. You just go on in with Cricket."

"Hey, Mom?" Cricket calls out, "what's *foreclosure* mean?"

CHAPTER TEN

Carrie

My head's a windshield wiper going back and forth on the drive
from Wendy's, listening to Cricket, who is the coolest and best
human being on the whole entire planet, and looking out at the
mansions we're passing. I sure do wish Emma was here so she
could see me going through neighborhoods like these. Momma
wouldn't like it much, but I bet her head'd be going left and right
too just like mine. You don't have to like what you see to want to
see it. Most places have bushes cut in squares outlining the yards
that are more like green carpets. The driveways are clean and
smooth blacktop, with mailboxes neatly setting at the end, their
family names in block lettering and what number the house is.
We passed one mailbox in the shape of a mallard duck, another
had a picture of two black dogs laying nestled into each other, and
a third showed a horse jumping over a fence. I cain't imagine what
the houses look like inside if they take so much care for the mail-
man.

The grass here is like the Emerald City when Dorothy sees it across the fields of flowers. At the Loveless there's a dried-up ring of spiky grass circling the old empty pool set behind the rusty chain-link fence that comes up to about my armpits. When no one's around I climb over it and the dead grass crunches hard underfoot. I have to wear flip-flops doing it because it's so parched it hurts to set my bare feet on it. At first I was sad the pool had no water but I've come to like laying on the bottom of it. I pick at the chipping paint with my fingernail, stopping only when a shard cuts under the quick. There's dead leaves, some empty cola cans that've been there so long they're rusty, and tangled up in a dirty old plastic grocery sack was a lady's brassiere, but I cleared a lot of it to the side so I could lay on my back and pretend I'm on a raft floating in the blue Bermuda sea. Lately though I been having nightmares of being down there, laying on the pool floor staring up at the clouds when someone turns on the water. I dream that they don't see me and the pool's filling up fast and I holler to shut it off but they cain't hear over the rush of the spigot and then I'm splashing around like crazy trying to keep my head over the waterline and . . . then I wake up. I tell myself I'm not going to go down there anymore but stupid me, I forget about the nightmares until I swing my second leg over and let myself fall onto the spiky grass, then it's too late and anyway I figure sooner or later my brain'll get tired of having the same old stupid dream.

It's like someone made a law against burnt-up spiky grass in Cricket's neighborhood. Here they got flower beds along front walks. They got garages connected to their houses and right two houses before Cricket's, I see a garage door open like magic and a car roll out all quiet, down the driveway out into a life that's probably got magic all through it. I cain't help but notice, as nice as these yards are, not one person's out in them. Not a one. They go to all that trouble making it nice and soft underfoot, planting and mowing and picking up after they-selves, and I don't see a single solitary person out enjoying what they worked so hard to make pretty. One place has a slope that would be perfect to roll down.

Cricket undoes her seat belt before we come to a stop, and that's how I know we've reached their house. Here's the God's honest truth: I ain't never seen a place like where Cricket lives. Not in real life at least. In picture books there are places with picket fences and new-looking front porches with rocking chairs and fern plants and hanging baskets of pretty flowers but I never seen them in person. But then I never knew folks like Cricket and Mrs. Ford, so I guess it figures.

Mrs. Ford says, "What in the . . . ," and Cricket runs to the front door and Mrs. Ford fusses but I cain't hear any of it on account of me being about to go inside the biggest house I ever been in before. The front steps don't even creak. They're swept clean. The porch wraps around the entire house like a moat around a castle. There's a metal sign next to the door that says WELCOME, VAGABONDS with a man's fancy top hat and cane spelling out some of the letters. The front door is thick heavy wood. When it closes you feel safe and sound.

The first thing I see is all the dolls. It's a doll museum maybe, is what I'm thinking. Dolls, dolls, dolls. There must be thousands of them, lined up in perfect rows on perfect shelves. And on the fireplace mantel. Ever-where you look, more dolls in all sizes. I never even seen a *store* with as many dolls in my whole life much less someone's real-life home. There's no sign saying NO TOUCH-ING like the one hanging by the fabric at Zebulon's, but the way these dolls are set out you just *know* not to touch them. And this is a home not a store for goodness' sake. I feel bad thinking it—them being so kind and all—but it don't feel much like a home in this front room. There's doilies on every chair back, even on the couch, like they're readying for company, but it smells like an attic and the pillows aren't dented so I'm thinking this is a room no one visits. Here's another incredible thing about it: the dolls are *boy* dolls, all dressed the same, all in black suits head to toe. With round hats—black. And canes. Some of the boy dolls hold canes up and down, proper, some swing them off to the side like to show they're happy. All of them have little bitty black mustaches. They're all kinds of sizes.

"What is this place?" I ask out loud without knowing who is there to hear me. There's something about the way the dolls are staring that keeps my eyes trained on them. One, in particular. He's bigger than the rest, about halfway up to my head if I stood by him I bet, and his doll eyes twinkle and follow me if I move. I try going left, they watch me. Right, the same. I tiptoe closer to him and wave my hand in front of his face in case it's a trick.

"So freaky, right?" Cricket says.

I jump at her voice—I hadn't heard her come up behind me.

"What *are* these?" I say. I whisper because I feel like I shouldn't be talking about the dolls in front of them. "What is this place?"

Cricket pulls at me and rolls her eyes. "It's kinda embarrassing. It must seem weird, I mean. Come on, let's go upstairs. I'll show you my room."

"Wait, what *are* these though?"

"It's my great-great-uncle," she says, shrugging. "He was a big movie star before they had sound in movies. When movies were black and white. Charlie Chaplin is his name. It's okay you haven't heard of him. He's been dead forever."

She says the name Charlie Chaplin in a grown-up accent like a butler in a movie, and makes a mustache with her finger under her nose, and waddles from side to side like a penguin.

"This is how he walked," she says, laughing. "My grandma's, like, obsessed with him. Everyone is. It's freakish. Before my grandma had a hard time getting around, she used to have tour groups come in to see all the stuff. Grandma had a lot more out than she does now believe it or not. I bet she's in the *Guinness Book of World Records* even. He was super-duper famous. Actually, he kinda walked like this," she says, splaying her knees out in a duckwalk, "and he always got in weird situations. Ugh, I don't know. My grandma will tell you all about him, trust me. Hey, come upstairs! Mom, we'll be up in my room!"

She takes the stairs two at a time and I hear Mrs. Ford hollering at her from another room to slow down. At the foot of the stairs in the hallway is a glass case with sparkly crystal glasses and silver plates and lots of expensive stuff in shapes I hardly know and all of it jingles when Cricket bounds by.

Each side of the stairs has old-timey pictures of the real-life man the dolls were made after. *Charlie Chaplin* doing all sorts of activities surrounded by all sorts of fancy people smiling at the camera. There's even pictures of people taking pictures of him. There he is without his hat on a horse. Here he is with rich ladies and nice-dressed men standing in front of old-timey cars. I wonder how other people say his name—I only hear Cricket with that accent making the name take longer to say. *Chah-lie Chap-lunn.* In the middle of the way upstairs is a movie poster for *The Kid*—they must've used that to model all the toys. Who is Charlie Chaplin? We ain't never heard of him where we came from. Momma would surely have mentioned a man who has posters and fans and dolls made after him.

"Carrie? You coming?" Cricket calls for me from down a dark hall. I follow the sound to a door with cutout words made into signs stuck to the outside: STAY AWAY and KNOCK BEFORE ENTERING and CRICKET'S CRIB tacked up alongside a poster-size butterfly in rainbow colors.

"Hey," I say, pushing the door open to a room full of pillows and stuffed animals enough for every kid in my school to have one and then some left over. It feels like I walked straight into a circus, what with so many *things* laying ever-where. I have to step over a stack of books to get to the middle of the room that's even got a window seat.

"Wow," I say.

"It's a total disaster zone," Cricket says. "My mom's going to kill me if I don't clean it up tonight. Ugh!"

I'm so busy noticing all the brightly colored clothes crammed into her closet I don't realize I'm saying out loud what I'm thinking inside until I hear my own voice say, "Y'all are *rich*."

"No, we're not," she says.

"Are too."

"I'm not usually this messy," Cricket says. She kicks some clothes into a pile in the corner then falls back onto her bed and puts her hands behind her head, staring up like she's counting clouds. "Hey, check it out: I put these up a couple of nights ago."

I lay down on her soft bed, careful to keep my grimy feet off her bedspread, which smells so clean and pretty. Ever-thing's clean in this house. I feel bad, like I'm tracking in the dirt from my life, messing up theirs.

"I like those stars you got on your ceiling," I say.

"Thanks. They glow in the dark. My dad gave them to me for Christmas one year. I had them in my room in my other house and I know it's stupid and all but I thought I wouldn't be able to fall asleep without them overhead so I peeled them off and stuck them up here. Watch."

She turns off the lamp by the side of her bed and crosses the room to untie the curtains so it's nearly nighttime dark.

"Look up," she whispers.

It's the prettiest thing I ever seen inside a home. Her whole room feels like the outdoors, like we're camping and sleeping under the big sky.

"It's nice, right?" she says.

"It's like a magic land," I say. "So pretty. I'd never have a single nightmare if I slept under glow-in-the-dark stars like these. You're so lucky."

The lights come back on and she moves around the room, picking up more clothes and tossing them into a hamper, putting her things in order.

"I love your room," I say. "It's so big! I cain't believe you have it all to yourself. Or, wait, your sister probably shares with you. Duh."

"My sister's, um, oh, never mind. It used to be my uncle's room when he was little. He and my mom grew up in this house. So did my granddaddy and his daddy before him. Lots of Chaplins lived here. Blah blah blah—booor-ring! Let's put on some music. What do you listen to? Here, let me find—I can't find my iPod— wait, did I take it with me today? Uh-oh. If I lost it I'll die a thousand deaths I swear."

I watch her zigzag around, dig through her backpack, open drawers, rifle through the hamper she just filled, looking like a dog digging a hole in the sand the way she flings clothes back out one by one in her search for what I don't know.

"Here it is! That was close. My mom would've totally *killed* me if I ruined another one," she says, moving lickety-split back over to her painted-pink desk. "Okay, what do you wanna hear? I got Gwen Stefani—wait, what about Miley? I bet you like Miley Cyrus, right? I used to love her when I was younger, that's why I still have her on here. No offense, I mean she's fine and all but— Ooooh, here! Maroon 5! Why're you looking like that? Don't even tell me you don't like them. Don't even say it. Everyone loves Maroon 5."

I don't have any earthly idea who she's talking about or what the thing in her hand is that she's looking down at. It's about the size of a box of cigarettes but thinner and it clicks every time she touches it. It's bright pink like just about ever-thing else in her room: the pillows, a blanket, the round rug in front of her bed, and, like I mentioned, her desk.

"What's that?" I ask her.

She looks up from it and glances around to see what I'm asking her about.

"What's what?" she asks.

"That," I say. "That pink thing you got in your hand."

She looks down at it then back up at me like she doesn't understand my question then something blooms on her face, like it just took her a minute to catch up with my words.

"Oh-Em-Gee, you don't know what *this* is?" she asks, holding it up just to make sure she's on the right path. "For *real*? You're kidding, right."

I shake my head no, I'm not kidding.

"It's an *iPod*!" she says. Like now it should make sense.

"What's an eye-pod?"

"Oh-Em-Gee." She keeps spelling out letters that don't make any word I ever knew. "Okay, *this* is an iPod. It's got music on it . . . Here, come sit on the bed and I'll show you. I never met anyone who didn't know about iPods. iTunes lets you store any song in the universe. Here in the music library."

She goes on to explain it ever which way she can and I nod and say, "Oh, yeah, okay I get it," but really I don't get it one bit. Then she goes and plugs it into this box on her desk, hits a button, and music's booming through the room from that one thin little thing she held in her hand just a second ago!

"So who do you like and I bet I have them on here," she yells over the song.

I find myself wishing I spoke her language and then I realize she's speaking English, just not in any kind of sense. She's watching me and I can feel my cheeks get hot. I'm gonna blow it. I want to cry because I know in a few minutes she won't like me anymore and I'll be back where I was in the mountains. No friends. I cain't let that happen again. She don't even know me yet—for all she knows I was the coolest kid in my whole entire school. Think,

Carrie. Think, think . . . say something. Anything, just say anything. What is wrong with me? Oh Lordy.

"You okay?" Cricket says, turning down the music. Her eyebrows tilt up in worry. "You look like you don't feel so good again. Here, I'll show you the bathroom in case you need to hurl again or whatever. Follow me."

I never had someone hold my hand like she is. And she doesn't think it's weird or anything—she took my hand like it's totally normal, and I for some reason, probably because I'm a *half-wit* like Momma says, I want to cry. From being happy! Things are all backwards and upside down in this house.

The bathroom is right next to her room. It's got flowered wallpaper and hundreds of different-size bottles of lotions and potions covering every inch of space beside the sink. Nail polish in every color. And the toilet seat has a sweater on that's the same pink as in her room. The toilet seat!

"There you go," Cricket says, moving aside to let me in. "Sorry you don't feel well. I hate that. You want me to get my mom? No? You sure? She's really good when people are sick. She doesn't mind at all, don't worry."

"It's okay," I tell her. "I'm okay."

"All right," Cricket says. "Just holler if you need me."

She closes the door. There's a pink robe hanging on the back of the door that must be hers because it smells like a rose patch. She is without a doubt my number one favorite human being I ever met in my whole entire life. She's so pretty and nice and her momma's great—even better than Mrs. Bickett, my old best friend Orla Mae's momma, who used to bake us cookies and sometimes even have me to supper. And look at all she has. I touch everthing, undoing the tops of some of the bottles and sniffing—most of it is pretty-smelling but some is like the pure grain alcohol Mr. Wilson took nips of back in Hendersonville. She's got tons of photographs taped up on all sides of the mirror. Her in sports uniforms. Her with a bunch of other kids. Her with her momma and a man I bet is her daddy and a girl—oh Lordy, that must be her sister, Caroline. The one they say looks just like me and you know what? She does. It's like *I'm* in the picture with them. I try to find other pictures of Caroline with Cricket. There's one of the two of them wearing matching dresses in front of a Christmas tree. I trace the outline of them and close my eyes to help bring up the piney smell of the tree. Caroline looks like she's a few inches taller than Cricket, which makes sense on account of her being older. I stand on my tippy-toes to see if maybe that makes us look even more alike. She's skinny, like me. She's smiling in every single picture. Real smiles too. Not the kind where the mouth's turned up in the shape of a smile but the eyes stay cold. Like the one picture I saw from when Momma married Richard. If you look real close you can see that even though the bottom half of Momma's face is in smile-shape the top half is stone-cold. Richard has his arm around Momma and looks like he just heard a funny joke. But Momma has empty eyes. Dead eyes.

Nothing about Cricket is empty. Cricket's the opposite of empty—I never seen someone so full of smiles and words.

"You doing okay in there?" she calls through the door. Her voice gives me such a start I nearly break the perfume bottle I'm smelling.

"I'm fine! I'll be right out!" I call back.

I give the toilet a flush to make like I used it and I wash my hands because Mrs. Bickett said to always wash up after *relieving yourself.* That's what she called going number one: *relieving yourself.* Oh my goodness, even Cricket's soap smells pink.

"Hey," I say, coming back into her room. She's at her desk bent over something.

"Hey. You all right?" she asks me.

I never seen someone wait for an answer to that question, looking like they really wonder after your health and all.

"Yeah," I say. "Sorry. Hey, I like all them pictures you got up of your family. Is that your sister and you? In front of the Christmas tree?"

"What? Oh. The one of us in matching nighties? Yeah. That's us about six years ago. Before she got sick the last time."

"Those are nightgowns? Wow," I say. "I thought they were dresses they're so fancy. Wait, your sister—she's sick?"

"What's that?"

"Where is your sister? Y'all don't hang out together I guess," I say. Dumb. Dumb dumb dumb. It's just that I cain't think what else to say to keep her talking about Caroline, the girl that looks exactly like me. There's a family picture in a frame by Cricket's bed and I pick it up to see it closer.

"My sister died," Cricket says. "Three years ago today."

No wonder they were staring at me like I was a ghost.

"Oh" is all I can think of to say. Another dumb comment from me. "Hey, what's that?"

"It's my laptop, what do you think?" She smiles and turns back to it, her fingers pecking at the machine. "Don't even tell me you never saw a laptop before or I'll die of, like, shock or something."

"This is the nicest place I ever been in, your house," I say. "Where I come from this is better than the White House even. The *president* could live here and not even know the difference. You're so lucky y'all are rich."

"Nuh-uh, we're not," she says. "If we were rich we wouldn't be living here at my grandma's."

"Look at all the stuffed animals you got," I say, picking up this real cute teddy bear holding a heart that reads "Get Well Soon."

"Oh, yeah, well, some of those are my sister's from all the hospital times," she says, glancing over her shoulder at them for a split second then turning back.

"Um, wait, let me just close this window," she says. "Okay, sorry."

"You're lucky you had a sister. I mean, for so many years. I dream of having a sister," I say. It's not a full-on lie since I *do* dream about Emma all the time. "So how'd she—? I mean, what happened with your sister?"

"My grandma says it's because God didn't finish making her," Cricket says, shrugging while she twirls her chair to face me. "She had this rare kind of cancer. A form of leukemia, which Grandma says is because she came out before He was done making final touches on her. So the doctors had to go in and try to finish the job. *God withdrew His hand too soon,* she says. It's so funny, the way she says it. She's great, my grandma. You'll meet her in a sec. She's right downstairs. This is her house. Wait, duh, I just told you that. Anyway, she says Caroline had to go back to her Maker and that someday we'll see her again. And then you show up."

I take care moving around Cricket's backpack that's wide open, books spilling out . . . Wait! Lookee here!

"You've got the *Encyclopaedia Britannica*? I *love* the *Encyclopaedia Britannica*. You think I could borrow it sometime?"

"What? Oh, no way. I love the encyclopedia too! It's, like, the best set of books *ever.* My dad got me and Caroline started on it when we were little. He said the Internet knows some stuff but you can't trust it and anyway the *Encyclopaedia Britannica* knows it all. He's such a dork, my dad is. But kinda in a good way, you know? Anyway, he used to read to us from it. Just weird stuff. Then, when Caroline, um, well— I just decided I'd keep doing it. Looking up and memorizing all the things I can so I can tell her all about it when I see her again. That's from the library, though. It's not, like, *mine* or something. And it's just the *L,* which I was *going* to take back today to trade for the *M* but my mom said we *couldn't* which is *ridiculous* because we *totally* could have, it doesn't take but a second but whatever. Hey, come here, I've gotta show you something."

She's a whirligig, twirling around in her chair, waving me over, hunching back over her *laptop.*

I bring the *L* with me. I love the thin pages. And the smell of it. It opens to "Lilacs," which are some of my favorite flowers ever. It's a sign we're supposed to be true-blue friends forever and ever, me and Cricket.

"Hey, don't tell my mother I just said that about Caroline and the books," she says. "I don't think she remembers that today is the anniversary, and I don't want to make her sad by reminding her. Okay, so, you've got to see this new music video. I wanted it to download all the way before you saw it. Wait, so you never told me what music you like. Did you say you like Miley Cyrus?"

Then she's curling her legs under her and calling out more names of singers.

"Okay, let's do it this way," she says, slowing down like her speed's what's the problem. "What's on your iPod? Er, I mean, um, your CD player? Where do you get your music? Wait, I've *got* to show you this YouTube video—have you seen that surprised kitten one? Where the guy holds up his hands like it's a stickup and the kitten does the same thing? The kitten, like, *copies* him."

I thank the Lord Jesus she's busy fiddling around with the letter keys, pictures popping up as fast as she names them, so she cain't see that I have no earthly idea what she's talking about. On the far side of Cricket's bed, which is high as Princess and the Pea, is a second nightstand chock-full of more nail polish in shades of pink and purple, a clock that's the shape of Snoopy from the funny papers, and a beat-up book. I cain't hardly take it all in.

And then I see it, which is funny because I think my eyes are closed when it lights up. It happens real fast, same as the other times. Like a flash. Or when lightning hits and you can see everthing for a split second before it goes dark. In my head I see a book with real thin pages and a lady-hand holding a match to the edge of them. Before it goes dark the flash picture shows the lady-hand tossing the book into the fireplace where it lands on top of already burning logs, the cover about to go up in flames. I squeeze my eyes closed tight to make sure and yup, yessir, there it is, plain as day written on the cover: *The Bible.*

"Earth to Carrie," Cricket's saying. "What happened? You feeling sick again?"

"What? Oh, sorry," I say. "What'd you say?"

"You okay?"

"Yeah," I say. I'm not gonna tell her what I just saw or what I've seen before. Heck, *I* don't even know what I just saw. Why would a lady burn the Bible? Lord, please don't let me turn crazy having these visions all the time. Please?

"Okay, it finally loaded," Cricket says, pulling me close to her side. "Scootch in so you can see better. Check it out."

I cain't believe she's being so nice to me. She smells like bubble gum and lemonade. When she's thinking on something she twitches her nose to the right and left, you have to watch real close for it. But what if she's just being nice because that's what her momma taught her to be? And because I look like her dead sister. Maybe she'll want to be around me for that but then when she sees I'm not as great as her sister was she'll get tired of me. She's just being polite is all. Oh Lord, please don't let good manners be the reason she's being nice to me.

But maybe it's not that at all. She does really and truly seem like she's glad I came over. Maybe she really does like me—after all, she don't know anything about me. She'll just know what I tell her. So from here on out I was the most popular kid in school back home. Who's to say different? She'd never find out the truth. Just look at her. She flicks her hair back like she's a model, not even knowing she does it. I wish my hair fell over back behind my shoulders like hers does. Mine's shorter but I'm gonna grow it long like Cricket's. I was going to anyway. I'll get the rat's nests out and I'll brush it lots before bed so it'll get silky like hers. People might come to think of us as sisters. *Cricket Ford went and found herself another sister,* they'll say. I can show her some of the fun stuff me and Emma used to do. Emma. I haven't thought of her this whole entire day practically! Usually by now I'd have turned her name over in my head at least a hundred times. Emma, if the ghost of you is floatin' around, reading my thoughts, don't be mad, okay? I promise I won't ever stop thinking about you. I'll show Cricket how to do that log-fence-balance thing we used to love. I'll teach her how to play marbles and jacks. Someday I might could take her to see our creek back home. I'll show her your favorite rock, but don't worry I won't let her set on it because it's yours. So if you're reading my mind right now or if some other ghost is telling you about what I'm thinking, remember that I love you best of all. Cricket comes in second, I swear. You'd love her just like I do. She's busy looking at pictures on her laptop right now.

"What's that?" I say.

She looks up and around the room to see what I'm talking about. "What's what?"

"That," I say, pointing to where her hands are resting.

"This? It's a MacBook," she says. "You're on a PC? You've *so* got to go Mac—it's way better."

"What's Mac?"

She looks up at me and cocks her head like Brownie the dog used to do when he thought he heard something off in the distance. "Huh?"

"What's a Mac? I don't know what that is," I say, pointing again to the thing with pictures she's been pecking at with her fingers. I hate it that my face gets red hot when I'm embarrassed. It's like I have a secret and it's being flashed on a neon sign above my head.

"Wait, you don't know what *this* is? *This*. This whole thing." She waves her hand in a circle over it. *"You don't know what a* computer *is?"*

My cheeks are on fire.

"I, um, I know what a computer is, Jeez Louise," I say, the red not getting any better—like it knows I'm lying and won't go away until I tell the truth. "I . . ."

"You don't know what a computer is," she says. She's not saying it mean. It's more that she's thinking out loud. As if she was at the zoo and the teacher told her monkeys like bananas and she's repeating it so she can understand it better. *Monkeys like bananas,* she'd repeat it to herself, to make sure she got it right.

"So y'all didn't have computers up in the mountains?"

I shake my head. No sense lying now that I know she sees the truth.

"Maybe other people did," I tell her, "but not us. And not Orla Mae—she's my best friend. And not Mr. Wilson who lived next to us."

I'm ready for the names to start flying. Dumbbell. Stoop (for stupid). Instead, she just shrugs her shoulders, turns back to the computer, and says, "Wow. Okay, well, this is a computer and the first thing you should know is that computers have answers to everything you could ever possibly want to know. You can do *anything* on a computer. You can listen to music. Watch videos. You can chat with your friends—if they have computers, I mean. Anything. Think up a question and I'll Google it and get you the answer. First I want to show you something: what was your old address?"

"Why do you want my old address?"

"Just," she says. "It's too hard to explain—I'll just show you. You'll see. It's so cool. What was it?"

Her fingers are hovering over the letter buttons, waiting for me to tell them what to press. "Twenty-two Turn River Road," I tell her. "Hendersonville, North Carolina. I don't remember the zip code, though."

She pecks the words in and says, "That's okay. I don't need it. Now watch this."

There on the screen is a picture of Planet Earth. Cricket taps something and it starts moving—like we're watching a movie or television right here at her desk! It shows the planet getting closer—like we're birds flying to Earth from outer space . . . getting closer . . .

"Whoa," I say, almost feeling carsick watching it fly.

And closer . . .

"What in the Sam Hill?" I cain't help cussing. I never seen anything like this *ever*. It's like a little movie.

"I told you!" Cricket says, and I can feel her watching my face. "Wait. It gets better."

Closer still . . .

And then you can see we're heading to America. We keep flying and I wince feeling like we might crash-land. Then I can make out trees—real live trees not cartoon pictures of them—and mountains . . .

"That looks just like . . ."

Now roads and buildings. I cain't be certain but it looks like . . .

"Here we are!" Cricket says as the bird slows down to land lightly. "Home sweet home! Twenty-two Turn River Road. Hendersonville, North Carolina!"

If my eyes were any wider they'd peel back from my own head.

"Told you it was cool," she says, smiling big. I know how she feels. I feel—I mean I felt—that good whenever Emma got tickled by something I showed her.

"Google Earth," she says. Like that's supposed to explain it. "I just downloaded it. It's been around awhile, I just hadn't gotten around to signing up and then we moved in with Grandma and everything. See? You can put in any address—anywhere in the world—and it'll fly you there and put a little red pin. Sometimes it's a bit off of the exact address. Like now. Here, let's sweep along till you see your house. Just tell me when you see it and I'll slow it down. See it yet?"

"No," I say. "Wait, go back a second. Oh, no. I thought that was it. Wait! There! That looks like Mr. Wilson's house! It is! No way—that's Mr. Wilson's house right there! His fence lost the two middle beams a ways back and he's always saying he'll fix it when the beams come out of hiding so I know for a fact that's his house. So if that's Mr. Wilson's ours should be right . . . there . . . on the other side of that thicket. Why ain't—isn't—why *isn't* it there?"

That's when I remember the rumors going around town before we left. They said they were gonna tear the house down. Momma said at the time it'd suit her just fine—*no good memories in this god-forsaken house*—but I guess I didn't think they'd really go through with it. Now what do I do? I cain't tell her *oh, I just remembered they said they were going to wreck the house* because then she'd ask how come and then what would I say? *Because my stepdaddy was murdered there and oh by the way I'm the one who murdered him?* Oh Lord, I promise, cross my heart promise, that if you help me figure out what to tell Cricket I will never ever ask you for anything ever again.

"You didn't really come from there, did you?" Cricket asks, her voice quiet and grown-up and serious. "It's okay. You can tell me what's up, you know. I'm really good at keeping secrets. Are you in some kind of trouble, you and your mom?"

Mr. White from the drugstore back in my first hometown, Toast, used to say *the truth may hurt but it hurts a whole lot less than a lie.*

"I ain't—I mean, I'm *not*, we're not in trouble, Momma and me," I start out. "And yeah we're from Hendersonville, but I think, well, I'm not sure but they might have tore our house down after we left. That's why it ain't—that's why it's *not* there."

"Oh-Em-Gee, this is exactly the kind of thing computers are perfect for," she says, sounding almost happy to have a mystery to solve. "We can check the town records and see if the house was condemned or knocked down or whatever. Let's see. Hendersonville Town Hall. Okay here's the home page. Now let's go to the tabs up top. 'Records.' Let's start there."

"You can do that?"

"Let's see, there's birth records, death certificates, zoning." She's talking to herself as much as she's talking to me. I realize too that she can read a whole lot faster than me. She can do everthing a whole lot faster than me. Words pop up on the screen then vanish. Pictures too. All before I can make anything out, it goes so quick.

"This is so cool," I say.

It's true. I never had any kind of fun like the kind I'm having now.

"You should come over like *all* the time," Cricket says. "Wait, what school are you gonna go to, you think? You shouldn't come to my school—I hate my school. They're all like *mean.* In bad moods all the time. You're in, what, fourth grade? Fifth? I hated fifth grade at my school. This one girl? Gummy Brainard? She would always cross something when you said *no crossies counts* but you wouldn't know it and then she'd steal whatever secret you told her and blab it all over kingdom come. That just tells you what kind of a person she is. I'm just saying. Oh-oh, before I forget, lemme show you that cat video on YouTube I was telling you about just now."

She's tapping away again. It's a *real marvel,* like my teacher used to say when Maisey Wells bent her thumb all the way back to show she was double-jointed.

"Can you find out answers to anything on that thing?" I ask her.

"Anything in the world," she says.

Even though I cain't think what a computer would have about her, I hear myself ask, "Can you look up my momma?"

Cricket looks over at me and says, "I can find out *any*thing about *any*body you want."

Mrs. Ford's voice reaches us from somewhere down below:

"Girls! Y'all come down here a second, will you?"

"When I come back up I'll Google her, m'kay?"

"Girls?" Mrs. Ford hollers again.

"Let me go see what she wants," Cricket sighs. "I'll be right back."

When Cricket leaves the room she takes all the air with her. I look around and for a split second I think I'd like to press a letter button or two on her computer but I don't dare because that'd be a *recipe for disaster*. Before we left home, before we sold near ever-thing we owned, before her stitches were snipped out even, Momma said if I told people both her husbands had died it'd be a *recipe for disaster*, but if you ask me, Richard *not* being dead would be the real disaster.

There are some things that are blurry in my brain and some that are crystal clear. Even though I try my hardest for them to get fuzzy, the minutes before Richard died are shiny and sharp when they cut into my thoughts.

It was a Tuesday. I had eaten supper over at Orla Mae's house that night and skipped home with extra biscuits I snuck into my pockets for Emma because Momma was having one of her not-coming-out-of-the-bedroom spells again and Richard was disappearing for days at a time so food was scarce. When I opened the door to the house the first thing I noticed was the mess— a chair knocked onto its side, broken glass crunching underfoot, the lamp laying on the ground without its shade, throwing weird light that made me think I'd walked into the wrong place. I can still hear my own voice calling out for Momma and Emma, but it was real quiet and my stomach twisted up with worry. When I crossed the living room I heard a groan and there, crumpled up against the wall with the peeling flowered wallpaper the people before us had left behind and Richard never got around to sanding off like he said he was gonna on the day we moved in, there was my momma, blood spreading out from her head like a spilled coffee cup. One of her arms bent like it'd been pulled out of the socket. Her housedress pulled up almost to her underpants.

I crouched down and whispered "Momma?" while I tried to keep my tears from falling straight into her bloody mouth and wondered if I could touch her.

She moved her head slightly, so the one eye that wasn't swollen shut could fix on me. Her lips—I remember watching them moving over her teeth like they weren't her lips at all.

"Git," she said, softer than a whisper, "out." She took in another breath but it wasn't deep—it looked like it hurt her to breathe.

"Now," she whispered, closing her eye back up.

I shook my head no.

"Momma, where's Emma?" I choked on the name.

"Hurry" was all she said.

Then I knew why.

Richard's voice reached me first, and even though it was slurred, I could just make out his words. Not that they made much sense to me. He hadn't heard me come in.

"Trying to provide for my *family*, such as it is," he hollered on his way back into the living room through the swinging saloon doors that separated it from the kitchen. I froze, still hunched over Momma, knowing it was too late to hide from him. "That's whut I'm tryin' to do."

He paused in the doorway and gulped some more beer and before I could talk myself out of it I sprang up like a jack-in-the-box and made a run—past him!—for the kitchen so I could get outside quick once I found out the one thing I wanted to know. Now that I think on it, I was almost as brave as Emma always was, trying to make an escape like that.

"Whut the hell . . . ?" He batted his arm at the blur of me running past but thank the Lord he had the beer in him 'cause his grip wasn't too tight when he caught hold of my shirt. I didn't even have to bite him that hard to get him to let me go.

"Piece of *shit*," he said when I pulled free and whirled around to face him.

"Where's Emma?" I asked. I like to think I said it like a cowboy would, all demanding and scary, but really I begged.

I can still see the corners of his mouth curl up on either side of the bottle he was pulling beer from. He swallowed hard but didn't answer me. Then he crossed the broken-up room to his ratty old armchair which was the only thing left standing and settled back, crossing his legs in the man way, with one heel resting across his other knee.

"Please? Where is she, huh?"

"Don't you 'huh' me," he said, uncurling his first finger to point at me.

"Tell me where Emma is," I said. Where I got the courage to talk to Richard like that I still don't know.

I remember running upstairs, calling out for my sister while Richard laughed from his stupid chair below, hollering for me there was no need lookin' for her. I remember how pleased he looked when I came back down empty-handed, like he was proved right.

"I told you," Richard said. "She ain't here."

Emma was so *real* to me then. Of all the things I remember, the sound of my blood rushing through my body, pulsing against my eardrums, stays with me most. I busted through the back screen door into the dark night.

Next thing I was racing through the woods, tearing past the saplings and scrub brush, over moss heaps, leaping like a deer over roots and pine branches to Mr. Wilson's house on the other side of the thicket. My heart beats out of my chest just thinking about how fast I went that night, praying to God the whole time for Momma to live long enough for me to get help, promising to be good if He'd just keep her alive a few more minutes.

Please, Lord, let me get to Mr. Wilson's. Please let me get Momma help before he kills her altogether, I prayed.

I tripped on rocks I'd forgotten about, got scratched by every tree branch known to man, and twice I fell but I didn't feel any of it. When Mr. Wilson's house came into view I hollered for him.

But Mr. Wilson wasn't home.

No one else lived as close so I had to turn back to check on Momma. And to find Emma. I near to threw up with the panic of worry over Em but then I caught sight of Mr. Wilson's gun shed and it all went away. I knew what I had to do.

I cain't believe I found the gun in the dark with only a sliver of moonlight to go by but I did. By that time Mr. Wilson'd taught me how to shoot targets like cans or bottles, how to brace myself against the power of the gunshot, and how to hold steady so I could hit a moving target. He showed me how to take it all apart and clean it carefully so it could last a lifetime. By that night I knew every inch of that gun by heart. In the dark I popped open the chamber and used my fingers, feeling first one, then two, three, four, five open holes then, finally, finding the bullet loaded into the sixth hole so I wouldn't have to hunt for ammunition. I remember being so happy about that. About not having to find the right bullets, on top of ever-thing else.

I didn't have time to spare so I took my chances and instead of cutting back through the woods and risking falling with a loaded gun, I ran fast as I could along the side of the blacktop road. I figured I'd hit the ground and flatten myself to it if a car happened by but I had the road to myself so I made it back home quicker than I would've if I'd have gone through the dark thicket. Before going in I peeked in the front window—Richard wasn't in his chair no more. I took a deep breath. At the foot of the front porch stairs I took hold of the gun with two hands, pointing it at the ground like I knew to do, and locked my elbows. I remember counting the steps, knowing I couldn't look down at them, I had to keep my eyes on where my target might be. I held the screen door open with my foot and, once inside, felt it at my back then easing closed as I moved in. My eyes swept across the broken glass and china to where Momma was still laying. Her head turned toward me and once I was sure she was still alive I became another person, someone you might could see in a movie.

I heard him popping open another beer, the ruffled-edge metal top clattering on the kitchen counter, the *aaaah* he made after swallowing his first sip, then the sound of the bottle setting down on the table. That's when I kicked the swinging doors open and leveled the gun straight at him.

I can still see his face absorbing what the gun was telling him. His shock twisting into surprise then pain before he folded into himself and slid to the kitchen floor.

CHAPTER ELEVEN

Honor

There's a stillness in the house. That should've been my first clue. Not that I needed one, what with the eviction notice on the front door. You know something isn't quite right when you find one of *those*. Normally when we come in the door I call *hey* and Mother will holler back *I'm in the den!* or *I'm in the kitchen!* but today, nothing. I find her sitting motionless at the kitchen table.

"Mom? What's all that on the front door? We're not going to end up on the street, are we? Ha ha."

My mother has a habit of fiddling with whatever is closest at hand when she's upset, and right now it's the Lucy and Ricky salt and pepper shakers she keeps on either side of the paper napkin holder in the middle of the kitchen table.

"That was a joke, by the way," I say, pouring myself some Crystal Light iced tea from the pitcher in the fridge then settling into the chair across the table from her. "You want some tea, Mom? Seriously, though, what's that notice about?"

Lucy and Ricky dressed as Charlie Chaplin. Salt and pepper

shakers. They're shaped so that they fit together: Ricky's elbow is bent to play a tiny drum in the spot where Lucy's bust would have been. Along the bottom of each one BABALOO is spelled out in mariachis. She slides them in and out this way and that, then slides them together again. Like a little boy tinkering with toy soldiers. Mom's looking like she can't hear but her hearing is fine—she's stalling. Which means two things.

One, there's more to the story.

Two, it will be worse than I think.

"Mom? Why aren't you saying anything?" I ask her.

I would dearly love to shake her silly, but of course I don't.

Good Lord, now she's crying—*crying*. This is Bad with a capital *B*.

"Mom, whatever it is we can fix it," I say. I stand up and hurry over to rub her back between her shoulder blades just the way she likes it.

"If you get mad I don't know what I'll do," Mom says in between sobs.

"I won't be mad at you, Mom. But you've got to explain what this is so I can help you. What's going on?"

She takes out a napkin and blows her nose. Her cheeks press against her lower eyelids, so when she cries her eyes practically swell shut.

"Can you tell me what's going on?" I ask her again. While I wait for her to answer, I scan the eviction notice. "I'm not going to be mad, but you know what this is here in my hand? It's an eviction notice, Mom. Oh my Lord! I'm reading through it and it says right here the house is being foreclosed on. Repossessed. Huh? They use both terms. It says: 'The bank will take possession' blah blah blah . . . lots of fine print. This is so weird because there's no mortgage—you own the house outright. I don't get it. There must be some mistake, right?"

"I honestly didn't think it would come to this," Mother says, sniffing and balling up the used napkin. "*You* know how much I love this house, how much it means to me—to all of us. I never thought it would come to this. We're looked up to all over town, for goodness' sake. We're the *Chaplins.*"

The only thing I can do is wait. For the shoe to drop.

"Just . . . just tell me what happened," I say.

Then just like that her tears stop. As quickly as they started.

"No," she says, straightening up and trying to put her shoulders back. "No. Come to think of it, I don't want to talk about it. I'll call Bud Milner in the morning, have him take a look at what we can do legally, but nothing good's going to come from talking about it now"—she lowers her voice and tips her head up to the ceiling—"especially with Cricket just upstairs."

"Oh my Lord in Heaven," I say.

She's avoiding my eyes. She's concentrating hard on the balled-up napkin she still has in her hand. Wait a second. Now she's back to fiddling with those dang salt and pepper shakers. She's studiously avoiding my eyes. I know what this is . . .

"Please tell me this is not what I think it is," I say.

"Now hang on there a second," she says, pausing with her game of dancing Lucy and Ricky around as if she is seven years old to glance up in case I'm bluffing. "Before you go jumping to conclusions just hang on there."

"Oh my good Lord in Heaven, it *is* what I think it is."

"Shhhh! Hush. Honor, now don't you be taking on the weight of the world," she whispers. "It's not what you think."

Lucy-as-Charlie tips over and salt fans out from her bowler hat.

"So you're telling me it's not Hunter," I lower my voice to ask her.

"Shhhhh. Stop it," she hisses.

My younger brother, Hunter, is the black sheep and he relishes every minute of it. He lives in Nevada, hot-wires Camaros, blows all his money on slots in Vegas, calls and says he's broke, yet somehow always finds enough cash to keep up the cocaine habit he swears he doesn't have. Hunter's the kind of guy who probably nurses a host of sexually transmitted diseases. The kind of guy who makes a beer run with your money and pockets the change. This makes perfect sense. Mother is blind, deaf, and dumb when it comes to Hunter. I wouldn't put it past her to send him the remainder of the money my daddy left her when he died plus her Social Security checks—all he'd have had to do was tell her he was in trouble, and she'd do anything to help him.

"Okay fine, but just tell me this." I scrape my chair over so now it's next to hers at the kitchen table, and I whisper, "Is it Hunter? Mom, did you take out a new *mortgage* to give money to Hunter?"

She hand-sweeps the salt off the table and picks Lucy up, tipping her side to side.

And now I know. It is indeed my brother who has pretty much bankrupted our mother, sending us all into the street. I take a deep *cleansing* breath and remind myself you catch more flies with honey.

"Well, did you call him yet? Have you told my dear brother about this eviction notice?"

Mom gets a faraway look in her eye and says, "No I haven't told Hunter and I don't plan to."

"Why?"

"He's got enough to worry about," she says, "and I don't want him worrying over me. I don't want you telling him, you hear me? Do not tell Hunter. Poor boy is struggling worse than me—we should really be focusing on him now."

I now know what Oprah means by *aha moment* because I do believe I'm having one now. Suddenly it all makes sense. I lower my head into my hands and take another deep breath. I open my mouth and just before words come out a tiny voice inside me says

Walk away. Don't get sucked in. Let it go. Walk away. Of course I won't walk away—I wish I could but it's my family we're talking about so walking away isn't an option. But still.

"Mom? How much have you been sending Hunter? Look at me."

"He's my son and I don't have to check with you on how to raise my boy," she says.

"Look, Mom, just tell me so I can know what I'm dealing with here. How much have you sent him?"

"I don't know and it's none of your business anyway. Stop meddling."

"So he's back on coke now," I say, trying to control my temper. "You've been paying for his drug habit, Mom, you know that? You have. That or his goddamn, sorry, his *gosh*-darn gambling problem."

"People were after him, Honor! Scary people! With *guns*! I would have done the same for you, missy, and you know it."

"Uh-huh," I say. "Sure they were. *Because he's a gambling addict, Mom.* He probably owes a dozen people money. And he knows he can manipulate you into giving him whatever he needs."

"He does not manipulate me and I don't want to hear you going on about your brother. If I want to send my son money I will, simple as that."

"Okay okay okay," I say. After all this time I know which battles to fight and this is a losing one if I've ever seen it. "Fine. But no more of that now, all right? You need every red cent that comes in to you and then some. I've just got to think about the *then some* part of the equation."

Ticking down an invisible list of ways to make fast money isn't much help. Short of winning *American Idol* or becoming a prostitute, I've got exactly zero prospects. Then again, hookers make a lot of money. The high-end ones, I mean. Those escorts make a killing I bet. I would never in a million years become an escort, but it's something. A Plan B. A Doomsday Plan.

I may be a mess, but at least I didn't bleed my mother dry when Eddie and I were facing *our* financial crisis a couple of years ago. *We* dealt with it like adults, unlike *some* people. Yes, it was a terrible blow to have to sell the house, but what else were we going to do to get out from under the suffocating mountain of unpaid medical bills we were left with after Caroline died? And yes, it was depressing to realize that every last cent we made off the sale went toward erasing our debt, but in life you've got to make sacrifices, not that Hunter would know anything about *those*. Cricket and I first moved into a tiny, cheap two-bedroom condo in a development so new the saplings were still sitting in their burlaped root-balls, unplanted and already wilting the day we got there. It was a short-term lease affordable only because the developer was an old friend of Ed's from grade school. He gave us a "friends and family" discount until we could figure out our next move. I'll say this for him, Ed wouldn't even hear about taking the deal for himself. Instead he bunked at the station house for a while and finally ended up renting a halfway decent one-bedroom apartment in a soot-colored building not far from the "sad" section of town that was his beat. Once our lease ran out Cricket and I moved in with Mother, which, again, wouldn't have been my first choice in life but I can look myself in the mirror at night knowing I took care of my responsibilities without putting my mother in the poorhouse. Hunter? The only mirror *he's* looking into has white powdered lines on it. So, once again, *I've* got to be the responsible one. I've got to take care of business. Just like Elvis. TCB. He had that painted on one of the walls in Graceland: *TCB* for "taking care of business."

"Where's that yellow legal pad I had over by the phone? Oh, there it is." I clear a space on the table to make my lists. "Okay. Let's figure out where we stand. I've got practically nothing left in my checking account. Well. I have a little over three thousand, but that has to cover this month's health insurance and food and clothing—Cricket's growing like a weed. Where's the calculator?"

"Honor . . ." Mother tries to interrupt me.

"My unemployment ran out and now they say I'm *able-bodied* so it should be easy for me to find a job. Like I haven't been applying for jobs all along! Like they didn't get the memo that the country's in an economic crisis. Can you believe that? I told you about that, right? The woman said it *should be easy* for me to get a job. Through her bulletproof window. Without even looking up. She sat there sifting through a stack of unrelated paperwork with her stupid desk fan blowing streamers right and left like she had everything else important to do but talk to me. Unbelievable."

"Honey, wait just a second," Mother says.

"I will say this, though: the glass at the unemployment window is bulletproof for reasons I now understand."

"Shhhh. Now hush up and listen for a minute. You're being just like your daughter with the flood of words words words. I'll figure something out, Honor. I will. This is not your concern."

"Oh, I'm sorry," I say, "you *want* to be thrown out on the street. I didn't realize that."

Okay, I do regret saying this but before I can say so, Mother tries to leap to her feet, only she's forgotten (a) she is too huge to do any sort of leaping, and (b) she is sitting at the kitchen table so her knees hit the table and the Big Chair scrapes away and Mother yelps and grabs the edge . . . *just* in the nick of time. She rights herself, pulls the chair closer, and settles back down (humbled but not wanting to show it), exhaling from the exertion before starting in on me.

"If you keep condescending to me with that tone like I'm a *baby,* I swear to Charles Chaplin in Heaven I'll march out of here right this minute," Mom hisses and waggles her finger at me.

"Okay okay okay," I say, surrendering. "Sorry. I don't mean to be mean, it's just that I can't wrap my head around this."

"Well, you don't *need* to wrap your head around it because it is not your business," Mother says. "I am the head of this household and I said I'd take care of it and I will. That's that."

"But you *haven't* taken care of it! Sorry, I'm not being nasty I'm just saying. Let me talk with Eddie. Maybe he can think of a way to help buy us some more time here."

"You leave Edsil out of this, please," she says, rushing to his defense because of my agitated sigh, which she thinks I'm making because of Eddie.

"I wasn't saying anything bad about him! But while we're on the subject, Mother, why are you always taking his side? That's what I'd like to know. You're always pleading his case."

"Shhhhh! Keep your voice down," she says.

"Fine," I say, barely at a whisper, "but will you please tell me why you're always sticking up for him? I'm your flesh and blood. You should be taking *my* side."

"Oh, for goodness' sake, put a sock in it and come over here and help me out of this chair," she says. "I am so sick and tired of this nonsense."

"Wow," I say, positioning myself behind her as she heaves herself to standing then waddles over to the counter by the sink.

I would have bet a million dollars that *put a sock in it* would be something my mother would never say even if her life depended on it. The surprises just keep on coming today.

"You can look as startled as you want but you really do need to *put a sock in it*. You're drawing battle lines that are unnecessary and just plain silly," she says. "There. I said it. I have kept my mouth shut this whole time but I can't stand it any longer, Honor. That man is the father of your child—he loves her just as much as you do—"

"I know, I know!" I say, holding up my hand to shush her. "I told you I didn't say anything bad. I just asked why you're always protecting him, that's all."

"You talk about 'taking sides' and I'm sick of it," she says. "You have a problem with the way he grieved for Caroline? That's on *you*, not him. Men don't mourn the way women do and that's just a fact. So you're going to have to get over it and move on, you hear me? Let's change the subject. What's the story with that child—Cricket's new friend. What's her family name? Do we know them?"

The fact of the matter is, she's right. Intellectually I know she's right: men and women *do* grieve differently. But *she* wasn't the one crying in the face of Eddie's stony silence the day he announced he was cutting short his bereavement leave and going back to work. *She* wasn't reduced to begging—*begging* her husband to open up, to go with her to the Grief Group, to show some kind, *any* kind of emotion. She didn't lie in bed next to her husband in the dark feeling for his hand to hold under the sheets only to have it recoil and readjust, along with the rest of his body, further away to the outer edge of the bed. Yes, men and women grieve differently. But not because they want to. The chasm between Ed and me became a gulf by the time the second notices on the medical bills started coming in. By the third and final notices, we were mere objects moving around under the same roof. The soul-crushing pain of losing Caroline coupled with Ed's emotional shutdown might have been surmountable if the financial strain hadn't completely worn us down. We went from shards to sea glass. But lately. Lately I've been thinking a lot about Eddie. A lot.

"Hel-lo?" Mother is waving her hand in front of my face.

"What?" I shake off a memory of Eddie laughing, speeding Caroline up and down the hospital corridor in a wheelchair, the blur of them whooshing by, ignoring my halfhearted attempt to get them to stop horsing around. *Faster, Dad, faster,* Caroline would squeal in delight.

"Cricket's friend? Upstairs? Your daughter's playing with her right now? Where is she from? Who's her family?"

"Oh, my goodness, that's right," I say, remembering the *other* problem facing us today. When will this damn day *end*?

"You've got to help me figure out what to do about this child," I say. "I think we've got a big problem on our hands."

"Why? What's the story?" she asks.

"You'll see," I tell her.

I go to the base of the kitchen stairs and holler up for the girls, and just like that, just hearing myself call out the word *girls* again, makes everything else—the looming foreclosure, my marital mess, Cricket's loneliness—all of it melts away when I call for the girls to come down. God, I miss Caroline.

One more time, Dad! Faster!

I miss her so much my heart hurts.

"Cricket? Girls? Y'all come down here!" I holler again, just because it feels good.

Thunder of footsteps overhead and Cricket bounds into the kitchen breathless with an excitement I haven't seen in her face in a long time.

"Mom! Grandma! Listen to this: *She's never seen a computer before. Or an iPod.* For real. She didn't even know what one was!"

"*I* didn't know what an iPod did until you showed me," Mother says, smiling at her then back at me. "Come give Grandma a kiss hello, sugar. How was summer school today?"

"Hey, Grandma." Cricket breezes over to kiss my mother on the cheek. "No no—it's not that she didn't know what an iPod *did*, she didn't know what an iPod *was*! She's, like, from another *planet* or something!"

"Where is she now, honey?" I ask.

"In my room. Oh, and she *loves* the stars on the ceiling—she'd never seen *those* before either! It was *so cute*—she said it looked like a *magic land* when I showed her how they glow in the dark. I want her to sleep over, Mom, can Carrie sleep over please please? 'Kay, I'm going back up."

"Wait a sec, Cricket. How's she feeling now? Is she feeling okay? Has she said anything about her family?"

"Was she sick?" Mother asks.

"Grandma, it was so nasty—she totally barfed in the car. But she's fine now."

"That reminds me, I need to finish cleaning that up. Poor thing had an upset stomach in the car on the way home—I think it's from eating as fast as she did," I say. "Cricket, honey, go get Carrie and bring her down to introduce her to your grandma. Y'all hightailed it upstairs so fast you never brought her in here."

"Oh, and Grandma, she doesn't know who Charlie Chaplin was," Cricket says, popping open a Hi-C, "so I told her you'd explain everything. Do we have any more of those Swedish Fish? I'm going back up."

She takes the stairs two at a time. There is no slowing that girl down one bit, and for once I'm glad to see it.

I make sure I hear Cricket's footsteps overhead before I start whispering to Mom.

"It's the spookiest thing you have ever seen," I say. "The universe works in mysterious ways. And before you go saying I'm getting carried away with psychic mumbo jumbo or whatever it is you accuse me of, just meet her and you'll see what I'm talking about."

"I have no idea what you're telling me right now," Mother says. "Are we still talking about Cricket's friend?"

"Shhh," I say. "It'll all make sense when they come downstairs. Just please keep an open mind, will you?"

"How can I keep an open mind when I don't even know what it is you're talking about?"

"You will, you will. Just promise me you'll keep an open mind and you'll help me with this," I say.

"Honey, I'd help you with anything, you know that. I can't believe you'd even say that. Sheesh."

"Do we have stuff for nachos?" I ask, opening cabinets to hunt for tortilla chips.

Cricket barrels back in, Carrie trailing close behind as if on a leash.

"There's cheese in the drawer in the fridge." Mother is directing me when they come into the kitchen.

"Hey," Cricket says. "Carrie, this is my grandma."

"Oh, good." I'm relieved to see a better version of Carrie. "You look like you're getting your color back, that's good. Carrie, come on over here and meet Cricket's grandmother Miss Chaplin."

"Oh my good Lord in Heaven." Mom's voice catches when she sees little Carrie. "Look at you. If I didn't know better I'd say someone upstairs was playing a pretty sick joke on us."

"Ma'am?" Carrie says, looking confused.

"What did I tell you?" I turn to Mom. "Can you believe it?"

"Your name is Carrie?" Mom asks. "As in *Caroline*?"

"Yes, ma'am."

"Pleased to meet you, Caroline." Mom reaches out to shake Carrie's fragile-looking hand. "Honor, I can't believe y'all met *today* of all days."

I check my watch. The tiny number in the date box says six. Damn, now it's stuck at 11:43. I really need a new watch. I don't know why I bother even putting this one on.

"What do you mean?" I ask her. I shake my wrist like a dummy, as if the correct date will appear like a Magic 8 Ball. "My watch says it's the sixth."

"You mean to tell me you don't know what today is?" Mother asks me, looking incredulous.

I glance at Cricket, who's silent and as sheepish as I've ever seen her.

"Why, it's August eighth, honey," Mother says, wide-eyed and somber.

If a great big giant came in and threw a heavy winter blanket over Mother, Cricket, and me, you'd have about the same hollow silence that chokes us right now.

"What's August eighth?" Carrie practically whispers the question.

I stand frozen mid-movement, unable to speak while a familiar wrenching ache sinks so deep it's in my marrow.

"August eighth is the day my sister died," Cricket says in a quiet voice, watching me carefully.

How could I have believed a watch I know to be broken? What kind of a mother doesn't realize it's the anniversary of her daughter's death?

"It was three years ago today she left us, bless her heart," Mother is saying, though her voice now sounds far away.

I gulp for air and somehow make it from the refrigerator to a chair at the kitchen table, though I can't feel my legs moving.

"I thought today was the sixth," I whisper to nobody. "All day long I've thought today was the sixth. My watch says it's the sixth."

"I know, honey," Mother says, reaching across the table to gently stroke my hand, which somehow feels like it belongs to someone else. I look down at it. Maybe it's the hand of a mother who knows the correct date. A mother who knows it's the three-year anniversary of her firstborn child's death.

Over by the sink, a worried Carrie wrings her hands and in a pleading voice says, "Y'all can call me something else. I never really liked my name anyway. I won't ever use it again, I swear. We can name me something else and then you won't be sad and I can come over again. I'm real good at remembering names so I won't forget my new one, I swear. Please."

Mother's chair scrapes the floor when she pushes back from the table.

"Cricket, could you help your old grandma up from the chair please," she says, figuring I'm in no shape to do it.

Faster, Dad! Push me faster!

This is just the sort of calamity I've tried to avoid. Being surprised by sadness is like getting sucker punched in the gut. It takes all the air out of you, and for a brief moment you think you just might die from the pain. In all my disaster preparedness I somehow overlooked the fact that we're still recovering from a disaster of the worst kind.

I look up to see my mother enveloping little Carrie in a hug.

"Oh, honey pie, aren't you just the sweetest thing," she's murmuring, stroking Carrie's messy hair. "You have an exquisite name and we are being so rude talking about this whole coincidence in front of you like we are. Come sit down and have something to eat. Cricket, get the chips out of the cabinet, will you, honey? Now, Carrie. Tell me a little about yourself, sweetness. Where are your people from?"

I can't crumble. Not now, at least. I've got to pull it together for Cricket. And Carrie. Oh, Jesus, Carrie.

I try to screw my face into a smile, but from Cricket's frown I can see I'm not fooling anyone. Eddie. I'll call Eddie. Just thinking about him right now makes me want to cry for some reason.

"I've got to take Carrie back," I say. "I'm sure her mother's worried sick."

"Oh no she ain't, I mean, she's *not*," Carrie says. "She's not worried sick."

"Okay, well, maybe a little while longer," I say.

"You were about to say where you live, honey," Mother says to Carrie.

They talk for I don't know how long, and I'm grateful for it. While I am truly pleased to see Cricket's coping better, part of me is a little shocked that she can so easily push aside her grief over her sister, pressing me like she is now, to take her and Carrie somewhere tomorrow (the mall? the library?) even. I make a show of considering it so I can buy a little more time with my thoughts.

Faster, faster, Dad!

Cricket would have loved those wheelchair joyrides Ed always took Caroline on during those last days but we curtailed her visits to the hospital because we thought it might be too scarring. We agreed she was too young to be hanging out with dying cancer patients all the time, even if her sister was one of them. We wanted to *protect her childhood,* such as it was. How were we to know it'd do far more harm to her by keeping her away? We didn't know how adept Cricket was at putting on a happy face to keep us from worrying about her. We never said as much but I think we both figured we'd make up our lost time with her after . . . when . . . Oh, Jesus, we just thought we would make it all up to Cricket someday. How could we have known Cricket was silently suffering just as much as her sister, maybe even more?

Her teacher was the first to point it out. Cricket withdrew into herself and was no longer participating in class, which, up until her sister got sick, she had done on a regular basis. Ed and I sat in numb silence in those too-small chairs, Ed's knees practically up at his chin, staring at Miss Jensen as she ticked off the changes she'd noticed in our daughter. I nodded yes when she referenced Cricket's obsessive nail biting ("and then there's the issue of her fingernails, but I'm sure you're already working on that with her . . .") and nearly lost it when I got home and noticed—for the first time—Cricket's nubby nails chewed off below the quick, dried blood where she had bitten off her cuticles, ripping the skin from some fingers all the way up to the joint.

The truth was that neither of us had noticed anything amiss with Cricket. We were too focused on Caroline and chemo and bone marrow drives to see anything else. Miss Jensen asked about Cricket's sleep, noting she often appeared exhausted at school, and sure enough, when we asked Cricket about it, she broke down and sobbed that she'd been having nightmares and hadn't slept all the way through the night in months. We're her parents—how had we missed all that?

Looking across at my little girl showing Carrie a flashlight, chattering away, I see that the difference in her is astounding. She is a rare gem, this child of mine. I just wish someone other than her family knew it. Then it occurs to me.

Carrie knows it.

CHAPTER TWELVE

Carrie

Ever-where you look there's something interesting to look at. They got so many *things* it'd be hard to count even if someone offered to pay you a penny for every item you made note of. So many that if Miss Chaplin had to move from here to a tiny map dot in the mountains—Hendersonville maybe—it'd take her weeks just to pack it all up. Don't even get me started on how much money she'd make if she decided to sell it all in a yard sale because she was turning the page by moving away. I'm telling you: there are a bazillion things under this one roof.

Miss Chaplin tells Cricket and Mrs. Ford that she's *borrowing* me for a minute. She stands behind me and with her hands on my shoulders she guides me like a shopping cart into the front room with all the boy dolls.

"It's taken me over three decades to gather all of this together," Miss Chaplin says, standing now in the middle of the room. "We have the premier collection of Charles Chaplin memorabilia in the United States."

I worry she thinks I'm staring on account of the way she looks. Her being so fat and all. She probably weighs a thousand pounds. I went to a county fair once and there was a booth where you could guess the weight of the person setting there and if you got it right you'd get a huge jar of gum balls and I guessed wrong but Tommy Bucksmith was close so he won the jar and he didn't share one single gum ball with anybody. Not one. That was the fattest person I ever saw—the man at the guess-the-weight booth at the county fair. Until today. So I try to make her think I'm not thinking about her being fat by asking her questions I didn't put any thought into.

"Where'd that one come from?" I point to a random doll that's no different from a million others lined up alongside it and I make sure to look her in the eye because that's what polite people do.

She looks as pleased as if I'd told her she won the Miss America pageant. Which, not to be mean or anything, she isn't likely to do anytime soon.

"Well, someone has a good eye," she says, putting strength behind the *some* part of the word *someone*. "That particular likeness is one of a limited edition put out by Madame Alexander on the occasion of what would have been Uncle Charlie's one hundredth birthday."

The skin on the back of her arm stretches into a wing when she reaches to bring it down from the shelf. She's as careful with it as Momma was with that glass pitcher we had to part with back in Hendersonville.

"Look at this," Miss Chaplin says, turning it over and holding the base up close for me to get a look. "See the numbers there? Read them out loud for me, honey, will you? My eyes aren't as good as they once were."

"There's a number seventeen," I say, squinting to make out the tiny marks stamped into the wood, "then a line then the number two hundred and twelve."

She nods like she'd known the answer and says, "That means there were two hundred and twelve dolls produced in total, and of that two hundred and twelve, this particular doll is number seventeen."

The way she looks at me I know I'm supposed to say something about this fact but I don't know—is this a good thing? Or is she kind of sorry she didn't get the number one doll? Me, I'd gun for number one.

I settle for "wow" and that seems to suit her fine.

"Now take a look at this and tell me what you think," she says, waddling across the room to a glass case I hadn't noticed before and pointing to a china plate ringed in gold with Charles Chaplin's face in the middle, hat and all. I try to imagine what a shock it'd be to the person eating, say, meat loaf off the plate handed to them, finishing it entirely and realizing the whole time they'd been eating on top of a fancy man's head.

"Wow," I say again because I'm too stupid to think of something different. Plus, she seems happy with just that one word so *why mess with success,* as my daddy used to say when Momma'd ask him why he never got the promotion he'd told us he was going for.

" 'Wow' is right," Miss Chaplin says.

She pulls a pretty gold necklace up from underneath her blouse and dangling from it is a tiny key she fits into the lock on the front of the case. "You may find this hard to believe, Miss Carrie, but see this gold line here? The one around the edge? That's real eighteen-karat gold."

"Really? It's real gold?"

"Yes, ma'am," she says. "And all the black in his hair and top hat? That's a layer of real ebony. Do you know what ebony is?"

"No, ma'am," I answer her while trying to keep my hands to

myself. I so badly want to trace the gold-circled edge. To see what real gold feels like.

"Ebony is a rare kind of wood," she says, lifting the plate off its stand over the cups and saucers setting in front and out of the case. "Just think how difficult it must have been for the manufacturer to put these pieces together. The china, the wood, the gold. It boggles the mind. You can hold it if you like."

Of course I want to know what this plate would feel like in my hands but then what if something happened and I dropped it? I'd never forgive myself ever and, worse than that, she wouldn't forgive me either. So I shake my head and say, "I'm scared I'll break it, ma'am. I'm pretty clumsy. Momma always says it too. Shouldn't it be in a museum or something?"

"Don't be silly, here you go," she says, simple as pie, putting it in my hands like it was a deck of playing cards. "I trust you."

Now I cain't recall anyone ever saying those three words to me. Ever.

I trust you.

"It's heavier than it looks, isn't it." She smiles, knowing somehow that's exactly the thought forming in my brain at that very second.

"Yes, ma'am. It's two temperatures too," I say, "the white china part is cool but the black is warm. Why's it like that?"

"Well, you'd have to ask a physicist to get the answer to that," she says, "but it has to do with the different textures. The different solids and this and that.

"Now, I know my granddaughter's waiting on you, but let me show you one more thing before y'all go off and play," Miss Chaplin says. "You're probably bored to tears by now."

"No, ma'am," I say. "I'm not bored at all."

It's true. If you'd have asked me an hour ago if I'd care to know about a bunch of dolls and plates all covered with a man's face and hat I'd have said *no sirree.* But it ain't as bad as you might think, learning about all this museum stuff.

I don't tell her that me and Cricket weren't going to play—that's something babies do. She's being so nice, calling me *sweetheart,* talking to me like I'm grown-up like her.

Miss Chaplin motions for me to come closer to get a look at a small iron statue of—you guessed it—Charles Chaplin, leaning on his cane in what looks like a small town. He's facing an official-looking building, like a post office.

"*This* is a real crowd-pleaser," she says, fanning her hand out to reveal something that don't quite look to me like it'd please a crowd but what do I know. "We used to conduct tours here, and this was usually what the kids loved best. Watch."

Miss Chaplin puts a penny in a slot at the base of Chaplin's cane and presses a lever like a pump for a well of water and suddenly the statue moves. Chaplin leans forward into a bow, and when he does, his cane pushes the penny and it slides down a ridge to the building, whose doors magically open to take it in. A little iron dog moves alongside the penny like it's chasing it and I wouldn't be shocked if it started barking.

"It's a bank!" Miss Chaplin says, watching my face be surprised. I never saw anything like this.

"See? Wait, the bank doors are a little slow to close back up. Shoot, I've been meaning to oil this for years."

When they do close up ever-thing stands still again and if you were to walk into the room right now you'd think it was just a boring statue. You'd never know it had come to life like it just did only a few seconds ago. I'm not a baby anymore but if I were I'd ask her to do it again. That was really something.

The phone rings and Mrs. Ford hollers "I'll get it" from another room.

I start to thank Miss Chaplin for showing me around but she

holds up her hand and shushes me, cocking her head toward the sound of Mrs. Ford's voice. She floats—if an incredibly fat person can float—to the doorway and turns to hold her finger in front of her mouth to let me know I need to keep quiet too.

From the other room we can both hear Mrs. Ford's part of the conversation:

"I know, I know . . ."

Silence.

"I feel the same way too, Ed . . ."

Silence. Then she says some stuff in a low voice no one could make out even if they had super-duper hearing. More silence.

"Well, I guess that'd be all right . . ."

Miss Chaplin cups a hand to my ear and whispers, "Why don't you run on up to Cricket's room and keep her company for a bit, 'kay?" and even though she didn't say to I tiptoe across the living room, through the front hall where we first came in, and then up the staircase. I know how it is when you're trying to listen in on someone—you got to be careful nothing around you makes a sound.

Cricket's door is open. She's at her desk typing on her computer thing. When I say "hey" from the doorway she turns and smiles at me *like finally now ever-thing is great. Now that* you're *here.* That's what her smile says to me.

"Sorry you got stuck with Grandma," she says. "I was going to give it another five minutes then I was going to save you, don't worry."

"It's fine," I say. "She's so nice. Your momma too."

"Yeah, well, they're okay I guess," she says, twirling in her chair. "They're always worrying about me and stuff. You know. Because of my sister. And, um, well, I guess they worry I'm going to turn into a loner who shoots up people because my friends kind of dumped me when Caroline died because they didn't know what to do and . . . oh, forget it. I sound like a loser and no one wants to hang out with a loser so whatever. Hey, weren't we going to Google something? When we got called downstairs?"

Without waiting for an answer she turns back to the computer.

"Huh," she says, "I thought we started on something, but it's not in my history."

I don't know what that means but I do know she said we could find out anything about anyone so I remind her. "You said maybe we could check out my momma?"

She lights up and gets her fingers ready over the letter buttons.

"Okay, spell your mom's name for me," she says, and I do.

"Hey, why'd you move here, anyway?" Cricket half-turns from her desk so the question can reach me better on the bed, where I'm flipping through the *Encyclopaedia Britannica*.

And that's how it starts.

I didn't plan on lying. I don't even want to do it. But like it sometimes does, my mouth starts moving without checking with my brain first, and before I know it, the lie is told and there is nothing I can do to change it. Taking it back would be the end of being friends with Cricket. She's probably got hundreds of friends, I don't believe they all dumped her like she said. She'd throw me back like a caught fish too small to keep.

She isn't even really paying me close mind, tapping on the computer keys like she is. I could say anything. There are about a hundred and one things I could do that would make much more sense, but instead, I lie. I cain't say I even give the words much thought before they come tumbling out.

"My daddy finally got my momma to say yes to marrying him again," I say, "and he's here so we came on to be with him."

I think this will be the end of it, I really and truly do. I figure that will answer her question and we'll talk about something else. I hadn't counted on her swiveling her head to me with her eyes all huge and bluer than ever, saying, "That's so romantic! That's like a movie! Start from the beginning. Tell me everything, leave nothing out."

And that's how come it keeps going, my lying I mean.

Cricket folds her legs under her in the desk chair, Indian-style, and shimmies deeper into her seat the way you do when you want to get comfy for a long spell.

"How long were they apart?" she asks.

She keeps prodding me to keep talking so that's what I do.

In the beginning I felt bad lying to her like that. My stomach felt like it did when Richard punched me in the gut, all twisted up and knotted with no room for air to get in. I know I shouldn't tell a lie but I also know that I cain't tell her the truth because she'd tell her momma and her momma'd never let her be friends with a girl who's a murderer.

"I was little when they split up but I remember what they were like together," I start slowly, my mind racing to try to come up with details I know she's wanting. Lucky for me, I have some real-life stuff to use—that really helps when you're telling tales. "Daddy used to swing Momma around the living room, dancing to the music on the radio, and Momma'd try to get him to stop but there's no getting Daddy to stop dancing when he starts. He's a real good dancer."

"Yeah?" Cricket says, leaning into my words, smiling and nodding like she can picture exactly what I am saying.

"Momma always gets real pretty for him—so when he twirled her around the room, her dress would fan out like a ballerina tutu. He'd say *pea-pop*—that's what he calls me. I know it's stupid but he calls me *pea-pop*—"

"That's not stupid," Cricket hurries to say, "it's cute! Go on. What'd he say? *Pea-pop* . . ."

"He'd say, 'pea-pop, your momma's the prettiest thing I ever laid eyes on,' and Momma would holler for him to stop spinning her around and for me to turn down the radio but Daddy'd wink at me to stay put and I'd watch him move her to the music, one hand on her waist, the other holding one of her hands arching up high enough for her to twirl underneath and out from him then back in close to his chest.

"He's got this laugh—he'd laugh and holler real loud over the music things like 'I love this woman!' and Momma'd get all mad and tell him to hush up but he'd keep going. 'Libby-Lou I love you' he'd call out sometimes. Momma's given name's Libby, but he likes to make things rhyme so he'd say 'Libby-Lou.' Momma'd get spittin' mad when he used that name and that's usually when I knew the dancing was over. She'd yank herself away, smooth her dress, and fix her hair if it was out of place and tell him to start acting his age. But she still loved him and all."

"Why'd they break up?" Cricket asks.

"Why'd they break up?" I say her question out loud.

Why'd they break up? Why'd they break up?

"Um, I don't know."

Again, my mind races to come up with something that makes sense but turns out *I don't know* is enough of an answer for Cricket.

"Don't worry, my parents are apart now and I have no clue why because as far as anyone can see they still love each other but it's like they're the only ones who don't know it. They're totally getting back together. I don't know when but they have to. Anyway, go ahead," she says.

Go ahead. Go ahead. Oh Lordy . . .

"Um, well, I don't know." I try that again, thinking it will cover the middle part of the story. I squinch up my shoulders and act real casual. "Then we moved here."

"Wait!" she says. "How'd they get back together? What happened?"

"Daddy left for a while," I say, picking at my thumbnail like I do when I'm thinking hard on something, "I guess for work. Yeah, he was away for work a lot of the time. But he'd always bring

Momma flowers and presents whenever he'd come back to town. When they were apart, I mean. Even when they were apart he brought her all kinds of things. And me too. He's always giving me stuff."

Cricket says "That's *so* romantic" again.

I don't know what happens, but somehow it starts getting easy. The more I talk about Daddy trying to win Momma back, the more I can see it. Like I'm watching a movie. I picture Daddy and Momma kissing hello when he comes in the door from being gone—even though in real life back when he was alive Momma'd always turn her head so Daddy's kiss would land on her cheek instead of her lips. My stomach stops knotting up the more I come up with scenes of my movie parents. Daddy and Momma getting all dressed up for going out just the two of them. Movie Momma tying a scarf over her hair to keep it from flying around in the convertible sports car Movie Daddy drives. Momma smiling and feeding him a bite of her supper because it was *so good it melts in your mouth.* My movie parents laughing at me playing with the new movie puppy they surprised me with on Christmas.

None of it happened in real life but it could have. If things were different I bet it could have.

Then, when it gets to where I'm good to keep going with the story, Cricket decides she's heard enough and starts fiddling with a little musical jewelry box.

"It used to play this really sweet lullaby when you opened it," she says. She holds it open for me to see. "And this ballet dancer would twirl and twirl. So cute. My dad gave it to me when I was little."

"Hey, is Cricket your real name?" I ask her.

"Nah, it's a nickname I got when I was a kid," she says, rolling her eyes. "Daddy says I talk so much I'm like a chirping cricket and they started calling me Cricket and it stuck."

"So what's your real name then?" I ask her.

"My real name is Hannah," she says. "After my great-great-aunt Hannah Chaplin, Charlie's mother."

I been fiddling with this tiny flashlight of Cricket's. It looks like a thin ruler, but when you pinch it in the middle a point of light shoots out the end.

"This is so cool," I say, pinching the light on and off.

"You can have it," Cricket says. "I already have something just like it and anyway it was free, so."

"Oh no, I cain't take it," I say. *Is she serious?*

"It's yours," she says, shrugging and turning back to the computer.

"Thank you *so* much!" I tell her. "The is the best present I ever got *ever.*"

She laughs but it is.

I wish I had something to give Cricket in return but it looks like she's got ever-thing anyone could need and then some.

But I bet she doesn't have Gideon's Bible.

"Here we go," Cricket says, tapping buttons. "We can start here. Wow, so pretty!"

She slides her chair over to make room for me alongside her at the desk. And there, smiling at me from the computer screen, is a picture of my momma when she was young.

CHAPTER THIRTEEN

Carrie

I stand outside the Loveless office and watch them drive away until I cain't catch sight of the taillights no more. After being in air-conditioning it feels good to get warm standing here in the sun. I rub the freezing out of my right shoulder, which was where the air in the car hit for the whole entire drive.

"Hey, Mr. Burdock. Hey, Birdie." I come in the door and pet Birdie the cat laying on the front desk right on top of the book Mr. Burdock writes in when people come and go.

"Here she comes, Miss A-mer-i-ca," he sings to me, why I don't know. He always breaks out into some song when he sees me. Then he musses my hair even more than it's already mussed.

I wish just once he'd fetch the key from the cubbyhole, hand it over, and let me be on my way right quick but that never happens. Mostly I don't mind but today I need to be up there to make it look like I been up there all along. The last thing I need is Momma coming in for the key right now, catching me sneaking back in when I was supposed to be here all along.

"Can I have the key, please?" I ask nicely and all but he's smiling in the way he does when he's settling in for a long talk. Orla Mae called long talks *gabfests*.

"Why don't you start by telling me how you came to be best friends with that rich Chaplin lady," he says. "I'd be real curious to know 'bout that. You know who they are, right? The Chaplins?"

"Um, I know they're real nice but I ain't—I'm *not*—best friends with them and anyhow I only just met them and I really need to get up to the room, so—"

"You think your momma would like knowing her baby girl's climbing into cars with strangers? Because me? Well, personally that ain't something *I'd* cotton to. Not at all. And don't even get me started on *Missus* Burdock. You got to take care not to just get in a car with anyone offering you a ride. The world's a scary place sometimes. Now, it just so happens the Chaplins are good people, but *you* didn't know that when you got in the car. You've got to be more careful than that, girlie."

"Please don't say anything to my momma! I mean, I only just met them and I don't think I'll probably ever see them again and if my momma finds out I'll never see the light of day so please don't tell her, please, Mr. Burdock."

Sometimes it's okay to stretch the truth if it's helping you keep the peace or if you don't mean any harm to anyone. That's what Mr. Wilson told me. I know I'll see Cricket and them again tomorrow, but for all Mr. Burdock knows they hated me and don't want to lay sight on me ever again. He doesn't know that already Cricket feels like a sister to me. I knew I could tell Emma any secret and she'd keep it and already I know I could do that with Cricket too. I knew Emma'd never hurt me *ever* and I know Cricket wouldn't either. But for all Mr. Burdock knows, Cricket doesn't want to have anything more to do with me.

"Um, could I please have the key to our room?" I ask again.

"You mind my words, girl. Oh, and you don't need a key," he

says, tipping his head up toward the second floor, "your momma got home a bit ago."

I holler "bye" and "thank you, sir" over my shoulder but the door closes on the words. I take the stairs fast as I can, two at a time up until the final four, when I get out of breath.

Please, dear Lord, if you can hear this coming from my brain, please let Momma be passed out already. Please, Lord.

I open the door real slow and careful in case the Lord's heard my prayer and put her into sleep before I got here.

"Well well well," Momma says, in her whiskey voice that melts words into one another. "Look who decided to grace us with her presence. Hurry up and shut that door 'fore all the bugs in the state of North Carolina start making nests in here."

"You never said you had a kid," says a man setting next to Momma on the side of the bed. "Lookee, lookee here. Aren't you just full of surprises."

The sound of Momma laughing along with him is so strange I barely know it's her. Then there's the fact that there's *another person* in our room—he makes the room feel tiny.

The man stares at me so hard I pretend there's something on the floor I need to find so I don't have to look at him. I feel my cheeks burning, though, and for some reason it makes me feel naked. His face is bumpy and red but not like a suntan, more like picked pimples. He's got a belly that, if he were a lady, people'd ask him when's the baby due. His arms have so many tattoos it's hard to know what his skin really looks like and the tattoos end in a perfect straight line at his wrists which makes it look like he has on a long-sleeve shirt. I glance up long enough to see his grin showing a missing side tooth.

"She's a shy one, that girl of yours," he says to Momma, passing her the bottle he just swigged from. Momma keeps her stare on me even when her head tips the bottle back. She swallows hard, like a man. Why they have to talk about me like I ain't standing right in front of them, I do not know.

"Shy isn't the half of it," Momma says to him and he acts like that's the funniest thing he ever heard.

Then Momma looks at me with her fake eyes and says, "Come say hello then go on and get yourself something from the vending machine, all right? Quit dawdling and come over here. Caroline, this is Mister . . ."

Momma's face turns to his and then the two of them start laughing all over again. *What is so daggum funny?* I want to say.

Looking at me the man says, "McNight. Hollis McNight. You can call me Rock, though. Everyone calls me Rock."

I look at Momma to see if this is another joke but she gives me that whiskey stare again that I know means I'm either in trouble big-time or becoming invisible and what she's *really* looking at is behind me or above my head. She looks back at him and then I nearly cain't believe it—she touches his arm. Momma hates touching anything and ever-thing. She runs her finger from his shoulder down almost all the way to his elbow. Slow.

"I bet I know how you got that nickname," Momma says to him. She's acting weird. If I only heard her and was blind to how they were sitting next to one another, I'd think from the way she's talking to him that she was in his lap. How in the Sam Hill would she even know how he got his stupid nickname? I wonder. She's being so fake and show-offy. I wish I could tell him he's a fool if he thinks she's being real right now.

"Cain't say," the man says to Momma, tipping his head toward me instead of saying out loud the rest of the sentence—*with her in the room.* I want to say *I'm not a baby, Mister Rock or whatever your stupid name is. That's how much you know. People say all kinds of things around me and I can take it just fine.*

"I can *show* you though," he says to Momma. He tilts his head back to get the last drops from the bottle then blows into it making a horn sound that makes me jump which they laugh at even though the joke's on Mr. Creepy Rock because I happen to know Momma's fake laugh when I hear it, not that I hear it all that often but still. She's fake-laughing. He's setting on the edge of my bed, probably smelling it all up and bugs from him are probably crawling into the covers and the sheets right this very minute. I look at him and in my head I'm yelling *get off my bed stupid Mr. Creepy Rock* but he's so dumb he smiles and says, "I think I'm making myself a little friend."

Momma looks at me then looks away and says, "Don't count on it. Girl's crazy as a three-legged cow."

"You know how to play a trombone, kid? What's your name—*Caroline*?" he asks me. I hate him saying my name.

"It's all right, I don't bite," he says. "I just asked you: *do you know how to play the trombone*?"

He says it slow like I'm deaf.

"No, sir," I say. I hate that my voice cracks when I say it.

"Look at you, little nervous Nellie," he says. "I'll show you how."

While he chuckles and holds the empty whiskey bottle out to me, Momma walks over to her pocketbook and pulls out a dollar bill. She don't say not to so I have to walk over to him. She'd kill me if I weren't polite. *We ain't animals,* she'd say.

"All you gotta do," Mr. Creepy Rock says, "go on and take the bottle. It's empty, don't worry. Now hold it at your chin and push your upper lip out like this"—he makes a monkey face—"and blow some air down into it. That's it! You got it! Now you can say you're a trombone player! Ha ha look at you, wiping at your mouth like you're gonna get cancer from the germs. Boy, you're a good little girl, aintcha."

I hand the sticky bottle to him and back away. I hate the way he smiles real wide at me. And the way he says *good little girl* doesn't make it feel good at all.

"Here," Momma says, shoving the dollar bill into my hand. Her back's to him. Her eyes are back to being cold and there's no sign of her laughing when she lowers her voice so only I can hear and says, "Now go on and leave us be."

"Where?" I ask her.

"We should send her on a beer run," Mr. Creepy Rock says.

"Well, now, wouldn't that be handy," Momma says back in the fake voice. I can tell she doesn't want to do whatever he's saying but she has to go along with it because she doesn't want to be *in-hospitable*. When Richard started hanging around back in Toast, Momma said we should do whatever he said because he was *our guest* and we needed to be *hospitable. If you don't make guests feel right at home you're inhospitable,* she said to me and Emma. *We ain't animals you know,* she said.

"Hey, kid, I buy you fly," Mr. Creepy Rock says, standing up to fish out his wallet from his back pocket. He's got a silver chain snaking from his belt to his front pocket and whatever's on the end of it jingles from inside his pants. He pulls a twenty out of his billfold and holds it out for me.

I look at Momma, who is staring at it like a stray dog looking at table scraps.

"What're ya, deaf? You a little Helen Keller, are ya?" He laughs and looks over at Momma who's fake-smiling so he keeps going, cracking jokes, trying to make her laugh a laugh he doesn't know ain't real.

"You need me to do sign language, Helen Keller? Look at her, just staring at it like she never saw an Andrew Jackson before. All right, now, this here's what we call money. M-O-N-E-Y. Take this—good girl, that's right put it in your pocket. Good. Now go on down to the corner place and fetch us a bottle of Jim Beam. Tell

Lenny—he's the guy behind the counter—tell Lenny it's for Rock and he'll sell it to ya. Go on. Scoot, Helen Keller."

I look at Momma but I cain't make out what all she's thinking behind the plastic mask she has frozen across her face. She just nods at me and keeps on grinning for him to see.

"She's a quiet one, that one," Mr. Creepy Rock says to Momma as he settles back down on the bed. This time he puts his arm around Momma, acting like it's *his* bed, in *his* room that he paid for with the money he made from selling ever-thing *he* ever owned.

"You like 'em seen and not heard, do ya?" he says to Momma, twisting a piece of her hair around his finger.

They're back to laughing when I close the door behind me. It's summer so the night hasn't fully taken over for the day yet. It's dark enough to where you couldn't read words but still light enough to where you'd know what's on a plate in front of you. My mouth is watering so much on my way to the candy machine, you'd think I was a dog or something. My fingers shake hard, I'm so excited for a candy bar, and I almost push the wrong button and end up with a Mounds, but phee-you, the right one falls to the slot after all. I eat my Baby Ruth real slow, pulling off teensy tiny pieces with my fingers, pretending I am a momma bird dropping worms into baby bird beaks. In my head I count to thirty and chew real slow to make it last longer. Leaning on the balcony rail in front of the candy machine, I watch the traffic light turn red, yellow, green—it stays green longest, red second longest, and yellow but a second or two.

It's hard not to eat the whole candy bar altogether but halfway through I make myself quit so I can have some for tomorrow.

"What in the good Lord's name do you think you're doing, going about your own sweet business without a care in your empty head." Momma's popped her head out the door to our room, hiss-whispering down the balcony to me and pointing to the spot right in front of her. "Git over here."

"Sorry, Momma," I say on my way hurrying to her. Thank goodness I swallowed the bite before she saw me chewing real slow.

"You're *gonna* be sorry when I get through with you. Now hurry down to the store and fetch up that bottle like the man told you to."

"He's scary, Momma," I whisper, my mouth moving before my brain can tell it not to. "I got a bad feeling from him."

Good thing there's a rail along the balcony or I would've fallen onto the blacktop parking lot when she whacked me. Instead I only hit my head on it but it don't hurt too much. Before I can pull myself back up to standing Momma appears over me.

"You get a *bad feeling* from him?" she hisses at me. The blood's warm trickling down from where I hit my head but I hold still while Momma whisper-hollers at me. The balcony lights flicker on and ever-thing turns orange, and orange is a scary color in a mad mother's face. "If you so much as make a squeak about him, I'll pull your arm out of the socket and beat you dead with it. You hear me? That man in there could be my meal ticket outta here. You mess this up for me and I swear to Jesus I will hunt you down and send you to Hell where you'll rot for the rest of your pathetic life. After all you put me through. Standing there. High on your horse. Telling me you got a *bad feeling* about him? You better hurry the hell up and get that liquor. And bring back the receipt and every penny of change, you hear me? Pull yourself together and *get going*," Momma says before disappearing behind the slammed door.

I cain't waste time rubbing my head but I have to pause a bit because when I stand up I see stars and I know if I'm not careful I might could faint. I got a *propensity for fainting spells*. Momma wrote that on the medical form parents had to fill out at my last school. *Caroline is uncoordinated, bruises real easy, and has a propensity for fainting spells*, she wrote. She used the dictionary.

I'm on my last leg with Momma I can just tell. I've got to watch myself and do ever-thing perfect from here on out. I'll *go the extra mile*. I swear I'm gonna be so good Momma won't know what hit her. Maybe I'll pick up some ice along with the Jim Beam. She loves ice. Clinking it around in her glass, shaking it into different positions. Momma used to say *without ice the world'd be hell*. That's the best idea I had in a long time, to get ice for Momma. That's *extra mile* material for sure. Wait, the ice machine's still broken—there's an Out of Order sign on the front flap of it. Dangit.

The man behind the counter at the liquor store nods like he knew I'd be standing there in front of him, telling him Rock sent me to buy a bottle of Jim Beam. When I ask him where's the ice he tilts his head toward the freezer at the back of the store and goes back to filling in the crossword puzzle. I fetch the ice while he sacks up the bottle then hands me the receipt and change without saying a word. Dang, this ice is heavier than I thought it'd be. Didn't look this heavy whenever Richard'd come in with a bag or two on his shoulders. Figure if I lay the bottle down on top of the ice and carry it with both hands like I'm rocking a baby I might could do it. Trouble is my arms get frostbit before I'm out the door practically. It *is* ice, after all. I push back out into the world, the bell jingling behind me, and I decide I'll count the steps it takes to get back to the room—that'll keep my mind from thinking about my freezing arms. Twenty steps to the sidewalk. At thirty steps I've got to stop.

I lose count somewhere short of the Loveless office. Mr. Burdock's not in there but Birdie's curled up under the potted plant in the window.

"Hey, Birdie kitty kitty kitty," I say through the glass, tapping to get his attention while I rest my arms one last time. Birdie looks up at me, meows, then tucks his head back into his curled self. I wish I was a cat that could sleep all day and night. "You're a good kitty cat, Birdie. Aren't you. Yes you are. Good kitty."

I pick the ice bag back up with the bottle laying neatly across the top and head to the stairs. Mr. Burdock put plastic grass carpet on all the steps. I make it one floor up and am three steps toward the second floor.

"You need a hand with that?" Mr. Burdock's voice comes out of nowhere behind me.

I didn't plan on dropping the ice—I swear I didn't. But it's dark and Mr. Burdock scared the living daylights out of me and before I know it Jim Beam is crashing onto the cement way down below.

He whistles through his teeth and I drop the ice and say *"she's gonna kill me"* over and over on my way hurrying down to see if what I think happened really happened. Maybe it was a bad dream. Maybe my mind played tricks on me again like Sheriff said back in Hendersonville.

She's gonna kill me.

The minute I see the broken glass bottle and the spray of wet coming out from it I know I'm in the kind of trouble I haven't seen since Richard passed. I can hear Mr. Burdock on his way down to catch up with me. *"Now, hold on a minute,"* he's saying, *"let me see what's what. Just hold on till I get down there."*

Between him and Momma I'm dead, plain and simple. I've got to run. I ain't got a choice. No way am I going back up there with less money and no Jim Beam. And Mr. Burdock didn't want a kid staying here in the first place—I bet he's been waiting on something like this to kick me out. My heart's pounding like a horse in the Kentucky Derby.

She's gonna kill me.

I can hear Mr. Burdock calling after me something about how he was sorry and only wanted to help but I'm already out of sight and halfway over the fence. I skin my knee on the way down to the pool floor but I can barely feel it for the thumping in my chest. No way'll Momma know to look for me here so I'm safe for now, heart, you can stop beating so fast and loud. I may be stupid but

I'm not so stupid enough to lay in the middle of the pool floor like usual. I curl up like Birdie over in the deep end, where I'd kicked most of the trash into a pile when I first started laying down here. Good thing the trash is still here because I use some of it to cover me up. In the shadows, no one'll find me and I can buy some time to put a plan together for what to do next.

Mr. Burdock's talking to himself from the maid's closet where he's fetching a broom I reckon. I feel bad—I should be up there doing that. He's been nothing but nice to me, Mr. Burdock. And here I go making trouble for him. I arrange a couple more handfuls of trash over me so now I'm completely invisible in the dark. It's not too smelly so that's good news too. Laying still like this my head decides it's time to start thumping from pain where it hit the railing. *Thump. Thump.*

I hear Momma hollering for me. I hold my breath. She ain't using the top of her lungs on account of it's a motel not just our house so I can say I didn't hear her. If she catches me, that is. Now her voice is mixing with Mr. Burdock's. I can just . . . make . . . out . . . the . . . words . . .

"I sure am sorry about that girl of mine, Mr. Burdock," Momma's saying. "I promise you she'll make amends when I get ahold of her. You can take my word for it. Caroline? Caroline! You better march yourself on home right now, girl!"

Thump. Thump. Boy my head hurts a little more than I thought it would.

In the quiet following Momma's calling for me, the sound of the broom pushing the tinkling glass into a pile carries across the air. I got good ears normally but tonight they're not working so good because of the pop I got from Momma maybe. They're still talking to each other, Mr. Burdock and Momma.

"Like I said, it ain't her fault," Mr. Burdock's telling Momma. "I offered to carry it all for her—she was struggling up them stairs and you can call me anything under the sun but you cain't say I ain't a gentleman. I ain't gonna stand by watching a girl carry something I could take off her hands with ease. Hap Burdock's a gentleman, through and through."

They say some things I cain't make out, then Momma says: "I best get back to my room. Sorry again for the trouble. Caroline? Time to come on home now," Momma calls out in her whiskey voice she's putting on for Mr. Burdock. From the click of her shoes it sounds like she's heading back upstairs.

"I'll keep an eye out for her and send her home, don't you worry," Mr. Burdock calls out to her. "I'll send a replacement bottle of Jim Beam up in a minute. Right's right, after all. I broke it, I bought it, you know."

Glass scrapes into the dustpan. Mr. Burdock mutters something I cain't understand. A door closes hard. His boots carry him back home. Another door closes. Now it's quiet but for the whoosh of cars passing. Headlights beam across the top of the pool, lighting up the side of the building, and it occurs to me we'd be up all night if our room faced the other direction 'cause more cars head into town than out of it and those headlights are pretty bright.

I must've drifted off because next thing I hear is the slam of a car door. An engine revs loud twice then three times. I bet it's Mr. Creepy Rock in a big old truck like a cowboy in an old Western movie. He peels out like Richard used to do on payday. If I time it right, Momma will be passed out when I come back in. 'Cept the door'll be locked. Dangit. I better go on and get it over with now or I'll be sleeping out here from now on.

I'm not too dizzy standing up thank goodness. The moon has turned ever-thing the dark purple of a bruise.

"Momma? It's me, Momma, open up," I say into the door. It's hard to be night-quiet when you need to be heard through a door. "Momma? Please, Momma? I'm real sorry."

When I hear something moving in the room, I squinch up my lady parts real tight so I don't have an accident all over myself like

I usually do when I'm this scared. I been trying real hard to keep from it. But it's too late—when I hear the sound of the metal latch turning, unlocking the door, I feel the warm wet down the insides of my legs.

"I'm sorry, Momma, I'm real real sorry," I say before I even set eyes on her.

The door lies open to the room but since it's pitch-dark in there I cain't make out where exactly Momma is. She can move quick when she puts her mind to it. Sure enough, I never even saw her arm until it was attaching itself to a fistful of my hair. Then she's dragging me into the room like I'm a sack of potatoes.

"I'm—*drowning*—and you—are the—*brick*—in my—*pocket,*" Momma says in between pops. Her foot does the rest of the talking, until the wind is completely kicked out of me and the air is all yelled out of her. I covered my head with my arms this time but now I'm thinking I'd have been better off holding my sides instead. I cough if I take too deep a breath. It's not so bad if I pant like a dog.

I'm smart enough to know to stay put when she finishes with me. Until she gets into bed I'm best where I am here on the floor. Momma doesn't like seeing me after I been punished. She doesn't even like to *breathe the same air* as me. She feels bad, is why. If I could I'd tell her I'm gonna be so good from now on she won't believe her eyes. I'm no brick in her pocket, she'll see. It'll be like magic. I'll get Cricket to help me work on carrying stuff and not dropping it. And maybe they could loan me the money to pay back Mr. Rock for the Jim Beam so Momma ain't *beholden* which she hates more than pickles. I'll take such good care of her she won't need Mr. Creepy Rock or anybody else but me. And if she needs me she surely won't go off and leave me with the state of North Carolina. Or in the loony bin.

In the morning light I realize I'm lucky: Momma mostly stuck to punishing my body and not my head so she didn't leave many marks for me to have to cover up. I get out of bed without making a sound but the way Momma's sleeping, I don't think an alarm clock could get her to stir. I tiptoe over to her makeup kit and pat some Foundation for a Youthful Complexion on my forehead *for good measure*. As long as I don't cough, I'm good. I just have to take care to move slow on account of my knee. I must have knocked it on something. The key to sneaking out of a hotel room your momma's sleeping in is to turn the door handle *before* you pull. Then, once you get on the outside of the door, you've got to remember to turn the handle before you close it or you may as well forget about the whole thing to begin with. It sure is bright and sunny out today. The kind of sunny that makes the day feel clean. Going down the stairs is tough but by the time I'm out front of the Loveless I feel a hundred times better. I found the rest of the Baby Ruth in my pocket so I ain't even that hungry. I make it last the whole of the time I wait for Mrs. Ford, sitting in the shade of the tree by the Loveless driveway.

Oh goody! Here they are now. I check over my shoulder to make sure Mr. Burdock don't see me getting into the minivan and sure enough, the coast is clear. Just seeing them waving at me through the car windows makes me know today is gonna be a great day. Ever-thing with Cricket and them is great.

"Hey, Mrs. Ford! Hey, Cricket!" I say, reaching for the seat belt so they know I'm a fast learner. I'm gonna make them want to have me around all the time.

CHAPTER FOURTEEN

Honor

What in the world?

"Hey, Carrie, how are you, honey?" I ask, trying not to stare at her as she settles into the backseat next to Cricket. "You need help with that seat belt? Cricket, help Carrie out, will you?"

"No no, I got it thanks," Carrie says, waving her off.

I guess in addition to letting children wear garish makeup, they refuse to practice basic vehicle safety up in Hendersonville because this child cannot operate a seat belt to save her life. Ha— literally. Good one, Honor.

"Well, don't you look *fancy*," I say, picking the word carefully, "with your face all made up. Did your mama help you apply it, honey?"

"Ugh, no offense, but I never want to wear makeup," Cricket says, as I had known she would. "*Everyone* wears makeup but me. I'm, like, the *only one* I know who doesn't."

"All right, Cricket, I think we've heard enough from you on the subject. Some of us enjoy putting on some makeup from time to time. And I'm sure Carrie's mother has parameters she hopes her daughter will keep to, isn't that right, Carrie?"

"Ma'am?"

"Your mother has rules about when you can wear makeup and how much?"

I don't know how else to say it: the girl looks like a clown with foundation gunked thick over her face. What could her mother be thinking, letting her go out in public looking like this?

"Oh, my momma doesn't care," Carrie says.

"*Really?*" Cricket asks her.

"I mean, she *cares*—she cares about ever-thing I do of course," Carrie says.

"Of course she does," I say. "Listen, honey, I've got to help Cricket's grandmother with some important house stuff, so y'all are going to have to find something to do at home, okay?"

"That's fine," Carrie says, shrugging while Cricket groans. "My momma? She doesn't care if I put on some of her makeup ever once in a while. But, like, about my friends? She cares about all of that stuff. Just like a normal mom. She's always asking me about all the mail I get, about all the phone calls and stuff. *Who's that on the phone?* she asks me all the time. It's hard, though, 'cause she cain't keep my friends' names straight. I got so many of them, that's why."

"You're so lucky," Cricket says. And my heart breaks.

"I don't know. My momma just wants me to be happy," Carrie says. "Just like all moms want their kids to be happy. She's always saying that. *I just want you to be happy, Caroline.* It's embarrassing how much she says it."

"We *do* want y'all to be happy! You're absolutely right. You hear that, Cricket? You hear your friend saying that? Just remember that the next time you say I'm trying to ruin your life."

I don't need to check the rearview mirror, I can *feel* Cricket rolling her eyes.

"Oh-Em-Gee, that is *so* not true," Cricket says, leaning over to tell Carrie about Layla Latrooce.

"Here we go again," I say. "When are we ever going to stop dredging up poor Layla Latrooce?"

"What? Jeez! I'm telling her about something else," Cricket says, faking an innocent face. "Quit *spying*."

I can just make out Carrie whispering to Cricket, "I cain't believe you can talk to your momma like that. If *I* did that? Who-ee, I'd be skinned alive!"

Layla Latrooce was in Cricket's class last year. A preteen with a woman's body and all the boys slack-jawed and nipping at her heels as a result. Which is not her fault of course but a girl like that has to be watched closely, something her parents never seemed to do. On the contrary, Layla's mother clearly subscribed to the if-you-got-it-flaunt-it philosophy, dressing in the lowest-cut tops she could find. Pretty soon, word got out that Layla Latrooce was playing some online video-chat thing and hooked up with a seventeen-year-old boy. Like I told Ed when Cricket first brought her over after school: her parents sure did set the bar low when they chose to give her a name like Layla Latrooce. Sounds like a stripper's name. The girl's going to get really good at taking off her clothes, is all I'm saying. Why not go ahead and install a pole in your living room right now? Oh, we sure laughed over Layla Latrooce, Eddie and me. Say what you will about Ed Ford, the man's got a great sense of humor. I'll give him that. Certainly better than his parents', who named their son Edsil but always appeared baffled by the laughter that broke out whenever Ed's full name was revealed. Layla lost interest in Cricket pretty fast, but unfortunately for us we'd already gone on record banning Cricket from going over to the Latrooce house so *we* were the villains in Cricket's eyes. Never mind that Layla flat-out ignored Cricket to her face. No. According to Cricket, Eddie and I were the *Worst Parents in the World.*

"Hey, Mom, where did Ferrin Albee move to?" Cricket asks from the backseat.

"Oh my goodness, Ferrin Albee," I say. "Poor Ferrin Albee."

"Ferrin Albee had both boy and girl parts," Cricket tells Carrie. "No one ever really knew if he was a boy like he said he was or if *he* was really a *she.*"

"So sad," I say. I can see Carrie's eyes big as saucers, taking in all our stories. "I wonder where they ended up. The Albees. I think they went up North. New York probably. I hope that child's all right."

If you ask me, there's yet another example of parents not doing right by their children in name choice. I mean, *Ferrin*? When your child clearly has some gender issues? *Ferrin?* Couldn't they have made it a tad bit easier and gone with, say, Charlotte. Or Catherine. Or James. Michael. Oh, well.

"So, was Ferrin a boy or a girl, Mom?" Cricket asks.

This is where it's helpful to have a child with attention deficit disorder. All I have to do to avoid answering a difficult question that, let's face it, will only lead to more difficult questions is wait about four seconds and Cricket is onto the next topic.

"Hey, Carrie, can you do this?" Cricket asks, rubber-banding her mouth into an ugly position not many can imitate. Her top lip curls to the left while the bottom heads in the opposite direction.

Ladies and gentlemen, my daughter the Subject Changer. The girls proceed to a timeless competition that is as annoying as it is humorous. In the rearview mirror I watch Carrie unsuccessfully try to copy Cricket's snarl.

"No, but can you do this?" Carrie asks, touching her nose with the tip of her tongue.

"Wow! That's really something," I say, smiling back at the two of them.

"Wait, can you do this?" Cricket says. "Wait wait, no, look. Wait, don't make me laugh. Okay now."

"Cricket, don't fold your eyelids up like that," I tell her, but it's too late.

"Ew, that's so scary looking," Carrie says, clearly charmed. "I wish I could do that."

"Oh wait, I've got a good one. Here, squeeze my hand for thirty seconds," Cricket says. "Mom, can you time us? Okay starting . . . now!"

"Girls, are you hungry?"

"Mom! Time us! Thirty seconds!"

"I'm about to pass the grocery store," I say. "Speak now or forever hold your peace."

"Mom!"

"Cricket, I'll time you in a second. Just tell me: are you hungry now or can y'all hang on until we get home? Carrie, honey, are you hungry?"

"Yes, ma'am. I mean, no, ma'am," the little voice says.

I can tell she is checking with her new best friend to see if she should be hungry or not.

"Y'all wait in the car, I'm just going to run in for two seconds. I'll be right back. I'm leaving the car running so you have the air-conditioning on. Cricket, are you listening to me?"

"Mom, I'm paralyzing Carrie's hand. Watch! Wait, Carrie. Don't move your fingers until I say. Keep squeezing my hand. Keep going. That's good . . ."

"Hannah Chaplin Ford, do you hear me?"

"On the count of three try to wiggle them, okay? Not yet. Not . . . yet . . ." Cricket directs Carrie.

"Cricket! I'm getting out of the car now. Wait here with Carrie, okay?"

"One . . . two . . . *three!* Okay now, try to move your fingers."

I unbuckle my seat belt and turn to watch Cricket beam at her triumph. Carrie is holding her still-clenched fist out, mentally willing her own fingers to move, clearly horrified that she cannot make the connection.

"I cain't move my fingers! Help! I cain't move them," she says, bursting into tears.

I had no idea this would lead to crying. I'm so glad I didn't leave them right then. Thank goodness I have a fresh packet of Kleenex right in the glove compartment for emergencies.

"Aw, honey, shhhhh, it's okay." I try to reach Carrie to console her from the front seat, but the headrest is in the way so I settle on her leg. "Cricket, what did I tell you about these stupid human tricks. See what happens?"

"Carrie, look, it's just a trick, see?"

Cricket gently takes Carrie's hand and opens it flat.

"See?" Cricket says, looking worried and, if I'm not mistaken, kind of sisterly. "It's okay. I'm sorry. It's okay."

"Cricket, don't do any more of those silly things," I say. "How many times have I told you to slow down and don't overwhelm people. Here, let me get you some more tissue, sweetheart."

"I wasn't trying to overwhelm her, Mom, jeez! Carrie, was I overwhelming you? I didn't mean to."

"Don't be silly, of course she's not going to say yes to that," I say. We talk at once, Cricket and I do, and I realize it can be a lot to take in. Especially for a lost little girl. "Let's just . . . let's just be quiet here for a minute, can we? Honey, let me wipe your face a little."

Carrie flinches at first, but I'm determined. The caked makeup comes off with each swipe of the Kleenex, revealing an angry bruise above her right eye. Cricket and I both gasp.

"Oh my Lord, what *happened*?" I ask Carrie.

Now I know why she had so much makeup on.

"Answer me, honey," I say, trying to keep my voice from shaking in fury. "What happened?"

I stroke Carrie's knee until her tears come to a hiccuping end.

"Carrie, I hate that silly trick too," I say, waiting on her to tell me about the bruise. One thing at a time. "Cricket did that to my hand a long time ago—I remember how scary it felt. I'm so sorry, honey. Does it hurt? Your hand? You all right, sweetie?"

Carrie looks in wonder at her now-recovered hand, opening and closing it as though she's just come out of a coma, then she nods up at me.

"You need to tell me about that bruise . . . Well, aren't you sweet . . ."

While I am talking, Caroline takes her hand that was, until a few seconds ago, immobilized, and places it on top of mine, which is still on her knee. For a breathless moment we look down as though they are disembodied, these appendages of ours. When Cricket reaches over and puts her hand on top of ours, Carrie, eyes full of wonder, finds her words.

"Y'all are the nicest people I ever met," she whispers. "In my whole life."

Well, that just about breaks my heart.

"Aw, honey, now you're going to go melt my mascara right off my lashes," I say. "It's not hard to be nice to *you*—you're such a sweetheart. Isn't she, Cricket?"

And then my daughter surprises me once again.

"So what happened to your forehead?" Cricket asks her sternly.

Carrie's hand flutters up to cover the mark and she tells us about playing catch with a kid who lives a few doors down from them at the Loveless and how since she's no good at baseball she got *beaned* and luckily it hadn't hit her in the eye.

"That's what my momma said when she came rushing over," Carrie says, "you know, when I got knocked down. She was real worried. She practically *cried* she was so worried about me."

"Of course she was," I say.

It does sound plausible. After all I went through with our Caroline and the Dressers, I've learned not to jump to conclusions too quickly.

Eileen and Whit Dresser moved to our neighborhood from Omaha soon after Caroline was diagnosed. In fact, at first I felt bad for not having the time to go over to welcome them with cookies or a bottle of wine like you're supposed to, but back then we could barely keep up with all the phone calls we had to return and all the other things that get brushed aside when you have a sick child in and out of the hospital. Ed and I spent our days as a tag team, spelling each other so that one of us was always with Caroline. I don't think I even laid eyes on either Dresser for their first few months on Witherall Drive. When I wasn't at the hospital or in a doctor's office I was picking up the slack at home or I was hunting down second opinions, researching treatment options, washing up and returning casserole dishes, or relieving my mother, who would come over to take care of poor Cricket, whom we barely saw. The Dressers were about the furthest thing from our minds.

Until we got a knock on the door one night from Child Protective Services. It was a Tuesday. I remember because Tuesdays happened to be the only nights Eddie had without the police beeper he'd been assigned. That particular night was a rare one that found all four of us under the same roof at the same time. Caroline was in between treatments. Eddie was upstairs reading to Cricket and I hollered up that I'd get the door. At that time it wasn't uncommon for neighbors to stop by with food or a stuffed animal, so I didn't think anything of it being late. We were a tight community there on Witherall Drive, a tree-lined cul-de-sac with a neatly planted island in the middle of the circle. In fall a neighborhood committee of gardeners planted mums around the edges; in May, impatiens. Thanks to an avid botanist a generation of neighbors ago, every spring dozens of bulbs shot two different varieties of yellow-headed daffodils through the thawing soil. We knew ten of the ten homeowners, nine of whom were young parents of young children who rode Big Wheels and tricycles freely in the street and ran through sprinklers in summer. The tenth home belonged to Mr. and Mrs. Hamilton, an elderly couple who had raised their three children in their powder blue vinyl-sided house and enjoyed watching ours run wild from wicker armchairs on their front porch. Most of the other homes had been updated to reflect changing and optimistically ambitious aesthetics. Front walks had *pavers*. Front doors had *porticoes*. Whitewashed brick and clapboard replaced siding. It was almost as if our houses were working in tandem with our careers to climb up the rungs of society. We had block parties twice a year, usually timed to coincide with a national holiday like the Fourth of July, where barbecues were wheeled out front and everyone pooled their food on a picnic table festively outfitted with whatever decoration befitted the occasion. Yes, the Websters were lax in taking down their Christmas lights (one year they twinkled back at me on Easter. Easter!), and yes, from time to time Jim Barnestable forgot to pick up after his dog, but on balance it was an idyllic haven in which to raise our girls. When Mr. Hamilton passed away, the grown Hamilton children returned to move their mother into a nursing home, and while it was the right thing to do—she had been showing signs of Alzheimer's—it was heartbreaking to watch. The Dressers bought the Hamilton home at the asking price and began renovating immediately.

Even when I saw that it was a stranger standing there at our front door on that fateful Tuesday night—*even then* I remember thinking perhaps they were dropping something off for one of our friends. Funny how the mind works. When you haven't done anything wrong, when you have a wide circle of friends and family supporting you, the last thing you would ever expect is for a complete stranger to accuse you of something so abhorrent it's almost comical. *Now,* of course, my suspicions are easily aroused, but back then . . .

"Mrs. Edsil Ford?" the woman asked me, checking the papers she held. If she saw the humor in my husband's name, as everyone else did, she did a great job of hiding it.

"Yes?" I answered.

I remember suddenly being aware of the fact that I had forgotten to put lipstick back on after dinner. A nice Southern woman is never without her lipstick.

"I'm Marcia Clipper, C-P-S," she said, handing me her business card.

Being unfamiliar with the acronym, I struggled to figure out what the letters stood for and was still puzzling on it when Ed came up behind me in the doorway.

"Can we help you?" he asked her.

"May I come in?" she asked.

Not waiting for an answer, she moved forward, knowing we, being polite North Carolinians, would allow her room. Looking back, I realize she was clearly so accustomed to being rebuffed that she had to make inroads before the gravity of the situation bloomed across the mind of whomever she was addressing.

"Whoa there," Eddie said. "Let's see a badge."

"Here, she gave me this," I told him, handing over the business card I had been staring at but not comprehending.

"What's all this about?" he asked, not even glancing at it.

The rest of that night is a blur of tears and bewilderment and, in the end, helpless fury. Bottom line: the Dressers had seen bruises on Caroline when she went to their door selling Girl Scout cookies, *which,* by the way, she had begged to be allowed to do because *that's what normal kids do,* she had said. Caroline had promised to come home when she felt tired. *Plus, I'll make a kill-*

ing because no one's going to turn away a Girl Scout with leukemia, she'd said. She was like that, our Caroline. Always making me smile. She got her father's sense of humor.

Instead of coming to us or to another of their neighbors, the Dressers called 9-1-1, and Child Protective Services rained down on us like we were running a day care in a meth lab. Even Eddie's being on the force didn't deter the *rigorous investigation* they said they were required by law to conduct. An investigation that culminated in Caroline being taken away—alone and crying—in an unmarked car to an unnamed location for questioning. To say I was apoplectic would be a massive understatement. I thought Eddie was going to have a stroke he was so mad. It was splashed across the front page of the local papers. CHAPLIN KIN INVESTI-GATED FOR CHILD ABUSE. That was all anybody needed to see. *Everybody* was talking about it. The stares and sneers kept me from going anywhere but the hospital for a long time. Ed was put on desk duty because too many people on his beat recognized him and that put his safety at risk. Someone even threw a bottle at him, though thank God they had bad aim. His captain told him the whole thing was *damaging the credibility of the force.* We stopped going to the neighborhood block parties and did our grocery shopping at night at the twenty-four-hour Kroger outside town. Our friends—our real friends—stuck by us, but many of the neighbors I'd considered friends evaporated. Which certainly made moving out a whole lot easier. In the end we were, of course, cleared of any wrongdoing, but to this day the whiff of "child abuser" trails me like cheap perfume. Memories of the turmoil it brought into our lives will remain with me for the rest of my life.

Good Lord, the heat is oppressive today. After scrapping the grocery store, we finally pull into the driveway at home.

"Now, girls, I've got to go run an errand, so I'm going to drop you off and do it now to get it over with. Y'all play upstairs and don't make any work for Grandma, okay?"

"Mom, we're not *babies,*" Cricket says, throwing a conspiratorial look to Carrie, "we don't *play.*"

"Fine," I say, pressing Door Unlock. "Cricket, I've got chips and popcorn for y'all to snack on if you're hungry. There's Cokes in the icebox on the door. Now y'all get that for yourselves—I don't want you asking your grandma or she'll want to wait on you two."

"Okay, okay, jeez," Cricket says. She slides the side door open and hops out.

I watch them bounce up the walk. And then, on her way up the porch stairs, Carrie slips her little hand into Cricket's and my heart just about melts. I wish Eddie could see this.

I sigh and reach around to collect the used tissues, the backpack Cricket forgot, a crumpled up Big Mac container, and the two empty Coke cans that've been clanking underneath the seat for days because I keep forgetting to clear out all this mess. It's a miracle I manage to make it up the walk, through the front door, and into the kitchen without anything falling off the pyramid of trash teetering in my arms.

And then the universe speaks.

I've barely emptied everything onto the kitchen counter and said "hey" to my mother when damned if Edsil Ford isn't rattling into the driveway. I'd recognize the sound of that old pickup truck anywhere.

"Knock, knock!" he calls out as he lets himself in the front door. "Anybody home?"

Mother looks at me defensively, eyes wide, mouthing *"I don't know anything about it,"* but lately she's been on a kick to get us back together, so that, coupled with her love of Nora Ephron movies, means I can't rule out a setup. Until Cricket flies down the stairs and into her father's arms, and then it's all clear.

"Daddy-O!" she says, as he swings her in a circle before putting her down and letting her out of his embrace. "Lemme go, Dad, jeez! Okay, okay, wait right here. I have something incredible to show you."

He laughs and watches her hurry back up the stairs, pleased too to see her so full of life for the first time in a long time.

"Hey," I say. I come into the front hall to prepare him, warn him, I don't know—I guess maybe even to protect him. I feel worried about his reaction but if I'm going to be honest, part of me is also curious to see what, if any, emotion he'll show. When he sees her. Carrie. Caroline.

"Hey, baby." He smiles when he sees me and I pretend to be bugged by it but secretly I'm glad he still calls me *baby* sometimes.

"I take it she called you over here?" I smile and glance up the stairs at the invisible wake Cricket left behind.

To build in a little time before he's hit with the shock, I hustle us both out the door, explaining I need to talk to him in private. He opens the passenger door of the truck and I clamber in, smiling for a moment at the familiar smell of McDonald's and diesel.

"Sorry it's so messy," he says, brushing trash off the armrest between us, then starting the engine. "Let me get the AC going. Man, it's hot. Speaking of which, what's our girl all hot and bothered about? She called me yesterday and said I had to come over right away but she said it wasn't life or death and I was pulling a double shift so—"

"Shhh, we don't have much time," I say, hushing him. "Okay, first of all, Mother had a foreclosure notice tacked up to the door yesterday. That's number one."

"What?" He turns in his seat to face me. "You're kidding me."

"No, unfortunately, I'm not. Apparently she's been handing all her money over to Hunter, though of course she won't admit it. But there's something else. I just want to prepare you. Cricket has a new friend. A little girl. We don't know much of anything about her yet—she's new to town, staying with her mother at the Loveless of all places."

"What's that got to do with the foreclosure?" he asks. "And what're they doing in *that* dump?"

"Well, that's the thing," I say, nodding. "They're barely making ends meet from the sound of it, but that's a whole other story. This girl, she looks—"

Before I can finish, Cricket knocks on his window and points to little Carrie standing next to her in the burning sun. I hadn't seen them come out. Ed is now plunged into the shock of recognition Cricket, Mother, and I had. He feels for the door handle and robotically opens his door without for a second taking his eyes off Carrie.

"I tried to warn you." I mutter the words as I hop out onto the driveway, but he doesn't hear me and what does it matter anyway?

"Dad, this is my friend." Cricket gently holds Carrie by the shoulders. It's unclear what other than monumental shock is going on in Eddie's mind.

"Caroline," he whispers the name.

"You can call me Carrie, sir," she says, searching my face to see if Ed hearing that name would count against her, poor thing.

I never would have predicted what comes next. Never in a million years. Edsil Ford, my stoic husband who barely showed a flicker of emotion after Caroline's passing, drops to his knees in front of Carrie. His knees!

"Your name is *Caroline*?" he asks her in an almost-whisper.

She nods.

Cricket comes to stand beside me, I put my arm around her, and together we watch in total amazement as her father bursts into tears. Tears!

Carrie looks at us panicked, but before I can reassure her or explain or even just smile, Eddie pulls her into him, hugging her, still sobbing like a newborn. After a minute or so Cricket stands on her tiptoes to whisper, "Mom, *do* something" in my ear, breaking my reverie. I clear my throat because, well, because I want to give Eddie a chance to regain his composure on his own. He's a proud man, Eddie. But throat clearing doesn't get through. He's that broken up.

"Um, Carrie honey, I'm sorry," I say, stepping forward to rest a hand on Eddie's back, feeling an ache of love and sadness and grief rush in at the contact. "Mr. Ford's just surprised at the likeness we talked about."

I lean down to quietly comfort Ed, who is still holding on to Carrie as if for dear life.

"Eddie, let's let poor Carrie here catch her breath, m'kay? Ed? Baby, I know. I know."

He releases Carrie and struggles to his feet.

"Of course, of course." He sniffs and mops his face with a red bandanna he's pulled from his back pocket. "Sorry. Jeez."

"Cricket, take Carrie on inside while Dad and I catch up, will you?" I smile to let her know he'll be okay, but will he? I don't know.

"Come on, Carrie," Cricket says.

Then I get the wish I'd thought of only a few minutes ago. This time, though, Cricket reaches for Carrie's hand and, with Eddie and me looking on, mouths hanging open, they skitter up the walk, up the steps, and into the house. The door closes behind them. We turn to face one another and once again, this man I'm so dang confused about stuns me. Now it's me he's pulling into him, burying his head in my hair, his words tumbling into my ear.

"I prayed to God for Him to give me more time with her." He chokes back sobs. "I swore I'd keep holding myself together, be a better husband and father, if I could just have more time. You fell apart—you did, and that's fine, Honor, you have every right. We couldn't both crumble, and anyway I'm the man. I'm supposed to be rock steady. But you want to know the truth? The truth is I've been holding out for a miracle. All this time, I've been waiting. I still pray for Him to let me see her again, just one more time. I pray so hard, baby, I pray so hard I've been worried I'm losing my mind."

I hold him, stroke his back, and whisper, "Shhh . . ."

"You just don't know," he's sobbing. "You just don't know."

But I do know.

Because I do the same thing.

CHAPTER FIFTEEN

Carrie

Things I Now Know About Momma

1. She had a best friend named Suzy Bridges. They got caught smoking cigarettes on school property. More than once.
2. She wasn't in any clubs in high school and she didn't play sports.
3. Momma was prom queen.
4. Mr. White was prom king. And he had hair back then.
5. Momma was voted Most Beautiful.

Things I Now Know About Daddy

1. His nickname in high school was Hef.
2. He drove real fast but never got speeding tickets.
3. He was captain of the football team.
4. He was good at getting free beer.
5. He was voted Most Likely to Be Found Dead in a Ditch.

Cricket's computer really does have the answer to any question you ask it. I've never seen a school picture of Momma—and I'm her flesh and blood!—but the computer has, and all Cricket had to do was push a few buttons to find it. Momma was about a million times prettier back then and she's real pretty now. Her yearbook shows her smiling, her hair almost reaching her elbow, curly at the ends. She didn't wear as much makeup as some of the other girls in her class—we could see their pictures too. The whole yearbook was there waiting for us. Momma wore a cross around her neck and a pretty pink button-down shirt that looked ironed. And from what some of the writing underneath the pictures said, she and Suzy Bridges did ever-thing together. They were *inseparable,* the *Panther's Paw* said. It also said my daddy had to do a *detention* for unscrewing all the tops of the saltshakers in the school cafeteria. It said *yet another* detention but it didn't say what else he got in trouble for. Oh, and it listed Mr. White as senior class president.

If it were up to me, I would ask Cricket's computer questions all day long. We spent days looking at all kinds of things on it—my favorite stuff is about Toast and Momma and Daddy but that gets boring to Cricket after a while so yesterday when she said I couldn't come over today after she got out of school I worried it was on account of me not being fun and not because she had a doctor's appointment like she said. If you could see the fuss they all still make over me you'd swear Cricket's telling the truth but that doesn't stop me from being scared I'll do something that'll make her stop liking me. These past days have been the best days of my entire life. I'd do anything not to lose her.

Momma won't say what her job is but they sure have her working lots. On her first day they got her a new dress but if you ask me I don't think it fits right on her. It's real tight and kind of embarrassing to see her in on account of her bosoms showing as if she was just wearing a bra. She wears it to work every night along with more makeup than I ever saw her put on. The only thing that's the same is her black pair of high-heel shoes I color in with Magic Marker when they get scratched up. They hurt Momma's feet because her boss makes her stand up and walk around in them all night but since I only know whatever bits and pieces Momma lets slip, I don't know why. All Momma said when she came in wearing her new dress was that she's finally getting paid for what she used to give away for free but Momma doesn't give anything away for free so I cain't figure it out. Plus, even though she was real nervous about job interviewing, she never looks that nervous about the actual job. From day one she looked sad about it. Like she was being punished. When I asked her why she wasn't happy about finally finding work, all she said was "This isn't the kind of work a decent woman would be happy doing."

Her boss pays her in cash and once she even came home with the first grocery sack we've had since Hendersonville, full of chips and soda and a carton of cigarettes and ready-made biscuits and sliced "deli meat." It felt like a feast but in a few days it was all gone and we haven't had another grocery sack in room 217 since. The good thing about Momma's job is she's away more so it's easier for me to come and go. Not first thing in the morning, though. Momma doesn't have to go to work until she feels like it (*not till I'm good and goddamn ready* is how she puts it) which is usually in the afternoon but when she leaves I know I won't see her for a long time. Once she didn't come home until noon the next day! Lucky for me I got Mrs. Ford and Miss Chaplin pushing food on me all the time. They pack up "goody bags" for me to take home, and I can make food last. Anyway, today I'm not going over there on account of Cricket's maybe-fake-maybe-not doctor appointment, so after Momma leaves for her secret job I decide I'm going to walk farther than I ever did before so I can make the time pass until it's tomorrow and I can see Cricket and them again.

I had no idea there were stores so huge you could fit five of our motels in them easy! And grocery stores with big baskets of fruit and vegetables *on special* right outside where anyone could walk by and steal them! Right out in plain view! And no one's taking anything. Oh, and people buy dirt here in Hartsville. Hand to God they do. Great big plastic bags of it. Sealed tight so the dirt won't mess up their cars. And the cars, they're all shiny clean. All prim and proper like they pick their way around mud puddles after the rain.

In Hart's Corner Shopping Center every single thing you lay eyes on is humongous. It's a clump of stores huddled together around a parking lot like they're warming themselves by a fire. If these huge stores were alive they'd be like the Godzilla movie Cricket and me watched a couple of days ago, they'd be able to step on motels and filling stations and even some office buildings—they'd kill ever-thing in sight. Instead they sit here with their mouths opening wide to swallow up anyone looking for TVs, food, books that are *20% off*. I'm walking to a store called Books Galore, passing Bedding Superstore, then Best Electronics to get there. In front of Best Electronics, out of nowhere, the doors fly open like they were expecting me, a cold blast of air comes out, and I have no earthly idea what in the world is going on. I walk back and forth a few times on account of me not ever seeing anything like what the doors are doing (how do they know to open?) until a man in a yellow collar shirt with a name tag reading BILLY comes out and tells me to *stop tripping the sensors*. I never heard of a grown-up with the name of a kid. How come he doesn't call himself Bill? Something more his age.

"Just what do you think you're doing?" Billy says. "Will you please—and I'm asking nicely here—please stop messing with the sensors. You kids are driving me crazy. We're not in the business of cooling off the whole town, you know."

"Yes, sir. Sorry, sir."

He fixes his squinty eyes on me and says, "You got nice manners. That or you're a smart aleck. You a smart aleck? You got friends out here waiting to cause trouble?"

I say "no, sir" even though he's not waiting for the answer. He's shading his eyes. Looking to the right and left. When he sees I'm alone, his shoulders relax and he stares out into the day.

"The parking situation is just out of hand, you ask me. It's ridiculous—people circling twenty minutes waiting on spots to open up . . ." He talks himself away back into the cold store.

The door stays open until I get a person length inside it. Someone says "Welcome to Best Electronics," but it could have been anyone—they're all smiling real hard and wearing matching shirts with name tags. This store is amazing with a capital *A*. There's a huge wall of a million television sets every size anyone would ever want. Racks and racks of music and stereos and other kinds of music players and a zillion other machinery—I don't even have names for some of the things they sell here. I'll come back and take a closer look later.

Books Galore is next door and oh my goodness this store is like a dreamland. It's like someone said *gee I wonder what Carrie Parker would like more than anything? Maybe she'd like a store with so many books to choose from she might could lose her mind being happy.* That's how great this place is. I never want to leave. I guess I ain't the only one who feels that way because people are all over the place, some even sitting on the floor and they don't get in trouble. And get this—you can buy drinks and food and *eat it right there inside the store while you read.* Most of all I love the big armchairs they got here. They're all over the place. It looks real easy to curl up in them. I pick a purple one by a window that has sun streaming through.

My purple chair's upstairs near the Young Adult section which has life-size cardboard cutouts of three girls supposed to be kids but wearing makeup and grown-up clothes. I figure I'll read later, I just want to close my eyes for a minute or two then I'll get going.

My daddy would have loved this place: the carpet goes on forever. He would've been a millionaire from this store alone. Daddy probably came to places like this all the time, selling carpet like he did. No wonder he always talked about us moving out of Toast.

Daddy'd come back from his trips and ask how my day was. Calls me *pea-pop*, like usual. He always smelled like new carpet and fresh laundry. His hair's wet but it's not raining out.

"The nurse came to school today in her truck, Daddy," I say. He's not paying attention. He's looking over my head for Momma who's pretending she hadn't seen him come in from being gone overnight.

"She checked all our heads with a flat wood stick," I tell him.

He squats down to face me and puts his hands on my shoulders. "How'd you like to live in a place they don't have to check you for head lice, pea-pop? How about living in a house fixed up real nice with a real front walk you could plant flowers up and down? Would you like that?"

For some reason he's talking loud and looking to the kitchen even though he's supposedly talking just to me.

"We're moving? Momma, we're moving we're moving we're moving Momma!"

I run into the kitchen to tell her the good news. She slams the lid back on the pot on the stovetop. She goes through cabinets like she's mad at them, and every time the cupboard door closes I want to hold my ears.

"Well isn't that just perfect," she says. Daddy tries to kiss her neck while she's at the sink but she pushes him off and crosses the kitchen to the stove.

"Hey, pea-pop, how'd you like to live in a place with eleven stoplights? Come 'ere, button," he says and without taking his eyes off Momma he opens his arms for me to jump into like I love to do.

"Eleven stoplights? How many cars? How many cars, Daddy?"

"Don't go getting your hopes up," Momma says to me. "We been down *this* road before."

Next thing they're over in the corner and Daddy's back trying to kiss Momma again, saying stuff I cain't make out but then she whips around and says, "You can't make this right by moving away from it."

"Lib, you always said you wanted to get out of this town. We're gonna do it, Lib. It's really happening."

That's when Momma says something about Garland, and that's not a good sign, no sirree. Garland was where Daddy promised we'd go the year before. I'm glad baby Emma's sleeping sound in her drawer-crib in the other room and not hearing this.

"It's not my fault Garland fell through, Libby," Daddy's saying. "We been over it. This is different, I swear. This is the real McCoy."

I called Garland Winktown because ever-time Daddy'd say its name he'd wink at me and Emma. Even Momma got real excited about it. She smiled all the time back then. She planned ever-thing right down to the nails and the floorboards, what we'd take with us and what all we'd leave behind. She said even the trash collector'd turn down the wobbly old chair with the busted leg and Daddy laughed and said we'd get new chairs and none of them would be wobbly.

Then one day the upstairs rattled like a stampede of elephants. Doors slammed and I scooped up Emma and went behind the couch to wait it out. Daddy stormed down the stairs with Momma at his tail yelling for him to *get gone.*

"Take one last look because that's the last you'll see of this place, you son of a bitch," she hollered at his back.

He pushed through the front door and she flew to it, locking it behind him. I watched as she took the stairs two at a time and, before I could decide whether I should follow her to the second floor, I heard the upstairs window sash being forced open. I peeked out the front window in time to see Daddy's dressy-up shoes, the ones I always helped him polish, flying out into the front yard, the first one tumbling onto the dirt not far from an old wooden peach crate Momma used to plant flowers in. The second one hit the smooth slabs of rock that made up our front walk. I cain't remember how long it took but Momma finally cooled down enough to where Daddy came tiptoeing back in and something was decided without having to say it out loud. It was understood. We weren't to talk about Garland no more.

I hope that don't happen this time because I dearly want to see a place so big it has eleven stoplights.

Momma pushes Daddy away from her again, telling him to leave her be.

"Lib, listen to me," Daddy says in a voice that'd quiet *Misty of Chincoteague,* one of my favorite books of all time. "Just listen. Remember we always said we'd blow this popsicle joint someday? Remember? You wanted out of here just as much as I did. Hell, you used to say that's why you married me, so I'd rescue you from rotting in the hills! Remember, Lib?"

Momma snorts, shakes her head, and says, "Lotta good that did me," and Daddy throws up his hands like *I give up.* No more *Misty of Chincoteague* voice.

"Then tell me!" he says. "Here I am telling you we just might be able to do it after all and you push me away. So tell me what you want, Libby. Tell me what I can possibly do to make you happy 'cause I sure ain't doing it this way."

"You know what would make me happy?" Momma raises her voice to match his. "It'd make me happy if you didn't *tomcat* around. Coming home smelling like tacky perfume from some second-rate whore—"

"You got some nerve saying *I* tomcat around," he says, back to hollering. "If that isn't the pot calling the kettle black."

"Don't you start," she says. "Don't you even start."

"Well? You think I'm blind, do you? You think I can't see with my own eyes the *uncanny resemblance* she has to a certain drug-gist? Why'd you go off to stay with your mother *who treats you like shit,* by the way, the whole time you were pregnant then? Why'd you keep the whole thing a secret, huh? No one even *knows* about her!"

"Don't be a damn fool," she says. "That child's yours and you know it. You're just trying to change focus from your cheating, and you know what? This time I ain't—this time I'm *not*—taking the bait. Unlike *some* people, *I'm* going to take the high road."

"Well, la-di-da aren't you just Miss High and Mighty. Pre-tending you and him haven't had a thing for each other ever since high school. Y'all mooning over each other like Romeo and god-damn Juliet."

"Oh, please," Momma says. "You don't know what you're talk-ing about."

The room is so quiet it's easy to hear the flick of the lighter she uses for her cigarettes.

"Oh really? So it's normal to spray on perfume and fix yourself up real nice just to go to the drugstore?"

"Stop it," Momma says, blowing smoke out the side of her mouth.

"Acting all surprised to see him—like he doesn't own the damn place! He's there every day and you put on the big fancy-meeting-you-here show like you had *no* idea you'd run into him, all gussied up like a tramp."

I want so bad to giggle out loud watching Daddy playact like a lady, fanning his hand in front of his face like he did when he said *fancy meeting you here.* And wiggling his hips.

"You're acting like a fool," Momma says.

"If I'm a fool then so is Rick Bulkeley who said he saw you and White driving down Riverbend Road in White's car. Which, as I recall, was a couple of months before you got up the courage to tell me you were knocked up again. And how long ago was that? A little over a year ago. And how old's the baby? Why, golly gee, she's a little over a year old. What an amazing coincidence!"

"Oh, Jesus Christ, how many times do we have to go over this?"

"You're saying Rick Bulkeley didn't see you two? You're saying—"

"I'm saying Rick Bulkeley's a washed-up drunk who would swear a UFO landed in the center of town if he thought you'd buy him a drink for telling you so," Momma says. "Rick Bulkeley, ha! Since when does *any*one place any kind of stock in what that buffoon says?"

"And then the baby's born with that mark—the same mark he has. And you got the nerve to stand here and lie to my face about it. *That kid is not mine and nothing you can say will ever make it so,*" he says in a mean voice I only heard once before when squirrels dug up holes in the front yard and hit a pipe that ended up freezing and cracking later on in the winter. He reminds me of a rattlesnake when he uses that voice.

"You know what?" Momma asks him.

"What?"

"I'll tell you what. I wish she *was* his." She spits the words at him.

Daddy recoils his rattlesnake head back up as if she'd slapped him in the face.

It gets real quiet.

"That's it," he finally says. "I don't need to take this in my own home *that I pay for,* thank you very much. I'm done."

"Daddy. Don't go, Daddy." I run to him and wrap my arms tight around his right leg. "Wait, Daddy, please!"

Momma points at me and says to Daddy, "See? See what you did? You see what I have to deal with day in day out? While you're out *making sales calls.*"

"I'm outta here," he says.

He slams the door on his way out and I want to scream at Momma—she was always scaring him away, being so mean to him like that.

Instead of hating on Momma, I go to check on my sister, figuring she has to have heard Momma and Daddy fighting. Figuring she's probably real upset over it too. But even when she was a baby Emma knew to lay low because there she is, awake but totally still. Smiling up at me like *hey, big sis, I been waiting on you to come in here!*

"Shhh." I smooth her baby blond hair. "It's all right, Em. Shhhh."

She reaches out and touches my hair like it's made of gold.

"You have beautiful hair. Maybe need to brush it a little but there's no two ways about it—it's just lovely."

Which is strange because Emma didn't talk then. Definitely not in full sentences. She was still only a baby.

"Time to wake up, honey."

I come out of a deep sleep to the sound of a soft voice above my head.

"Time to wake up."

My neck is so stiff I cain't move and for a second I think maybe there's been a horrible accident and I broke my neck and this place I'm waking up in is a hospital. The person behind the voice stays stroking my hair and part of me wishes she'd keep doing it forever. The other part of me's sad to realize I'd just been dreaming. I get hit with a wallop of missing Emma and Daddy and Momma the way she used to be.

"Just lovely hair. We're closing, sugar, it's time to wake up," a lady's saying. "You need to go find your mom."

"What? Where am I?"

"You're at Books Galore. Don't worry. People fall asleep in these chairs all the time. You were having some real bad dreams. Who's Emma?"

"Ma'am?" I can finally sit up and turn my head to the sound of the voice that belongs to a lady with a stack of books in the crook of her arm and eyeglasses dangling from a string around her neck.

"You were calling out for Emma," she's saying. "I keep telling them the chairs are too comfy. Not that it's bad you fell asleep. Just that some people take advantage. *You* know."

"Sorry. I'm sorry, ma'am." I put my flip-flops back on. "What time is it? I've got to get going."

The lady's already half gone down a row of books. I have to pee. I feel like I'm still asleep. Like I'm sleepwalking. If they're closing up it must be past five but it's summer and there's no telling time in summer with it being light out so late. I hope I have enough time to use the washroom before they lock up.

I've got to hurry—I may have been here so long Momma might be on her way home from work already. If she's coming home to-night, which she may not be but I cain't take that chance. Stupid me! If I'm not there she'll be red-eye mad. She'll pace back and forth mumbling to herself how she's gonna tan my hide with her belt. How she's gonna show me how it feels to be disrespected like I'm disrespecting her. That's always worse than a whipping—because Momma knows a lot of ways of disrespecting so when she *teaches me a lesson* it could be any number of disrespectings.

Off in the distance I hear a man's voice announcing *Ladies and Gentlemen, we are closing in five minutes. Please move to the front of the store.* I wish I'd eaten something earlier, my stomach's growl-ing loud. I missed getting to the trash bin out back before the gar-bagemen came and I already ate the "goody bag" Miss Chaplin sent home with me yesterday, dangit. I really don't want tonight to be a clay night.

There's a kid, Kenny's his name. He lives with his grandpa one floor down and two doors over from us at the Loveless. Their room is the same as ours but every inch of their window is covered with stickers so it's more like a wall than a window. Kenny eats pieces of a clay pot broke into tiny bites. He said it gets warm when it's inside your belly and when it's warm it grows back into Silly Putty clay. Then you're not hungry because your stomach's filled up completely. Kenny said you feel fuller than at Thanksgiving.

So the other day I did just like he said. I worked up a gob of spit and held it in my mouth so it was waiting for the hard clay. Before biting down I used my tongue to swish it around and give it a *spit bath*. That's what Kenny called it: *a spit bath*. He said you do that inside your mouth and after you been rolling it around you feel better about biting down on it. *Pretend it's chocolate M&M's*, he said. It wasn't so bad but it wasn't M&M's either.

It must be my lucky day because I get back to the Loveless and Momma's not home yet. Phee-you! I close the curtain and quickly get ready for bed in case she comes in. Here's another way I'm lucky: taking off my shorts I find five packets of ketchup in my pockets. After squeezing every drop of ketchup from them I crawl into my bed. I wish I had borrowed one of the books Cricket offered me but I couldn't because what if Momma saw. I try squeezing my eyes shut to remind them it's time to go to sleep but I'm not tired. Then I remember I hid the bookmark flashlight under my mattress. I pinch it and the room turns silver. I love this dang thing. I pretend it's a beam from a spaceship and I sweep a ray of light across the floor. That's when I see it.

The light flashes on something sparkly from behind a square metal air vent about a foot off the floor. Me and Emma used to love this baby book about a family of mice who lived in the tunnels behind an air vent in the wall that looks just like this one. I cain't believe I never noticed it there before. I crouch down in front of it and pinch the bookmark and what do I see but Momma's travel case! So *that's* where she hid it. My fingers are small enough for me to slide the edge of my fingernail into the grooves of the screws holding the grate in place. I've got to be fast about it—Momma could come in any minute. My heart's thumping so hard I can feel it in my ears. In my head I keep hearing this old bluegrass song Mr. Wilson used to hum while he whittled: "Time's A-Wastin'."

Those are the only words of the song he'd sing out loud—the rest he'd just whistle or hum. Those words, though—they're bouncing from ear to ear across my brain like a pinball machine while I turn the last screw.

Time's a-wastin'.

I lift the metal grate away so I can pull the travel case out. It's real dusty and I almost sneeze but I hold my breath and count to ten like Mr. White told me you could do if you need to keep from sneezing. Like in church.

Time's a-wastin'.

I need to make haste. *Hurry up,* I tell myself. Funny how you stop being hungry when you're in a hurry and you're scared you might get caught doing something you shouldn't be doing.

Momma probably figured she didn't need to lock the case if she hid it real good from me. Inside it smells like Momma from when she used to wear perfume. There's a clunky wood bracelet I never saw before. A small packet of papers rubber-banded together—letters maybe—but I don't have time to read them. A silver flip-top Zippo lighter. A neatly folded *diploma* that shows Momma graduated from high school. A dirty old braided friend-ship bracelet made of rope. Some ticket stubs.

Time's a-wastin'.

Now I can practically *taste* my heartbeat, it's going so fast. I've got to hurry up but it's hard since I don't know what I'm looking for. This might be my only chance so I've got to make sure I check ever-thing. Good thing I've got *eagle-eye vision* like Mr. Wilson said because anyone else might've missed seeing the paper-thin tear in the fabric lining. I get up real close and blow some air at it and there it is. The thing I didn't even know I was looking for.

You know how sometimes you could swear you were someplace you never could have been just because you've seen it in pictures so many times? Or how you feel like you know someone you've only just heard a lot about? It's like your brain playing a trick on itself. Well, when I shimmy the small square of a photograph up from its hiding place, I get that feeling. Only this time I know it ain't my mind horsing around. I don't know how to explain it so I'll just say that I am one hundred percent sure I am holding in my hand a real-life picture of my baby sister. Emma. It's her! With her face all scrunched up like someone pinched her leg and she's about to let out a holler. After all this time being told she wasn't real. After a town full of people told me I was crazy. After swearing to Momma I would never say her name again. After promising the state lady I didn't ever have a baby sister. After all that I now have real live *proof*!

I thought it would feel different, finding out she existed, proving I'm not crazy. I figured I'd want to show someone or shout it from the rooftops or just say *Ha! Told you so!* to the kids at school who called me Scary Carrie but turns out I don't care about any of that right now. All I care about is seeing her little face again. I smile looking at it and even though I'm so full of happy I might could burst, part of me wants to cry.

Emma. I'm holding Emma! Yeah, it's only a small picture of her not the real thing but that doesn't matter. It's her! Emma. Emma Emma Emma.

I forgot babies don't have teeth—the picture shows tiny pale ridges lining her gums, holding the places where teeth will grow in. I can practically feel her soft baby blond peach fuzz when I trace her head with my finger. Studying the picture up close I see that she looks a little different from how I remember, and then I see why. At first I thought it was a shadow cast on the side of her face by the person taking the picture (Momma?) but then I realize it's a birthmark. Which is weird because it's just like Mr. White's.

His was on his forehead, though, and Emma's is on her cheek, but still. It's weird.

My sister.

Emma!

Then *pow*! Sitting here cross-legged in front of the open vent, I have another flash shoot across my brain and it's what I've seen before but with a little more added in this time. A pudgy baby arm reaching out to me from over a grown-up shoulder then—this is the new part—then I see two big hands shaking shaking shaking something like you'd shake a snow globe. *Pow!* The something being shook? For a second I think it's a doll but then it dawns on me it wasn't a doll at all. It was a real live baby! And I don't know how it took me so long to catch on that the pudgy little arm reaching out? It was Emma's. The flashes have been trying to tell me something only I haven't been paying them any mind! Shoot, I'll have to think on this later.

Time's a-wastin'.

I hurry to slide the picture under my mattress, taking care not to bend or fold it, then I push the fabric lining up against the inside wall of the travel case and it stays put. Momma won't notice the picture missing. Not for a while I bet, and by then I'll have figured out what to do. The braided bracelet was halfway out from under the packet of papers when I opened the case but maybe Momma doesn't remember leaving it that way so even though it was her that did it she'll think it's me. I better straighten it up the way she'd want it straightened. But then maybe it's a trap. Maybe she's left the bracelet like that on purpose because she knows I would set it right and then I'd be caught. *What should I do what should I do what should I do?* What would Mrs. Ford do?

Time's a-wastin'.

Mrs. Ford would hurry up, that's what she'd do.

I leave ever-thing exactly like I found it, click the case closed, and slide it back into the tunnel, all without making a sound. The metal grate fits back into place, and just as I'm turning the second screw tight I hear Momma at the door. I scramble up into my bed and squeeze my eyes closed so she'll think I'm asleep.

With the sound of Momma bumping into things and cursing under her breath in the background, I let my mind go on a field trip. Sometimes, like tonight, if I'm real hungry or if I cain't easily fall asleep, I close my eyes and take a ghost tour of our old house in Toast and how we looked in it.

What worries me, though, is I'm starting to forget what Daddy looked like. I go real slow, moving from room to room, making sure to notice ever-thing that crosses in front of my ghost self so I can hold on to the memory of it. In my mind's eye I can see the teensiest details but lately, no matter how hard I try, I cain't picture Daddy's face. I remember the last time I laid eyes on him, but that's exactly what I don't want in my head.

He looked smaller than usual, laying facedown on the ground just inside the front door the way he was. I remember thinking he was doing a magic trick, because a flower of deep dark red bloomed out from a tiny circle near the middle of his back, below his left shoulder, right in front of my own eyes. The petals, bright red against the white businessman shirt he was wearing, blossoming wide open while I stood there looking down at him. Momma got real cross and said for me to go to my room when I came in and asked where Emma was—I can hear her voice still.

"God dammit, go!"

From the top of the stairs I watched Momma huffing and puffing trying to move Daddy and I remember wondering why he didn't wake up with all her pulling when Momma finally gave up. I was still there when she squatted down beside him, put her head in her hands, and started to cry. Through her sobbing she was talking to him but he kept on just laying there.

She didn't seem to care that Daddy was sleeping through all her questions and tears. I tiptoed away to go find Emma.

Later that night Momma, all red-eyed and puffy, called me to her room and told me to sit next to her on the bed because she had *something important* to tell me.

"I don't believe in sugarcoating things so here it is," she said, tapping ash into the overflowing saucer she used for an ashtray. "Your father's dead. I was pinning clothes on the line out back when a man banged on the door—"

"Daddy's dead?" I remember turning the words over in my head, not really understanding what they meant at first.

"Listen to me," she said. "I'm trying to tell you. A man banged on the door hollering for him and then I heard a pop and came running in time to see Selma Blake's husband walking back to his truck with a rifle, cool as a cucumber now that he went and killed the man who'd been sleeping with his wife."

I cried so hard I couldn't hear the rest.

It was a small house, our house in Toast. The kitchen floor was always clean as a whistle—Momma liked ever-thing *clean as a whistle* back then—and I never knew how hard it was to keep it that way until Momma stopped coming out of her room and left it all up to me. I remember listening to Momma crying, thinking for a time that even the *house* was sad Daddy died because Momma sobbed so hard in her bed it made the walls shake. I spent lots of time wishing and praying to God that she'd come out of her room and that Daddy would come back to life and take us all out for ice cream.

My ghost tour takes me past the front hall table with the dish that Daddy tossed his keys into whenever he came through the door. They'd clink into it, covering up the three blue *K*s. When Momma found it at a yard sale she said *well, I'll be! Isn't this just the funniest thing* to the lady selling it who told her it wasn't what she thought—the KKK was her sister's initials or something. But how she knew what Momma was thinking and why Momma said it was funny is still a mystery to me. Momma gave it to Daddy for Christmas that year, saying *I didn't know y'all had a gift shop—I may have to come to one of those meetings y'all're always holding,* and he laughed and said *now that I'd like to see.*

That time is fuzzy in some parts, clear in others. Like I can see myself mixing flour and water to make flapjacks or hunting through emptying kitchen cabinets for any kind of crumb to keep me and Emma and Momma alive. Momma needed to eat just like ever-body else. I'd leave whatever food I made or could find outside her bedroom door. I can even see the pile of dirty laundry that started forming at the bottom of the stairs when Momma was hiding in her room. That pile was super-duper cool—I would jump onto it from the third stair, pretending it was a trampoline in the circus.

After Momma came out of her room and started moving around in the world again, she'd come into my room to wake me up in the middle of the night. I never got used to it. It scared me silly ever-time. The worst part was not knowing when it'd be. I'd go up to sleep not knowing if it would end up being one of the nights she'd burst in. It always turned out that just when I'd forget to worry about being woken up in the pitch dark, I'd feel a shove and then *click!* the lightbulb hanging from the ceiling would switch on and Momma'd be standing over me, unsteady on her feet, swaying like the black folks in church, popping me quizzes I didn't have answers for.

"Tell me how it happened," she said that first time. Her voice was a day voice that seemed louder because she was using it at night.

I remember rubbing my eyes and squinting against the brightness. I thought at first she was sleepwalking. She was making no sense at all. She wore eye makeup back then—I remember because it'd be all smeared from her crying.

"Tell me what happened to him, god dammit!"

"I was asleep, Momma," I whispered, hoping she would soften

her voice to match mine. That first time I didn't know to cry. "I don't know what happened—I was just sleeping."

"I ain't talking about *now*," she said and then she hauled off a good pop across my face to prove it wasn't no dream.

It took me a few times to figure out what she was talking about and then I landed on what she wanted to hear and what I needed to say to be let alone and for her to feel better. All I ever wanted was for Momma to feel better.

"A man came and banged on the door," I would answer.

"What was I doing at the time?" she'd ask.

"You were pinning up wet clothes on the line," I'd answer. She'd nod and say, "Go on."

"You heard a pop and came running in time to see the man with the rifle going back to his car."

"It was a truck," she'd correct me, "but keep going. Who was the man?"

"Selma Blake's husband," I'd answer.

"Anything else?"

I learned to time my answer perfect. If I answered too quick she'd slap me and tell me to *think on it real hard* before I opened my *pie hole*. If I took too long to answer she'd shove me, saying *don't you be keeping anything secret—you tell me what you're thinking right now.* Finally I knew I had to wait the time it took to say one-Mississippi-two-Mississippi before I'd say:

"Nothing, Momma, I swear."

"You're right," she'd say. When she nodded I knew her better mood would last a few days. If she didn't nod? Well, then I knew anything could happen. "You remember that now."

"Yes, ma'am."

"Go back to sleep now."

"Yes, ma'am."

I'd close my eyes for her to see so she'd think I was falling back under, but no sleep would ever come back to me on those nights.

I'd lay awake listening to myself breathing, thinking about Momma's questions and how strange it all was, and when the sun would rise and it'd be time to get out of bed I was almost sick at my stomach from being tired.

By the time the police came around and asked me about the last time I saw my daddy alive, I could practically see Selma Blake's jealous husband climbing back into his truck. At first they were real interested in ever-thing I said—they asked what he'd been wearing and did I notice anything else. Momma seemed worried but I don't know why. The police left us alone after that.

I remember all of it clearly, like it happened yesterday. But no matter how hard I try I cain't see Daddy's face anymore. Laying here on the scratchy sheets at the Loveless, I squinch my eyes closed to try to picture him but nope. Nothing comes. I have to put all thought of the picture under my mattress out of my head because otherwise I cain't sleep. I tell myself I'll get to be with it after Momma leaves for her secret job.

The next morning I hear Momma shifting in her bed which means she's thirsty. It's quiet enough to hear her swallowing a sip of whatever's left over by her bed from the night before. Usually it's whiskey and Tab.

"Momma?" I ask the sleepy lump of her. "Do we have any pictures from before? Like, of Daddy or anything?"

She doesn't stir under the covers but I know she's awake. After all, she just poked her head out and sipped some whiskey and Tab.

"Or from when I was little maybe? Do we have any pictures from back there in Toast?"

Toast was the magic word. Funny, because the second I said it the room felt different and I knew Momma would answer me.

"Why are you asking me that?" She peers at me from above the covers. Something about the way her voice sounds tells me I was stupid to bring it up. Now she's going to suspect me of doing exactly what I did! "What are you up to?"

"I don't know," I say, not meeting her eye. "Nothing."

But I *do* know. I bet I'd be asking her about it anyway, because I been seeing all the zillions of pictures of Cricket's life and even before I found the picture in Momma's travel case it got me to thinking how I wouldn't mind seeing a photograph or two of me from when I was a baby.

"The answer is no," she says. "We don't have any pictures."

"How come?"

"What?"

"How come we have no pictures of us?" I ask her.

"Well excuse me, sorry we're not *rich enough* to own a camera for you," she says. "Little Miss Fancy Pants." That last part's muffled on account of her head being back under the covers.

A few minutes later we both shock at the sudden banging on the door. Mrs. Burdock. Again.

"I know y'all are in there," she hollers through the thin door. "Don't think I don't know it."

She bangs again.

I've gotten real good at holding my breath. When Mrs. Burdock first started coming up and banging on the door Momma would put her finger to her mouth for me to be quiet and I'd hold the air in so long I'd make noise letting it out, but now I know when to breathe out in time to do it quiet-like so no one can hear, not even if they were standing right up next to me. Both Momma and me, we learned quick that Mr. Burdock hadn't been telling Mrs. Burdock the whole truth because he saw us come and go ever-day but he must have told Mrs. Burdock we hid in our room and never came out so she wouldn't fuss at him for not collecting rent.

"Open up and we can settle this like adults. You think you can cheat us, living here rent-free like y'all are? You think that's the way we do business? They may let things slide up in them hills y'all come from, but down here in the *real world* we've got a business to run. You hear me?"

Mrs. Burdock uses her whole forearm so the entire door rattles when she hits it.

"You may have sweet-talked my husband into turning a blind eye but enough is enough," she says to her side of the door. "He isn't going to stick up for y'all forever. Open up and we can talk about this like civilized human beings. Y'all are still civilized human beings, aren't you?"

I look across at the lump of Momma laying in bed. She's got to where she pulls the covers over her head if she's home when Mrs. Burdock comes to call.

"This can't keep on, you know," Mrs. Burdock says.

I peeked out from the window once when she first started coming at us, and what she does is she cups her hands around her mouth and puts her face right up to the wood of the door to talk through to us. It's smart of her—the sound comes straight to us without bothering any of our neighbors.

"Don't make me call the po-lice"—she says the word like it's split in two. "That's what's going to happen next, y'all hear me? I'm calling the po-lice if you don't settle up the bill. And I got a news flash for you: they'll haul y'all out of there so fast it'd bring tears to a glass eye."

Mrs. Burdock talks whether someone's near or not. She doesn't mind carrying on a whole conversation with her own self. If you come upon her when she's in the middle she'll just turn up the volume of her words so you feel like you've been a part of it from the beginning. I can hear bits and pieces of her talking and then I make out Mr. Burdock's deep voice mixing in:

"What's all the commotion up here?" he asks Mrs. Burdock.

"I don't know who they think they're fooling, acting like the room's empty," Mrs. Burdock says.

"Calm down, calm down," Mr. Burdock says. "Let's leave it be for now."

"We've *been* leaving it be," Mrs. Burdock says, "and look what that's gotten us. Standing here with a fistful of nothing, that's what. This is unacceptable. I want them out of here, Hap. I want them gone."

"Bess, now come on," he says, "those two got nothing."

"Then they shouldn't have rented a room!"

"What happens to the girl, huh? If we turn them out on the street, what happens to the little girl?" Mr. Burdock says. "It ain't *her* fault, them having no money—"

"Well, that's some kind of mother, isn't it," Mrs. Burdock says. "Letting her daughter forage for food like a goddamn *ferret* . . ."

Mrs. Burdock keeps talking but Mr. Burdock must be leading her away because their voices get hard to hear before disappearing altogether. After I'm sure they're good and gone I sit up in my bed.

"Momma? Why's Mrs. Burdock coming at us if you got a job now?" I ask.

She doesn't stir.

I look around our room and wish I could ask the man whose name's on all the bottles laying around. I bet Jim Beam would know why Mrs. Burdock's so mad at us. I'm not supposed to clear them out because the clinking makes too much noise and the dumpster is right outside the Burdocks' window. Mrs. Burdock peeks out whenever anyone throws anything away, wanting to catch whoever's been forgetting to latch the flat plastic top of the bin closed. She put up a sign saying there were raccoons in the area and to *please be mindful* about the bin lids but someone (not me) isn't paying it any mind.

CHAPTER SIXTEEN

Honor

I realize now why Mother was so keen on getting the house land-mark status. I wish to God I'd paid more attention and helped her go about it a better way, but how was I to know she was being fore-closed on? And anyway, I'm not so sure being of historical sig-nificance would have saved it. Well. We'll see.

I drive down to City Hall, a building that always disappoints me in its cement-blocked blandness. It looks like a community center in Provo in the 1970s. It depresses everyone who works there too, judging from the slumped demeanor of nearly every cubicle inhabitant.

After twenty agonizing minutes watching a Mr. Sylvester, the slowest-moving human being I've yet to encounter, try to locate our file, we settle in for the brass tacks. Which in this case means a lot of self-important sighing, scanning of paperwork, and head-shaking.

"Yeah, it's like I thought," he says, closing the file folder and looking up at me. "The historical claim was unverified. And without verification and proper authentication, we cannot proceed. Looks like a caseworker even went out to talk to your mother and explain this to her *again* a few days ago. As a courtesy. And frankly, we were getting a little sick of the calls."

"Calls from whom? We haven't called you," I say.

"Ma'am, your mother's been calling over here every single day, sometimes multiple times a day," he says, sighing for emphasis. "All due respect, it was getting a little old. The pestering."

"First of all, I think you're mistaken," I say. "You got her mixed up with someone else. That doesn't even sound like my mother. She wouldn't pester a flea. And furthermore the caseworker was the first she'd heard from y'all . . ."

I trail off because he's begun vigorously shaking his head, clearly not listening, just waiting for me to finish so he can shoot down everything I'm saying.

"Ma'am, I have a record here of all the interactions we've had with your mother regarding the matter," he says, triumphantly referring to his silly little folder again. "I can document for you all the times she contacted us about this. Looks like we first told her the case had been rejected last year. Well, nearly a year ago. Nine months ago. She applied again and it says here she submitted *supplemental papers* though it doesn't say what those were. Huh. They were returned to her and she was again rejected. That was seven months ago. Case notes—I'll read it aloud since we're not allowed to show you official documents but I can read this part out loud. The caseworker writes—and I'm quoting here—'told her the genealogical research she provided was incorrect. Showed her the independent research we conducted proves unequivocally that she is not related to Charles Chaplin. Told her all genealogi-cal research corroborates our findings. Even hers.' "

He closes the folder and takes off his reading glasses.

"Wait, wait just a second here," I say. "*What?* We're not related to Charles Chaplin? That's absurd."

"Mrs. Ford, can I speak candidly?"

"Yes, of course."

"You ask me, your mom knew all along," he says.

"That's impossible," I say. "If you saw her house, all the memorabilia. She's collected it all her life. Family heirlooms. Dolls. Collector's items! We even had tour groups coming through. Well, more like local school field trips and the ladies' auxiliary. But still!"

"Ma'am, I could collect Princess Diana stuff, but that wouldn't make me royal," he says. "Anyone can collect anything. Y'all have the same name is all."

"With all due respect you don't know what you're talking about," I say, looping my purse strap onto my shoulder and standing up to go. "But I appreciate your time."

Chaplins always take the high road.

"I'm telling you: it's a pure coincidence." He sighs and sits back in his chair. "I'm sorry."

Why do people say they're sorry when they're not?

"You know, I told your mother all this when she came in," he says. "The way she reacted? My guess is she knew all along."

Out in the parking lot I'm shaking so hard I press the Panic button instead of Unlock on my car remote and the alarm is set off. A Freudian slip if there ever was one.

Chaplins always take the high road indeed, Mother.

I can't wrap my head around this. This is huge. This changes *everything*. *Think.* I have to think. I'll have time to figure this out after the bank, and God only knows what I'll find out there.

Turns out, it is worse than I thought.

"Your mother took out a sizable mortgage on the house," says the bank officer named Clifford. Clifford is intent on bending a paper clip straight, and once he does, he tries to get it back to its original shape. I guess Clifford here is a fan of lost causes.

"Unfortunately at this point there's nothing we can do. She has defaulted on both her mortgage and the personal loan she took out last May. She owes a lot of money. We're talking thirty thousand and change. Our only option is to take over the property. I wish I had better news for you."

"How much time do we have? To raise the money." I shimmy to the edge of my seat and press my arms into my sides for exaggerated cleavage. A girl's gotta do what a girl's gotta do. I wish I'd thought to wear something low-cut.

Clifford clears his throat and says he can hold off a little while but not too long, and instead of asking him to clarify the amount of time I decide it's better this way. Down the road I can refer to this vague answer if the screws start to turn before we come up with a solution. Clifford's clammy hand bends on contact without sliding all the way into the V of mine, turning our handshake into a prissy half shake with only fingers touching, not the traditional kind where thumbs meet and palms press together in a clean grip. Poor Clifford.

The only other customer in the bank is an overweight woman in an electric wheelchair that has a mini American flag attached to the back and is plastered with ethical bumper stickers encouraging people to forgo meat, to vote, to drive slowly, to take one day at a time. Centered among them is a yellow diamond-shaped warning that she brakes for aliens. Then I notice a mop-headed dog sitting patiently in a towel-lined front basket. Wearing a sailor's cap. *It could be worse: I could have a dog wearing a jaunty sailor's cap.*

My mother has no money.

My mother is in deep debt.

We are living back home in a house that will be foreclosed on.

We are in big trouble.

Yet here I am, starting the car, cranking the AC, going back to the memory of Eddie holding Carrie and sobbing three-year-old tears. Here I am, turning onto Elm Avenue, smiling at the thought of him pulling me close, holding on to me like he used to, years ago, back when we were dating and being separated even for one day felt like torture.

The irony isn't lost on me: everything around us is falling apart but our family—Ed's and mine—feels like . . . I can't let myself even think it, but maybe I'll get it out of my system now, while I'm alone. This ridiculous idea. Maybe if I say it out loud I'll realize how ludicrous it is and then I can refocus on fixing this ever-growing mess. So here it is:

For some reason, while everything around us is falling apart, our little family is coming back together.

There. I said it. But now that I have, it doesn't seem so ridiculous at all. We're healing, Eddie, Cricket, and I. And I know why.

I used to tell myself (and Cricket) that sometimes when parents bury a child they're so broken nothing can put them back together again. They're Humpty Dumpty parents, I'd say. But then I went to Wendy's and found that troubled little girl bearing such an uncanny resemblance to our pain it was impossible to ignore. Standing there with her hand in a bowl of croutons, for goodness' sake, was our missing link. We need that child as much as she needs us. And while I'm on a roll I might as well admit it: I want to patch things up with Eddie, dammit. I want him back. I want *us* back. But right now we all need to have a roof over our heads, so I've got to focus on nuts and bolts.

I step on the gas and turn up Rascal Flatts on the radio. Look out, Mother, here I come.

CHAPTER SEVENTEEN

Carrie

By now I'm real good at fastening a seat belt. I say *hey* to Cricket
and Mrs. Ford and strap myself in, easy as pie. Mrs. Ford asks me
again if she can meet my momma and how did I sleep and am I
hungry. She turns on the radio and I lean over to whisper with
Cricket. Just like me and Emma used to do. We'd whisper with
each other even when we didn't need to keep quiet just because it
was fun. Sometimes we'd whisper in codes, like saying ever-thing
in opposites ("I'm *not* even the teensiest bit hungry" or "I *loved*
school today") or saying every other word backward ("I love *stib-
bar*"). Me and Cricket should do a game like that of our own, come
to think of it.

"I had the freakiest dream last night," Cricket whispers to me.

"About what?" I whisper back.

"That's the thing," she says. "I don't remember and when I try
to remember I almost do but then it's gone. I hate when that happens! Oh-Em-Gee we have got to play Tetris when we get home—
I just did my first T-spin and I'm, like, obsessed with it now. Don't

worry, I'll show you. It's actually not that hard once you get the hang of it."

When we get to the house Miss Chaplin shows me some more Charlie Chaplin stuff. She makes a big deal over some award he won for a movie he did called *The Circus,* only the statue is embarrassing to look at because it's a naked man. She says it's an *exact replica* of the real thing and while she's talking I want to tell her she's holding it right where his private parts are but decide against it at the last minute. Then Cricket finally says *let's go up.*

We're about to settle in at her desk where I now have my very own place to sit. Cricket brought in a folding chair Miss Chaplin had in some closet *for overflow* and a few days ago we put a couple of *throw pillows* on it to make me taller and moved it right alongside hers so we can both share the desk and I can see the computer better. Cricket's as great about sharing as Emma.

"Actually, first I have to go pee because once I start playing Tetris I'll never get up," Cricket says, already halfway out the door of her room. "I'll be right back."

" 'Kay," I say, looking around, picking up a cute teddy bear wearing a raincoat and hat. I fold his stiff arms to make like he's typing on the computer. *Dum-dee-dum-dee* . . .

All of a sudden the computer screen goes from being black (I thought it was turned off) to showing a picture of a newspaper with my daddy's face right there on the front page!

LOCAL MAN MURDERED: POLICE QUESTION LOVER'S JEALOUS HUSBAND.

The teddy bear tumbles to the floor. I stare at the picture in shock, my belly twisting into a knot, my head exploding—Cricket knows my daddy's dead! She knows I lied! Did she tell her mother and Miss Chaplin she caught me in a lie? And where'd that picture of Daddy come from? I never saw it before. What'd they say about him in the newspaper? I tiptoe to the door to look down the hall. The bathroom door's still closed so I've got time to try to get the picture to go away so she won't know I know she knows. Maybe I can confess before she calls me out so she doesn't hate me. But how do I turn the picture off? I'm trying to find the On/Off button when she comes back in and catches me looking wild-eyed and guilty as sin.

"Oh, jeez, um, I'm, I mean," she stammers, hurries over, and presses something so my daddy disappears. "I was going to tell you I swear. I guess I just didn't know how to bring it up."

"I'm real sorry I lied to you," I say, hanging my head because I'm so ashamed and saying it out loud makes me feel even worse. "I'm really *really* sorry, Cricket. I'll just go down and see if your mom can give me a ride back and you won't have to see me again."

Now I know what they mean by a broken heart. Mine feels like it was made of glass and someone dropped it, smashing it to pieces. But then Cricket says, "Wait, what?" and puts her hand on my shoulder to keep me in my chair when I get up to leave. "You're not going *any*where! I was just about to say *I'm* sorry. I snooped around behind your back but I swear it wasn't because I didn't trust you. When we Googled your mom and dad the other day that weird headline caught my eye and I made a mental note to go back and check it out after we looked at the yearbook but I forgot and last night I was looking in my history for another link to something totally different and when I saw the Google search I remembered there'd been some reason I wanted to go back. That's how this came up."

I understand almost none of what she's saying but I can tell she's feeling guilty.

"Can I ask you something?" she says.

"Yeah," I say.

"I'm not asking to make you feel bad but . . . I mean, why didn't you want to tell me about your dad being dead? It's not like it was your fault or anything. Why'd you tell me all that about your parents getting remarried and stuff?"

She kicks off her flip-flops and climbs onto the bed, settling

Indian-style up by her fluffy pillows, waiting on me to answer. I have to come clean. Now's the time I have to come clean. I know that. But knowing it don't make it any easier. I get up from my desk chair and climb up to join her on the bed.

"There's something I've got to tell you," I say. "Something worse."

I take in a deep breath and say the words as I'm blowing it out because if I don't do it now I'm scared I might chicken out altogether.

"I had a sister," I say. "I had a sister and her name was Emma."

Cricket cocks her head to the side and wrinkles show up between her eyebrows. "But . . . how come you never said?" she asks. "I mean, why didn't you ever mention it before? Did she die? You said you *had* a sister . . ."

"Sorry I didn't tell y'all," I say, feeling butterflies in my belly, "but it's more than just *I had a sister* and I didn't know how to explain it and then I worried y'all would think I'm crazy and not want me to come over here again plus then with my daddy being dead it all sounds made-up and weird and I thought you wouldn't want to be friends anymore . . ."

I trail off because I start crying. Cricket reaches down to the foot of the bed where I'm sitting and touches my leg, something I bet her mom would do if she was here. It still takes getting used to, the way they touch each other all the time in this family, hugging, patting, Cricket drapes herself all over her momma—and her momma doesn't even mind!

"Carrie, it's totally okay," Cricket says, straightening back up, "and just so you know, no way would we think you're crazy—that's ridiculous! And no way will we ever not want you to be here. Are you kidding me? Let's pinkie-swear so I can promise you that, okay?"

I smile through my tears and we hook our pinkies together and you know what? That does make me feel a little better.

"So tell me," she says.

Before I start back up again, there's one other thing that's been bothering me so much I don't even let myself *think* on it anymore much less write in my notebook about it.

"If I tell you," I say real slow because I almost cain't say the next words, "um, if I tell you and my momma finds out? If she finds out I said anything at all she'll have me sent away."

"Sent away?" Cricket's eyes get big. "What's that mean, *sent away*? Like, to live with relatives?"

"No no. Sent away to the loony bin for kids where they can lock you up forever if your parents say to. And Momma would definitely say for them to lock me up if she finds out I told you all I'm about to tell you."

"Okay, first of all there's no such thing as a *loony bin for kids*," Cricket says. She looks sure about that but how does she know? "And second of all, I swear I won't tell anyone what you tell me so your mom won't know."

I hold out my pinkie again for her to promise and she does so I keep going.

"Emma's my baby sister," I say, not knowing where else to start. "She's opposite of me. She had hair near-white blond, and it was tangled most of the time because she hated combing it. She was real little with tiny bird bones. I could make a finger bracelet around her wrist and still have my fingertip to spare. Her eyes turned the color green when she was mad but normally they were the pale blue color of this robin's eggshell we found one springtime.

"Back when I used to go to school my clothes fit right and if they didn't Momma would take us to our neighbor's house to get hand-me-downs from Maisey Wells, who was a few years older than me and *grew like a weed.* Her mama called ever-one *sugar* and said Maisey didn't mind letting me have her old clothes but I know for a fact she did mind. A lot. She would act all nice in front of grown-ups but then she'd tell ever-one at school we were poor white trash. Anyway, Emma being so much littler than me, she went around in nothing but a nappy. Momma said there was no sense buying her baby clothes when she'd outgrow them in five minutes and also in the hot summer Emma was happier just being naked. And that's another thing: Momma didn't mind talking about Emma back then when she was a little baby. She didn't mind hearing Emma's name at all. But then I wasn't to say the name Emma ever again. That's how it is now. I cain't ever talk about Emma or even say her name."

"Wait wait wait hold up. Where is Emma now?" Cricket asks.

I don't know how to answer that so I look down without saying anything.

"Carrie? Where's your sister now?"

I take another deep breath—this is harder to explain than I thought.

"Well, see, that's the thing," I say. My mouth gets dry, which is probably on account of me being at the tricky part. "Momma said—she still says—there never was an Emma. Momma says I made her up out of thin air after—well, um, after . . ."

"After your dad died?"

I'd been looking down at my hands but when she says that my head snaps up like Pinocchio's father lifted an invisible string on the top of it, to see how she said it. Like, did she have a mad look on her face or was she making fun of my stupid lying? But she was just . . . Cricket. She was saying the words out loud so I wouldn't have to.

"I'm really sorry I lied to you about that," I tell her again.

"Oh-Em-Gee, it's totally okay," she says, batting away my words like they were flies. And then she pauses, which she never does once she's started talking. She picks up a stuffed giraffe and hugs it close, nuzzling its spotted neck. "You know, for a long time after my sister died I lied when I met anyone new. Anyone who didn't know. I'd tell them I had a sister and that she went away to boarding school. If it was summer I'd say she was at sleepaway camp. I made up whole long stories about what she was doing there, her activities and stuff. So don't worry, I lied too. But wait, so, your mom says you made up that you had a sister because you were so sad your dad died?"

"Yeah. Momma says she felt sorry for me having no daddy so she *humored* me for a while and let me have an invisible friend—that's what she called Emma. My *invisible friend.* But then I kept talking about Emma and soon—this is the part where you'll say I'm crazy—but soon I got to where I just believed Emma *was* real. I cain't explain it good but I saw her, talked to her, played with her. Ever-thing. Most times I felt like Emma was all I had going for me, you know? You wouldn't know, actually. You got the best family in the world and loads of friends and all."

Cricket looks down at the giraffe in her lap and traces circles around his little glass eyes.

"That's how much *you* know," she says, still fooling with the giraffe. She looks up at me. "You're not the only one with secrets. You think I have a lot of friends?"

I nod at her and she snorts.

"Yeah, well, I don't," she says. At first I figure she's trying to make me feel better but then she goes on. "I've got, like, none. Zero. Zip. Caroline—my sister, Caroline, I mean—she was, like, my best friend. When we were growing up I copied everything she did so, like, if she wanted to go swimming at the Y, I did too even though deep down I've never really liked putting my head under-water. She was a fish, she loved it so much. Any music she lis-tened to, so did I. I copied everything she wore, her handwriting, the way she talked—she had this way of making everything funny, you know when people do that? Like if Mom said she was going on a diet but we knew she was still eating whatever she wanted, Car-oline would say *how's that workin' out for ya?* and Mom would laugh, but if it were me, I'd probably have said something awful like *but you're still eating like a horse* and then I'd get in trouble for being mean.

"Anyway, Caroline was the popular one," she says. "*Everyone* loved Caroline. She had so many friends her room at the hospital was practically wallpapered with get-well-soon cards and posters everyone in her class signed. I didn't get to see her that much when she was in the hospital at the end because my parents were trying to protect me or whatever—like I didn't know she was going to die."

She pauses, then her eyes water up and she looks away to try to keep from crying.

"I knew. Of course I knew," Cricket says, sniffling. "All anyone did in our house was whisper and if I walked in a room they'd stop and make these fake smiles to try to cover up what everybody knew, including me. Lots of times my parents would leave me at the Cutlers' house because their daughter, Lucy, was in my grade at school and you know how grown-ups think just because you're the same age you'll be instant best friends? Well, I hated Lucy mainly because Lucy hated me. She couldn't say so because her parents told her to be nice to me because of Caroline, but when we were alone it was like I was invisible. I'd start trying to talk to her about something—not something about Caroline but just, you know, *anything*—and she'd literally pick up a book and pretend to be really engrossed in it. I spent the night over at the Cutlers' lots of times and they were polite to me but we were all relieved when my mom or dad would pick me up. I'd have to hug them to say thanks and goodbye and Lucy would just stand there with her arms down at her sides, not hugging me back to make me feel even stupider. I never told my parents I hated going over there because I knew they needed me to be out of their hair so they could be with Caroline. When she died, you know how many kids from my class came to the funeral? Two. And that was just because one was the son of the school principal and the other had an older sister in Caroline's grade so their whole family came."

I don't know what I can say to help Cricket feel better so I just blurt out the first thing that comes to mind.

"*I'm* your friend."

She looks up from the giraffe with tears in her eyes. "You *are* my friend," she says, not smiling. "You're like my *only* friend. And since we're confessing, I've been wanting to tell you I'm sorry about yesterday. I told you I had a doctor's appointment but really I was going over to my dad's and I didn't want you to come but I didn't want to hurt your feelings."

"That's okay," I say.

"It's not that I haven't wanted to bring you to my dad's," she says, "I totally have! And obviously, as you could see, he's like in love with you. It's just that it's so *sad* over at his place, you know? It's like he doesn't know how to take care of himself without my mom. Half the time I'm cleaning up for him—doing the dishes he's got piled in the sink and wiping the counters, throwing out empty pizza boxes, stuff like that, but I have to do it when he's busy or not paying attention because I know he'll feel bad if he sees me, like, pity him or whatever. Plus, all he wants to talk about is my mom and does she ever talk about him. I mean, he doesn't come right out and ask point-blank like that. He thinks he's being cool about it. Like, we'll be talking about summer school and out of the blue, as if it's just occurred to him, he'll say *hey, by the way, how's Mom doing? What's she been up to this summer?* So anyway, it's just that I didn't want you to see him all broken like he is. I don't want you to know that version of my dad. He's so great when he's, you know, regular."

"You think they're gonna get back together, your momma and daddy?" I ask her.

"I want them to," she says, "but I don't know. I wish they would."

Seems like this is a good time to tell Cricket the last part of my story and I figure the best way to do it is to show her.

"What's that?" she asks me as I carefully put the picture on the bed facing her.

"That's Emma," I say. "My sister."

"But, wait, I thought you made her up?"

"That's what my momma says but then I found this and there's this other thing I haven't told you yet. See, I get these pictures? In my head? I been getting these flashes of memory or something—I don't really know what they are but they show a baby being shook hard and a Bible in flames. I know it makes me out to sound crazy but when I found this picture Momma was hiding from me suddenly I knew."

"What? What'd you know?"

"The flashes are of Emma," I say, waiting on Cricket to understand. But she's staring at me like she doesn't. "Get it? The flashes of the baby—they're of Emma. She *was* real! I didn't make her up after all! I think she died and *that's* why Momma says she was only imaginary and not to talk about her. I think Momma's covering up for something."

"Whoaaaaa." Cricket finally has the face I thought she would have: shock mixed with scary mixed with wow-what-a-story. "You think your mom killed her?"

"What? No! I mean I don't know." I cain't think of what to think and plus I never thought of it so simple like that. Did Momma kill Emma? Or Daddy? No. No way. "Is that what you think? I mean, from what all I told you, is that what *you* think happened?"

Cricket hops down and gets a pad of paper and a pen from her desk. Then she climbs back onto the bed.

"Here's what we should do," she says. "Let's make a list of all the facts we have now, then we can figure out what we need to search for online. Wait, how come you didn't tell the police about this?"

"They'd never believe me," I say, hoping she'll leave it alone and get back to the list making. *Please leave it alone Cricket please please please* . . .

"How do you know? You could tell my dad—he'd totally believe you," she says, holding her pen ready above the paper. "We should tell my father. I'll stay with you the whole time so you don't have to be scared and plus my dad's not scary at all so. Wait, what's the matter? Why're you crying?"

I'm crying because now I've got to tell her about Richard and I may be stupid but even *I* know she's never going to look at me the same way again.

"What is it?" she asks, scootching closer to gently pat my back. "You can tell me."

I sniff and wipe my snot and tears with the back of my hand. *She is never going to look at me the same way again.*

"There's something else," I say. But I hold off because maybe there's a way to answer her without telling about Richard.

"Tell me, Carrie," Cricket says.

I wish I could wave a magic wand and disappear from here into a time machine that could take me back to the car ride, back to before I went and opened my big fat mouth and got myself trapped in the truth. Or it could fly me into the future, way after today, when Cricket and them are long past the part we're at now. When they've learned to not think of me as a murderer. But my own momma hasn't learned that yet and she's my momma. So I'm a super-idiot for thinking Cricket will ever get past it.

"Carrie, seriously," she's saying. "You've got to tell me what it is."

All of a sudden it hits me. She's right. I've *got* to tell her because she's *got* to know ever-thing because I've *got* to find out what happened to my sister.

"Okay, well, there was this man"—I start from the beginning—"and his name was Richard."

The sun's starting to go down when I finally come to the end of the story. Cricket's laying on her belly, chin in her hands, feet making lazy circles in the air behind her. I'm still cross-legged and I'm pretty sure both my legs are asleep by now. It's going to be pins and needles when I stand up.

"Aha!" she says. "So *that's* why you say the police won't believe you."

I nod and wait for her to give me that I-didn't-realize-you-were-a-murderer look. But she goes and surprises me again.

"Okay then," Cricket says, sitting up then hopping off the bed. "Let's get started."

"Huh?" I ask, watching her turn on the computer. "Ow!"

My legs are asleep after all. Cricket pats the pillow on my desk chair for me to come set beside her. I don't tell her *thank you for not looking at me different now that you know the truth about me.* I don't tell her that I'm so lucky she's my friend. I don't burst into baby-tears and hug her.

I want to do all that, but I don't.

"Come on, we've got work to do," she says. "Wait, where did you say your mom came back from when she came home with Emma?"

"I think she was at my gammy's house," I say. "I don't remember much about where I was when Momma was there. Maybe I went and stayed there too, but I don't recall."

"Where does your grandma live again?"

"A small place near Asheville is all I know. She used to send us stuff from a store in Asheville she drove to all the time so it's somewhere near there."

"Okay, so, let's try this," Cricket says, clicking on something. "I think the county site is our best bet. Shoot. I don't know why they don't have anything under 'Public Records.' Seems like it should be— Wait! How come I didn't see this link? It was right there all along."

I'm excited because she's excited. That's why Cricket's so great. She knows this is something I need so it's like *she* needs it too, now.

"Here it is!" She says it like she's won a prize, twirling in her desk chair with her arms waving in the air, singing. "I found it, oh yeah, I found it I found it oh yeah . . ."

I rub my eyes and read it again to be sure I ain't seeing visions.

"And that's the only thing they got with my momma's name on it, right?" I ask her.

"Yup. Just the birth record. Nothing else. *Anywhere.*"

And then I copy it down in my notebook, word for word.

CERTIFICATE OF BIRTH

Buncombe County Hospital
Buncombe County
North Carolina

This certifies that Emma Margaret was born in this
hospital at 9:33 A.M. on Tuesday, the seventeenth of February.
In Witness Whereof this birth certificate has been duly signed
by the authorized officers who have caused the Corporate
Seal of this hospital to be hereunto affixed.

"Now we can go to my dad with this," Cricket says, bouncing in her seat while I'm racing to get the words right. "My dad's the best police officer there is. He can find out what really happened to your sister. Hey, I'm starving. Have supper with us tonight, will you? Please?"

"What time is it anyway?" I ask her, putting the cap on my pen and closing the notebook.

From out of nowhere it hits—I'm so tired I feel like I could sleep standing up. Saying my whole life story out loud sapped me of my syrup and now all I want to do is crawl into Cricket's bed here and sleep till I get it back. But I cain't risk spending the night—it could be the one time Momma comes home before dawn. "I kind of need to go back now."

"Okay," she says, making a frown. "You sure?"

I nod and follow her down the stairs to the kitchen to find Mrs. Ford for a ride back.

By the time we pull up to the Loveless my legs feel like they've been dipped in wet cement and dried into blocks. The door to the front office seems like it's locked shut, it's so heavy to open. Now I know what Momma means when she says she's *bone tired.*

When Mr. Burdock opens the door and sees it's me he hurries to close it so Mrs. Burdock doesn't catch sight but not before I hear her hollering at him from somewhere in the back. He looks as tired as me and I'm betting he's losing whatever fight they're having. Instead of mussing my hair or singing some weird song at me, he just shakes his head, points in the direction of room 217, and says, "I think ya got company."

What? Momma's home from work already? I knew it! Oh Lord, am I gonna get it. I get to the top of the stairs just in time to see a man in cowboy boots coming out of our room, still buttoning his rodeo shirt closed. He hurries past me, down the stairs, carrying a whiff of Momma with him—cigarettes and Jim Beam and the old lily of the valley perfume Momma's almost used up entirely. I watch him from the balcony railing. He looks over his shoulders, right then left, before getting into a brown car, revving the engine, and pulling out into the night. I get the feeling he didn't want to be seen here at the Loveless.

I try to come up with a reason why I wasn't there when Momma got home, listening at the door before knocking to be let in. Momma unlatches the door but leaves it to me to push open. She's at the sink when I step in, ready for whatever she's got in store for me. But she doesn't seem to notice I'm standing there in the middle of the room.

"Hey, Momma," I say, keeping my voice quiet and casual. "You're home from work early."

She's unsteady on her feet, scrubbing her face, splashing handfuls of water onto her soapy skin, so I guess Jim Beam saved me this time. Every once in a blue moon Momma has just the right amount of it to where I'm invisible to her. That's when I love Mr. Jim Beam.

I get into my bed quickly and hope for the best. Sure enough, Momma stumbles to her own bed, falls into it and, minutes later, she's sleeping. Easy as pie. I turn off the lamp that sits on the nightstand between our beds and wait for her to snore. Phee-you, I got lucky tonight.

There's nothing to do in the quiet but read and write and tonight I'm glad for that. After making sure Momma's out good I use my flat flashlight to stare at the words in my notebook and let my mind turn over the news. Emma was real! Emma was real. I knew it, I knew it, I knew it. But why did Momma say she wasn't? Why did she say I made Emma up and that I wasn't to ever talk about her again? Maybe Momma's so sad from her dying that she just cain't bear to think about it. But then Mrs. Ford and them are sad from Caroline's dying and *they* talk about *her* all the time. Cricket says we should talk to her father about all of it but I ain't so sure. I believe her that *she* doesn't think bad of me after learning the whole story, but Cricket's parents are grown-ups and there's never any telling what grown-ups will do. Her daddy could send me to the loony bin for kids just as easy as Momma could—he's the police.

I been reading Mr. Gideon's Bible and I have it on hand now in case Momma stirs and asks me what I'm looking at. If she wakes up I'll drop my notebook flat and grab the Bible like that's what I'm reading. I've been real careful not to crack it too wide open in case Mr. Gideon comes back and claims it. I want it to look spanking new for him, the way it does now. I lie on my bed and turn the pages quiet-like and read about the baby Jesus only it's not at all about the baby Jesus. At least not the part where I am—I'm a slow reader and lots of these words don't make any sense.

"Stupid . . . dirty . . . ," Momma says from her pillow about an hour later.

I sit up to try to get a better look at her talking in her sleep again. No telling what this dream's about.

"Goddamn . . . stray . . . dog," she's mumbling.

Her eyes are still closed. I hide the notebook under the comforter and walk around to the far side of her bed because I cain't see her face good from my bed.

Getting up close to her, I realize Momma don't smell too good. There was a girl in my old school named Penny and she never washed herself *ever*. After a couple of months Penny started smelling so bad no one would sit next to her. Or if they did they'd make a big show of pinching their noses closed. The teacher had to talk to Penny's parents who said they'd given up hoping she'd get over her *aversion to water*. One day I got to school real early on account of wanting to be out of the house away from Richard, and I saw a teacher out in back of the school over by the playing field holding Penny while the old black lady who cleaned the school scrubbed Penny's arms. Penny was crying and struggling to twist her way out of the teacher's arms. I remember seeing the hose laying there and wondering if grass ever drowns.

"So stupid, you don't even know," Momma says, her hollow eyes blinking at me. She's using her I'm-awake-for-good-now voice. "You, beating that Bible of yours . . . that precious Bible."

Suddenly she's wild-eyed and setting straight up in her bed.

She clears her throat, and without any notice she spits in my face! Trying not to think about how gross it is, I wipe it off my cheek with the back of my hand.

"Look at you, standing there with nothing but stupid to be," she says, looking like the sight of me turns her stomach.

"But I didn't do anything, Momma," I say. *Don't cry. Do not cry.*

"Let me see that book." She tips her chin in the direction of my bed.

For a second I panic, thinking she's talking about my notebook.

She holds her hand out and I see she means Mr. Gideon's Bible. I don't want to do it but I cain't tell Momma no.

Slowly I place it in her hand. I figure once she sees up close how the letters are carved into the cover then painted gold, once she feels the super-thin pages, she'll know it really is precious and she'll be just as careful with it as I am.

But Momma doesn't even spare Jesus her bad mood. She pries it open like butterfly wings, the spine cracking before I can remind her it don't belong to us.

"Where is it?" She races through the pages in search of what I do not know.

"Where's what, Momma?"

"Where is it?" Her hands shuffle pages madly back and forth.

"Aha! Here we go," she says, looking up to make sure I'm paying mind. "Love is patient, love is kind . . . blah blah . . . Here we go, here it is. *Love bears all things, believes all things, hopes all things, endures all things.*"

Slamming the book closed, she looks at me like she's won a bet. Maybe I had a forgetting spell again because it seems like she's waiting on me to say something.

"That's *your book* talking about love," she says.

"Yes, ma'am?" I say, hoping she'll say more so I can know what I'm supposed to be doing right now.

"Let me spell it out for you." She talks slow like to a baby. "I can't *bear* you, I don't *believe* you, and I sure as *hell* can't *endure* you another minute. I. Never. Loved. You! And I never *will* love you and yet you *still* keep at me like a goddamn stray dog, following me everywhere, watching me. Even when I'm sleeping. Everything I do. You watch me like you know something. You know what? I can't take it anymore."

"Momma, don't," I say. Dangit I hate when I cain't stop the tears. And trying to stop crying only makes me cry harder.

"Go on and cry," she says. "Right on cue. Where's the movie director, drama queen? Bring on the cameras."

"Please don't, Momma . . ."

"Momma please don't," she says in a high voice. "Just listen to yourself. You hear yourself? *Momma don't.* Just go on and get gone from my sight, you hear me? Oh, and don't forget your precious *Bible.* You can't hardly understand a word but there you are carrying it around like you and Jesus have found each other. The two of you judging me every livelong day. Take this damn book and *get the hell out of here!"*

The onion-thin pages crackle through the air when she throws the Bible across the room and at first I think they're ripping but phee-you, they're fine. Some are crumpled but I can flatten them back down later. I hurry to pick it up and while I'm at it I scramble for my notebook. The last thing I remember thinking is:

Getting kicked hurts just as much when Momma's barefoot as it does when she's wearing shoes.

Momma slaps me good and hard before shoving me out onto the balcony, kicking my notebook and Bible out too, then slamming shut the door to room 217. Clicking the lock just in case I try to come back in, which I won't. I drag myself to sitting up against the outside wall to our room, swallowing the metal taste of blood in my mouth. I don't know how long I'm there—I think I fall asleep but I'm not sure. The moon's bright enough for me to see my way down the stairs and over to the chain-link fence at the empty pool. I've jumped this fence a million times before but never when I'm this banged up so it takes me a few tries before I'm safely at the bottom of the pool, where I can curl up and sleep. I know Momma won't come looking for me so I let my brain turn off and slip away.

I don't know how long I sleep but it couldn't have been hours because the night is still velvet dark when I wake to the sound of someone stepping on an empty Coke can then cursing under their breath. I feel around for my two books and clutch them to my chest.

It's a man's voice. And he's standing right over me.

CHAPTER EIGHTEEN

Honor

I stir artificial sweetener into my tea and pull up a seat at the dining room table in front of stacks of file folders crammed full of Mother's financial records and God only knows what else. It's a mountain of papers so high my mind wanders every time I try to tackle it so it never gets tackled.

Over and over I replay the image of my former boss ushering me out after the firing—after my position as office manager was *eliminated,* I should say—his hand on my back as if I suddenly forgot the way to the door. Before I turned to face him to say goodbye I heard him stifle a burp then felt the mouthful of gaseous onion-scented air at the back of my neck.

"Damn economy," he said, patting my shoulder. "I'm real sorry about this, Honor. Real sorry."

"What're you thinking about?" Mother's voice startles me back to reality.

"I'm thinking we're between a rock and a hard place, if you

really want to know," I say. "And I honestly don't know what to do. I know you don't want to hear it but I could wring Hunter's neck."

"Oh, Honor, please," Mother says, opening the swinging door that leads to the kitchen and with her foot pushing a Charlie Chaplin doorstop into place to keep it open. "I don't want you bashing your brother over this. Over anything, actually. This is not his fault."

I hear the icebox opening. She's rummaging for something to eat. I put my hair into a hasty ponytail and scan the piles—for what I don't know.

"Of course it's his fault," I say. There are several unopened letters from the county office—I'm almost afraid to open them because I know they'll ratchet up my anger. "Whose else would it be, Mom? Jeez."

I'm surprised to see Mother reappear empty-handed in the doorway. She normally doesn't move that fast.

"Honor, listen to me and listen well," she says, pointing a finger at me. "Because I'm not going to say this again. You leave Hunter out of this, you hear me? You don't know what you're talking about and besides, he's your *brother*. He's your family. Your blood. When I'm long gone he is all you'll have left of our family. This is the sort of thing that can drive a permanent wedge between siblings and I simply won't abide that, do you understand me? That would kill me."

"Okay, okay," I say, holding up my hands in surrender. "I got it."

Something's not quite right about this but I can't put my finger on it. While she was talking I realized I'm never going to get anywhere by arguing with Mother, so I'll just call Eddie and go over it with him. He can figure it out with me.

"Mom, I know you don't want to hear this, but we've got to sell all this memorabilia, you know that, right?"

"No I do not," she says, "and I will not, so you can take that right off the table."

"You've got to be kidding me," I say. "*Mom*. These things could really be worth something—we're sitting on a gold mine and you want to plug up the hole? Why? Why hang on to all of it?"

"Honor Chaplin Ford, this is your legacy, for goodness' sake," she says, horrified that I'd dare mention parting with it. "This is your daughter's legacy. I would think you would want to keep it intact for her at least."

"Oh, Mother," I sigh. It's tempting to tell her about my meeting at City Hall with Mr. Sylvester. But I need to tease that whole thing out in my own mind before I tackle it with her, and I might just run it by Ed, see what he thinks. So instead I say, "Cricket doesn't need dolls and posters and letters to know she's a Chaplin. Seriously. Let me noodle around a little and see what we could get for—"

"No."

"Just one or two things. What's the harm in finding out the value of one or two things? Just pick out what you think you could part with and I'll take care of it."

"No!"

"It could buy us some more time in the house," I singsong to her.

To my great surprise, she's actually thinking it over. *Come on, Mom. You can do it . . .*

"I'm not selling the Madame Alexander ones," she says grumpily. "Or the signed stills. Or the Oscar repro."

"Okay, fine. You don't have to! Start with a few of the things you don't care too much about and we'll go from there, how about that? Oh, I'm so proud of you. This is great. Just bring me a couple of dolls you can live without and I'll take it from there."

"Oh well fine," she says. "But don't go sneaking things out behind my back, do you hear me? *I* will choose what to sell."

"Absolutely."

"I don't want to get any grief over this," she says.

"No grief. I promise."

"Now let's get our priorities straight here," Mother says. "You need to go get our little girl."

"She's upstairs in her room," I say.

"Not that one," she says. "Our *other* little girl."

I call up to Cricket and we head over to the Loveless.

After waiting in the parking lot at the Loveless for almost twenty minutes, I go in to use the house phone to call up to Carrie's room, see what's taking her so long and maybe even speak with her mother. It's not like Carrie to be late—usually she's waiting on the curb for us. The pine-tree-shaped air freshener hanging from the office door is no match for the kitty litter, and while Mr. Burdock clucks at me I start to wish Mrs. Burdock would show herself so I could drop a hint that she might want to water that pathetic-looking ficus in the corner.

"The phone was the first thing to go," Mr. Burdock's saying. "Hell they ain't paid rent in two weeks and Mrs. Burdock's about to have herself a stroke. She tallies up their bill every hour practically, it burns her up so much. You think I like hearing about them Parkers day and night like I do? Day and night I got to hear about how they're stiffing us. Day and night. It's all I can do to keep her from letting herself into their room to haul out their shit pardon my French and change the locks. I ain't the bad guy here! I know things ain't exactly right but let's not go flying off the handle here."

"I'm not flying off the—"

His hand flies up to shush me and he says, "All right, all right now. Let's say something *is* wrong. What do you expect me to do about it when her own mother ain't fretting? I'm supposed to call nine-one-one any time that girl decides to forage in some new place? 'Cause I'd be dialing them three numbers every day in that case. She hunts and gathers—that's who she is. That mother of hers only opens the door for Jim Beam. *She* ain't putting food on the table so the girl's gotta do it. I actually like the kid, it's true. I don't want to see harm come to her, or anybody for that matter. I'm a law-abiding citizen and I love my country."

"What's loving your country got to do with it?" I try to contain my anger. *Chaplins always take the high road.* "Look, all I'm asking is for their room number, not the key. I think you know by now I'm not here to bother any of your other—ah—guests. I just want to see if she's up there, let her know we're down here waiting on her. She's probably running late and you said yourself their phone's been cut off, otherwise I'd simply call up there."

This gives him pause.

"No hotel manager worth his salt would release a room number," he says. "It's rule number one of hotel management. But if I were to, say, step away from this ledger here, *this ledger with the room numbers and names in it,* and you were to, say, glance down at it, I guess that'd be out of my control now, wouldn't it?"

"Oh, Mr. Burdock, I could *kiss* you right now—"

His hand flies up again so I hush.

"So I'm going to step away," he continues, "check on things in the back. Might take me a couple of minutes. Maybe I'll see you when I come back, maybe I won't . . ."

As he's talking and without looking down at it, he turns the book upside down so it's now facing me. Before retreating to the back room he looks at me. "You tell anybody about this, I'll deny it," he says.

I silently pantomime locking my lips and throwing away the key.

"One more thing," Hap Burdock says. "Get that kid outta there, would you?"

And then he's gone. And I'm worried sicker than I was when I first came in. My panic sends a shot of adrenaline up my spine—it's like my blood drank a six-pack of Red Bull. It only takes a second, he's right, to find "Parker" on the guest registry. Room 217. I bust back out into the afternoon heat, give a fake everything's-okay wave to Cricket in the car and, once out of her sight line, I rocket up the stairs to the second floor.

At first I knock gently. *Tap-tap-tap-tap-tap,* pause, then *tap-tap.* The universal "friendly" knock.

Nothing happens.

I check to the left and right, and when I'm sure no one can see me I knock again and put my ear up to the door to hear if there's any sound of movement inside.

Still nothing.

"Carrie? Mrs. Parker?" I call out through a fake smile so I sound breezy and casual. "It's Honor Ford. Just wondering if anyone's home."

I knock again. Harder this time.

"Hello?" I call through the door. "Anybody in there?"

Please God, don't let me be too late. Now all pretense is gone and I'm banging on the door. To no avail. The shades are drawn so I can't see in through the window. Please God.

"Carrie? Honey, it's Mrs. Ford." I listen again. Nothing.

Now I know what I need to do. I go back downstairs to the car, fasten my seat belt, and pass Cricket my cell phone.

"Call your father," I tell her, shifting into drive, feeling like the Terminator, ready to kick some ass.

"What happened?" Cricket asks, full of fear. "Where's Carrie?"

"Just get your father on the line and hand me the phone."

A half hour later Eddie and I are at home, sitting at the dining room table, Cricket and Mother tucked safely out of earshot in Mom's bedroom watching TV because I don't want either of them overhearing the come to Jesus I'm about to have with my husband.

"Christ, Honor, I thought someone was getting murdered, the way you sounded on the phone," Ed tells me. "What's going on? What's all this?"

He tips his chin at the piles of dolls Mother has started making. Given how sparse they are, I suspect it will take more convincing to part with enough Chaplin memorabilia to raise the money we'll need.

"By the way, I've only got an hour," Eddie adds. "I told the desk sergeant I was taking an early break but I've got to get back so—"

"I'll get right to it," I say, pushing stray hair behind my ears and taking a deep breath. "Frankly, I don't know what to do about the Carrie situation. I thought somehow it would resolve itself or something would be revealed that would answer my questions— oh, I don't know what I thought. I didn't want to jump to the same conclusion the Dressers jumped to about us."

"What's the Carrie situation? The Dressers? Honor, get to the point for God's sake."

"Okay, okay! Jeez. Here it is. Carrie is clearly neglected. You can see that too, right? I mean, I know you've only been with her for a few minutes and it was emotional and all but surely you could see that she's neglected at the very least. She's malnourished, her clothes are far too small for her, she turns up with bruises and strange marks. And now she's missing."

"What do you mean she's missing?" he demands, leaning forward and putting his elbows on the table. I see the fierce protective streak that has made my husband such a damn fine police officer.

"Well, I went over to the Loveless to pick her up and after waiting awhile in the car I ended up going up to their room—"

"It's just her and her mother, right?" he interrupts.

"Yes, and I *still* have never met her mother," I say, "which is another thing. Wouldn't you want to meet the person your child is spending nearly every waking minute with? How could this mother let her nine-year-old daughter go off with strangers every day? For all she knows, we're child molesters!"

"What happened when you went up to their room? I take it no one was there."

"No one was there," I say, nodding.

"So how do you know she's missing and not just out with her mother, running errands or something?" he asks.

"Ed, I'm telling you, something's wrong," I say. "I'm looking you in the eye and telling you I can just feel it. Maybe it's a mother's intuition, maybe it's some cosmic sign, I really don't know. But this is me and I'm asking you, I'm begging you, to help me get to the bottom of this."

"Baby, you know we can't file a missing person report unless someone's been gone for—"

"Don't even finish the sentence. I know. But this is *me* talking to *you*. This isn't some nervous Nellie stranger who doesn't know diddly about what goes on out there in the world. It's *me* and I'm telling you I've got a really bad feeling about this."

We lock eyes for just a moment, but it's long enough for me to know he still loves me. He still loves me! *Focus, Honor. Focus.*

"What about Cricket?" he asks, looking down at whatever random pile is sitting in front of him. "I assume you've asked her where she thinks Carrie might be."

"She was with me, waiting in the car when I went up to the room at the Loveless," I say, "and she looked worried sick—panicked almost—when I said Carrie wasn't there, so I just tried to calm her down and then I called you."

"Let's get her in here," Ed says, standing up to call for her. "Cricket? Come on down here!"

"They're in Mother's room with the TV on, so let me go get her," I say.

When I come back Eddie looks up from reading one of the foreclosure documents.

"This is unbelievable," he says, shaking his head and looking back down.

"I just had a very illuminating talk with Mom about it this morning," I say, with a hint of sarcasm. Illuminating it was not.

Eddie's head jerks up.

"So I take it she told you," he says, missing the sarcasm.

Instead of displaying my confusion, I just sigh, fall into the dining room chair I'd been sitting in, and wait for Eddie to elaborate.

"Honor, I swear I didn't know, and by the way, she came to me," he says. "I don't want you to think it was the other way around. She came to me."

It's the oldest trick in the book: pretend you know what someone's talking about until you *do* know what someone's talking about.

"She came to you," I say, careful to clear my voice of accusation.

"Not long before we . . . before we split up," he says, "your mother came to me and said she had a sizable nest egg and wanted to help ease the pressure on us. I guess she thought our problems were all money-related, what with the medical bills and all. I didn't want to take her up on it—I downright refused her the first time she brought it up. I figured you'd hate me even more if you thought I was taking handouts from your mother. But then she said you wouldn't have to know. It could just be between the two of us, your mom and me, until—oh, I don't know, until I could somehow get my head back above water financially."

So she hadn't sent the money to Hunter after all. That's why she didn't want me blaming him. She didn't want me telling him about the foreclosure because it truly wasn't his fault. Oh my God. The medical bills bankrupted my mother. Oh my God.

"How long did y'all think you'd be able to keep this from me?" I ask. "Don't even answer that—I know the answer: forever. You thought you'd be able to keep this secret from me forever. You made it this far so I guess you thought you were almost home free. You've always played it close to the vest, Edsil, so this shouldn't come as any real surprise."

"Honor, please," Ed says, his eyes pleading with me. "You think I wanted to be in this position? You think I wanted your mother to put her life on the line like that? I didn't know! She said she had a lot in savings and I promised her I'd pay her back . . ."

I should control my temper. I know I should. But I don't. Sue me.

"This is exactly the type of thing that tore us apart," I spit the words at him like a snake. "You don't let me in, Ed. You've never let me in. You're so goddamn stoic and proud and private. *I'm your wife! I'm* the one you should have come to with the money problems! Not my mother. *Me.* Your *wife.* Every time you opened the mail or sat down to pay the bills, every single *fucking* time I'd ask you how we were holding up you'd say *fine, just fine,* until it was too late!"

"Honor . . ."

He can't stop me now. No one can.

"And every time her name came up, *every single fucking time her name came up,* a cloud would come over your face and you'd leave the room," I yell. The tears are cracking my voice. "Or if you couldn't physically leave the room, mentally you would just shut down. Locking me out entirely. Going back to work when you didn't need to because you couldn't stand to grieve with me!"

"I went back to work because we'd been accused of *child abuse,* Honor, remember? I went back to work because the longer I stayed away, the guiltier we looked! I went back to work to try to hold on to my job, Honor, Jesus!"

There are tears in Ed's eyes now too.

"You could have shown some emotion when she died," I hiss, not ready to accept his rationale, sensible though it is. "Would it have killed you to have squeezed out a tear or two when she died? You didn't cry! You didn't cry once. Until . . . until . . ."

"Until Carrie."

We're both startled by Cricket's sudden appearance. I'd been so overwhelmed with anger and hurt and sadness I'd completely forgotten about Cricket. Again.

"Why can't you guys just let the past be the past?" Cricket cries at us. "Why can't you *move on*? You think Caroline would be happy to know you split up after she died? You think she'd feel good about knowing her death *caused* you to break up? Huh? Because that's what happened. Caroline died and *I'm* not reason enough to try to stick it out."

When Eddie and I start protesting, Cricket shushes us. Shames us, really.

"Look. You both love each other, right? *Right?*" She looks hard at both of us, like a headmistress doling out detentions.

Then Eddie looks me in the eye and answers her, "Yes, honey. Yes, your mother and I love each other."

"Mom?"

I don't need to look at her to know she's turned her burning gaze to me. I look into Eddie's eyes and goddamn it all. Goddamn it all to hell.

"*Mom?*" she presses me.

"Fine! You win!" I holler at both of them. "I love your father, okay? I love him but he drives me crazy and if he thinks . . ."

The rest of my words are muffled because he has leapt out of his seat to come around and gather me into his arms, laughing at my pride in not wanting my anger to dissipate, kissing the top of my head, murmuring my name, knowing that now we can fix this. It'll take a lot of work but now we can fix *us*.

"So, Dad? Did you find Carrie yet?" Cricket, the inveterate subject changer, brings Eddie and me back down to earth.

"Oh my God, Carrie," I say, fixing my hair and straightening my blouse after our movie moment.

Ed is similarly discombobulated, but his rearranging has to do with his trousers and that's all I'll say.

He clears his throat and sits down in the chair next to mine.

"Cricket, did Carrie ever mention any favorite hiding places? Anything she liked to keep secret?"

Now it's Cricket who's squirming, which I must say is surprising. I assumed she would answer no, otherwise why wouldn't she have brought it up earlier? But her silence is telling. I know my daughter well enough to know she's holding something back.

"It's okay, honey, you can tell us," I say.

"You've *got* to tell us if you want to find Carrie," Ed says.

Cricket looks frightened but doesn't say a word. Which just proves she knows something.

"Cricket, it's not breaking a promise if it's a matter of life and death," Ed tells her. "Now, I know you want to be a good friend to little Caroline by keeping secret whatever she's asked you to keep secret, but a *real* friend would know that any little detail will help find her, so whatever it is, you need to tell us."

"It's a matter of life and death?" Her eyes widen in pure terror.

"It could be," I say.

Ed nods.

After agonizing over it some more, Cricket finally says, "So, um, Carrie was asking me all kinds of questions about the computer, you know, because she hadn't ever seen one before— remember how she came over that first day? It was like she was from another planet. I mean, who's never seen a computer?

"She was all *could you ask it anything* and *what about family history* and on and on. I just kept saying *yeah* and asking her what she needed to check out but she didn't say at first. Not that day, at least.

"Fast forward and it comes out that, um, I guess her father was murdered back when she was little. Then she said she had a little sister but there was something secret about it. She wanted me to look up birth records for her. She said her momma says she never had a sister but she knows for a fact that she did. She made me promise not to talk to anybody about it. I had to swear up and down to Tuesday I wouldn't breathe a word of it to y'all or anybody."

"Her father was *murdered*?" Ed and I speak at once in near unison.

"I asked her if her mom had files or pictures she could look through and Carrie said no." Cricket ignores our question and continues. "I think her mother's mean or crazy or something but I don't know. Carrie never really says anything bad about her—it's just a feeling I get. Anyway, I found her sister's birth certificate online. We were so psyched. It was awesome. She copied it down word for word in that notebook of hers. I asked her why her mom would tell her she didn't have a baby sister if she did but I don't think she knew the answer to that any better than I did."

Ed cannot sit still a moment longer. "I'm going to call this in," he says, getting up while dialing his cell phone.

"Why? What do you think happened to her?" Cricket asks. "Mom? She's okay, right? I'm so scared now."

I reach for her and, still a little girl at heart, she comes over and sits on my lap even though she's way too big for it, and buries her head in my arms while we listen to Eddie talk to the station house.

Where are you, Carrie? Where are you?

CHAPTER NINETEEN

Carrie

When you're hurt and away from home ever-thing seems scary. Car horns sound like they're aimed at you and you only. Lights look mean they're so bright. Footsteps are all heading your way, about to discover wherever it is you're hiding. No one smiles. Every smell makes you want to throw up.

When the sun of the following day sets about scorching the ground and anyone stupid enough to walk barefoot on it, I take cover under the bramble bushes in an empty lot a couple hours' walk away from the Loveless, squinching myself small enough to fit in what little shade they throw. If I had my flip-flops I might could keep going but I don't so I wait for the sun to ease up before setting out again. I scan the dirt for anything looking like food and catch sight of some trash toward the middle of the lot that might be something. I pick my way around the broken glass and abandoned tires and find there are still some potato chip crumbs at the bottom of a bag called *Lay's*, so I tip the whole bag into my open mouth to be sure I get every last one. Someone walks by. I panic and race back to my bramble bush but they don't see me. Phee-you. My heart slows back down. I don't want to be a scaredy-cat but Momma always says *you can't always get what you want* and I guess she's right. I am a scaredy-cat. At least today I am. After listening to my belly growl one too many times I give up and scrape some dirt into a pile so I can take pinch bites. It's not as bad as you might think and it quiets my stomach. That's the good news. The bad news is now, instead of thinking about food, I cain't help but think about what happened in the dark back at the pool. Waking up to a man standing over me. His grunts as he pinned me down. The stink of his beer-breath as he tried to pull off my pajama shorts. The ache in my legs as I kicked him off me before he could. The crinkle of trash underfoot when I scrambled to the ladder of stairs. The cool metal steps leading me up, up, up, up to the edge of the empty pool I thought no one else knew about. The thump-thumping of my heart beating in pure fear. The slap-slap-slapping sounds of my bare feet against the pavement, running me away from the man in the pool, away from room 217, away from Momma.

I fall asleep, wake up, then fall back asleep again. By the time I wake up for good, the sun's gone down but night hasn't entirely taken over yet so I set out from the empty lot feeling dizzy and sore but I've got to keep going. I keep telling myself that the whole way there. *Keep going. Keep going. Keep going.* My eyes are giving me trouble but I figure that's the least of my problems.

At the exact second I press the doorbell I realize it's probably later than it looks and I shouldn't be bothering them. A light comes on over my head and the front porch comes into focus when I squinch my bad eye closed and blink with the good one. On the porch swing, a book is splayed out and it looks familiar but like I said, I cain't see all that well right now. If I had air-conditioning like they do here I'd never set outside in this heat ever. Even if the book I was reading was real good.

"Oh my goodness, Carrie! We've been looking all over kingdom come for you, honey," Mrs. Ford says, pulling me into her body for a hug then pushing me back an arm's length to see me better. "You've had us worried sick. Oh my God—what happened? Sweet baby Moses in the rushes, *what on earth happened to you?* Come inside here, come on in, there you go. One more step. Eddie! *Mother!* Someone come out here, will you? There you go, honey. Oh my God, just look at you."

I hear her voice calling out again for help and that's about the last thing I hear before I run out of batteries altogether. Next thing I know, blurry faces are staring down at me and someone lifts something cold off my forehead then puts it back again in a way that feels cooler.

"Here she is," a voice is saying. "Here's our girl. Honey? Can you hear me? Carrie? Can you tell us where you've been?"

"Don't bombard her with questions," a man's voice says. "Let her come to before you set in with the third degree."

Seems like there are a dozen people in the room. Voices come from everywhere.

"We should take her to the hospital . . ."

"Let's see what's what first, why don't we . . ."

It takes a lot of blinks to bring them into focus.

"Looks like she's got something in her left eye," the first voice says. I see now it's Mrs. Ford. "She's favoring it. Mom, call up to Cricket and tell her to bring me a washcloth from the linen closet, will you?

"Keep them closed for now, honey," she says to me in a softer voice. "I think you've got something lodged in your eye—if you keep opening it like that, it could scratch your cornea."

From somewhere that feels far away but probably isn't, I hear Miss Chaplin hollering for Cricket. Then the booming of footsteps overhead. Then the mix of voices talking at once.

"I'm sorry to be a bother," I say. At least I think I say it—Mrs. Ford is sitting right here next to me on the edge of whatever I'm laying on but she don't hear me so I try to get my mouth moving again.

"I'm so sorry to put y'all out like this," I say.

"I think she's trying to say something," Miss Chaplin says.

"What's that you're saying, honey lamb?" Cricket's mom asks me. "You trying to tell us something?"

Why aren't they hearing me?

"I'm sorry . . . ," I start again, but up and suddenly I feel too tired to make any more words.

Jumbled sentences fill my ears:

"Where's that washcloth?"

"Cool water—not too cold, cool."

"Mom? Dad? What's going on? Oh my God, *Carrie*? What *happened* to her?"

"Shhhh, we'll get to that but first we've got to get her cleaned up."

"Is she asleep?"

"Cricket, bring me a bowl with some ice."

I'm trying hard to stay awake, to make my brain work along with my mouth, to figure out why they're looking at me funny, but I cain't fight sleep.

So I don't. I float away from them and let my brain turn off again. Until, a while later I think, it comes back on and this time it's clearer. The thump and thwack of Momma's foot then the sting of her hand across my face. The prickly dead grass ringing the pool. That's all clear in my brain until it turns itself off for sleep. When I wake back up I hear them saying stuff about me and I don't know what it is but I know it ain't good. I think I'm being blamed for something and since I don't know what it is and I cain't exactly make it right, I know the best thing for me to do right now is to be scarce so's not to be more of a burden. I want to holler at the top of my lungs *just tell me what I did wrong and I swear I won't do it again. I'm real good at never doing wrong stuff again, you'll see.* That's what I'd holler out but the words stay in my throat to almost choking.

"Look at her fingernails," the man's voice says. Then I realize the voice belongs to Mr. Ford. "You see that? They're packed with dirt."

Mr. Ford looks different in his police uniform. Official-looking. If I hadn't met him when I did and the way I did, I'd be scared of him for certain. Then again, Mr. Ford's got a Yosemite Sam mustache that curls up at the ends so he looks to be smiling even when he's not.

"Look look! Shhh. She's waking up," Mrs. Ford says. "Shh, y'all be quiet for a minute. Honey? Carrie? There's our beautiful girl. You remember Mr. Ford. Cricket's daddy. He's here too."

"Hey there, sweet Caroline." Mr. Ford steps in closer so I can see his face better. He smiles and gives a little wave.

"Honey, Mr. Ford's got a few questions he needs to ask you, okay?" Mrs. Ford says. "You feel up to a couple of questions?"

It hurts on my side when I push sound through my mouth so I near to whisper "yes, ma'am," and Mrs. Ford looks relieved. I feel so grateful to them I want to jump up and hug them all close. I cain't but I want to. Maybe in a bit I can get over to a sink so I can wash my hands. Get the dirt out from my fingernails.

"Honey, what happened to you, can you tell us?" Mr. Ford asks.

Cricket is craning her neck over her father's shoulder.

I want so bad to answer them but my tongue feels heavy and thick in my mouth and my side feels like a log split open with an ax.

"Did your mama do this to you, Caroline?" Mr. Ford asks. When his eyebrows crinkle together with worry he looks exactly like Cricket. He moves closer and tilts his head so my voice can get a straight shot to his ear. "You can tell us anything—nothing bad's going to happen to you I can promise you that."

I cain't keep from resting my eyelids but I'm still awake.

"I swear, that woman is a monster out of a horror movie . . . ," Miss Chaplin says from somewhere off to the side.

Mrs. Ford hushes her.

"Shhhhh, *stop* it, Mother. She won't say a word if she thinks we'll do something to the mother."

"I'm just sayin'."

"Well, *don't*. Not now. Not in front of her."

"Why don't y'all leave Caroline and me alone for a minute?" Mr. Ford says to them, lowering his voice then raising it to jostle me awake. "We could use some sweet tea, I bet, right, Caroline? Wouldn't that taste good? Some nice, cold sweet tea?"

"Coming right up," Miss Chaplin says. "Come on, Honor. Cricket, you too, honey."

"But, she's *my* friend," Cricket's saying.

"Grandma's right, let's let Dad talk to Carrie alone for a bit. You can come back and check on her later."

"Aw, man," Cricket groans and lets herself be led out of the room. "Carrie, I'll be in the kitchen, okay? You need me, you just tell my dad and he'll get me. Dad, be gentle, 'kay?"

"Always am, princess," he says. "Now go on. All of you."

Both my eyes are back working okay and I watch him watch them leave the room.

"That's better," he says, turning his head back to me, letting his brows relax while his mouth puts a smile on. A smile that feels like the sun is shining on my face. A smile like Cricket's.

"Finally some peace and quiet around here! That's much better, isn't it? Listen, Caroline, I want to tell you something real important here. I'm a police officer which I know you know and police officers are real good secret keepers which maybe you don't know. We are. You can tell me anything at all and if you say I can't tell anybody about it, well, then I won't. But it's real important you tell me the truth, okay?"

"Yes, sir," I say with my tongue so fat it comes out "yeth thir."

"Now, I can see it pains you to talk so what I'm going to do is ask you yes and no questions so all you've got to do is nod or shake your head. You don't even need to say the word *yes* or *no* if you feel you can't. All right?"

I nod my head.

"Good," he says. "That's real good. You're a smart little girl, I can see that. Sometimes smart people find themselves in not-so-smart situations, you know? Or maybe they do not-so-smart things. When I was your age I got up to lots of not-so-smart things. Hell, let's just call a spade a spade: I did some pretty dumb things. Who-ee, my mama sure did have her hands full with me. And I had eight brothers and sisters so you can imagine how tired my poor mother was. I'm worn out just dealing with that one in there!"

He smiles and tips his head in the direction of the kitchen so I know it's Cricket he's talking about.

"It's just you and your mama living over there at the Loveless, is that right?"

"Yes, sir," I say out loud.

"Um-hmm, yeah, your mama probably worries herself sick about you, I'm guessing," he says. "That's what mothers do. They worry."

He's pulled over a gray metal folding chair like they got at church for when too many people show up for services. The way he's eased back into it you'd think it was the most comfortable chair in the world, man-crossing his legs, one ankle over the other knee.

"No sisters or brothers? Ah, here we go," he says, looking up at something past the couch, then standing, "sweet tea for a sweet little girl. Thank you, Miss Ruth. That looks like just what the doctor ordered. Here, let me take that from you."

He's reaching, then sitting at the edge of his folding chair, then holding a straw to my lips.

"There you go, a little hydration'll do you a world of good," he says. "When was the last meal you had, sugar?"

I've only been gone and on my own for one day but you'd think it was a year the way my mouth waters hearing him say the word *meal*. I guess he can tell how hungry I am because he says, "Been that long, has it? Miss Ruth? Excuse me a minute, Caroline. I'm going to see if we can't rustle up some food for you. I'll be right back."

"Yeth, thir."

I'm tired. I'm tired of twisting my brain into knots to think what to do. If I tell him Momma got mad and threw me out, if I tell him she hurt me, he'll go over to arrest her and if he goes over to arrest her she'll tell him I'm crazy and if she tells him I'm crazy he'll have me sent away. But then I remember.

Emma.

"Hey, kiddo, I'm back," Mr. Ford says, resting a tray of food on his lap. "How about a piece of cinnamon toast? That sound good?"

After eating catalogs and clay and ketchup packets in between the goody bags, I don't need to tell you how I feel about buttered toast with cinnamon sugar sprinkled on it. Miss Chaplin even cut off the crusts.

"That's it," he says, holding the other triangle out for when I finish chewing this one. He smiles and says, "I guess you *were* hungry," and I nod and try to smile back at him while I chew.

"While you're working on that, there's something you need to know, Caroline," he says. I figure he's about to tell me again how he's not gonna let anyone hurt me. Or that I can tell him anything. The last thing I ever thought he'd say is:

"Honey, we know about Emma."

I stop working on the toast in case maybe I heard him wrong.

"Now, I know you didn't want anyone to find out, but Caroline, there are some things that shouldn't be kept secret. And when you went missing Cricket and her mom and Miss Chaplin—well, they were worried sick. And they did the right thing calling me. Don't go getting mad at Cricket, I forced it out of her. She didn't want to betray your confidence but she also knew what we all now know: you're in way over your head, baby girl. You need to let us help you. And in order to help you, I need to know where you've been and what happened that made you look like the losing end of a prizefight. I know I sound stern—I don't mean to come down hard on you—but if you don't tell me I'm going to have to go over to the Loveless and find someone who will call a spade a spade. Your mama, maybe."

"No! It ain't her fault!" I hurry to stop him and I cain't sit up easy but you can bet I'm trying.

"So tell me, then," he says, and while I quickly finish chewing what's in my mouth, he sets the food tray on the low table at the end of the couch. The glass table with a lamp that has a Charlie Chaplin hat for a shade.

"I knew she hated it when I studied her"—my thick tongue slows me up but it looks like he can understand me so far—"but she was having one of her fever dreams and I went to tell her it was just a nightmare and she saw me standing over her, staring at her—but the thing is, I wasn't studying her right then, I swear—"

"Slow down, peaches," Mr. Ford says. "I can't understand you when you talk fast like that. Take a deep breath and slow down."

I do as he says.

"I was crowding her and Momma hates me crowding her and I knew that but I guess I wasn't thinking it at that exact time."

"What happens when you crowd her?" he asks.

If I tell him the rest, he won't understand. He doesn't know Momma like I do. If I tell him the rest—

"Go on, Caroline." He says it like he's reading my thoughts, and just in case he *can* read thoughts I better just call a spade a spade, like he said to.

"I got punished," I whisper the words. Then I remember something. "Mr. Ford? Did y'all find a Bible when you found me? I mean, I think I was carrying something when I got here. A Bible that belongs to someone else but I been borrowing it and I meant to bring it with me."

He nods. "We found a notebook and a Gideon Bible out front on Miss Chaplin's porch swing, don't worry. We got them both safe and sound here for you, honey."

I settle back against the couch cushions.

"We also found you clutching on to this pretty tight," he says, holding up . . .

The picture of baby Emma.

I close my eyes, and for the first time since right before I stuck up for Momma and shot Richard, for the first time since we turned the page and landed at the Loveless, for the first time in what feels like forever, I feel Emma here with me. And *that* gives me courage. I take as deep a breath as I can and then spill the beans.

"Emma's my baby sister," I start from the beginning. "She's opposite of me. She had hair that was near-white blond and tiny bird bones . . ."

CHAPTER TWENTY

Carrie

"Honey, remember our deal? You promised to stay out of the way once you got her to open the door," Mrs. Ford says to me, "so come on out onto the balcony here so the police can do their work."

Momma looks her up and down and says, "Calling her *honey* already—isn't that just perfect."

The policeman is talking to a black lady in a suit holding a clipboard. He's using words like *child services* and *fostering* and *safe houses.* Mrs. Burdock is in her bright-colored housedress pacing on the balcony in front of our open door, muttering to herself about *cleanup crews.* Ever-body's talking at once.

Another policeman pushes past Mrs. Burdock, talking into his radio. He stands at the far side of Momma's bed, across from Mr. Ford.

"What's going on? What're y'all doing?" I ask Mr. Ford as he's pulling the covers off Momma. "Wait, stop!"

I wish all these grown-ups would just *leave her alone!* Don't they know this is gonna make it worse for me later, when they leave? Momma's gonna skin me alive for this.

It's all going so fast. Mrs. Ford keeps waving to get my attention so I'll go out by her but what about Momma?

"How long have they been living like this?" the lady in the suit is asking Mrs. Burdock.

"Too long, I'll tell you that much," she says.

"Fifty-one-fifty," a policeman's hollering into his radio but it keeps breaking up so he says it over and over again.

"Place needs to be fumigated," Mrs. Burdock's saying to no one in particular.

And then I see room 217 like they must see it. The trash is stacked up pretty high in the far corner—I'm sure they think it's Momma's fault but it was *my* job to empty the trash. *I'm* the one who forgot to do it, not her. The flies settle—*they're only buzzing around because y'all are going through our things*, I want to yell out. I want to tell them *it's not always this messy.* I want to cover up Momma's too-skinny body—I hate ever-one seeing her like this. *She's so beautiful,* I want to holler. *Y'all just don't know. She was voted Most Beautiful in her high school.* Suddenly ever-thing feels naked and ugly and tiny with so many people in it.

"It was only supposed to be until we got ourselves situated," I say out loud. In case anyone's listening. "Until Momma found work. Why're y'all going through ever-thing like that? Wait, don't hurt her! Momma? Please, Mr. Ford, please don't hurt her."

"Honor, you've got to get Carrie out of the way," Mr. Ford says. "This isn't something she needs to see."

Momma's picked now to laugh good and hard.

"Honey," Mrs. Ford is saying, "Carrie, come on with me, now. We'll just go down and wait in the parking lot."

"Momma, I'm sorry." I wriggle away from Mrs. Ford and run over to Momma, who's being held up to standing by two policemen, one on either side of her. "Momma, please don't be mad.

I'm sorry. I know I never should've left the room. You're hurting her! Wait, Momma? Momma, this is Mrs. Ford and she's real nice. She's been so good to me, Momma."

By then the policemen have Momma in the middle of the room. She's swaying to music that ain't playing.

"Ma'am, we're looking for your daughter Emma," Mr. Ford says. "Any ideas where she'd be?"

"Ask *her.*" Momma slurs the words, tipping her head in my direction, then tapping out a cigarette from the pack.

"We'd like for *you* to tell us, ma'am," the other policeman says. He shines a flashlight at her face but Momma just looks away and blows smoke to the sky. Cool as a cucumber.

Then she looks over at me.

I look from her to Mrs. Ford to Mr. Ford to the lady in the suit to Mrs. Burdock. *What's going on?* I want to scream.

"Go on and tell them," Momma says.

"Carrie? Do you know where your sister is?" the suit lady asks. She's using my name like she knows me. And acting like I lied to her when *I haven't ever met her before thank you very much.*

"Momma?" I cain't make any sense of all this. "Momma, what's happening?"

I'm in more trouble than I ever thought I could be. The best thing for me to do right now is try to make it right with Momma because I'm gonna have to face her when they leave. No one can save me then.

"Tell them, Momma," I say. I just cain't help it, the tears come whether I want them to or not. "Tell them we've been through that before. I know I only imagined her, remember? You said she wasn't real, Momma. Tell them."

"Tell them what?" Momma says, dragging on her cigarette. "You think you know what happened, you tell them. You with your eyes boring holes in my head . . ."

"Momma, I'm sorry," I cry.

"You were there, that's right, but you were a child. You weren't awake in the middle of all those nights, hours of crying crying crying enough to where I nearly pulled out my own hair from the sound of my own sobbing. Your dear *daddy*. Ha!"

"Momma don't talk bad about Daddy—"

"You think you can sit in judgment on me? You think I don't see your eyes guilting me over it? Well here it is. Here's the moment you been waiting for. Drumroll, please! Your dear daddy shook her and shook her—to make his point he just *had* to shake her."

When a new policeman takes up the doorway and says, "Hey, Ford-o, we got the go-ahead," ever-one stops picking through our things to surround Momma.

"You have the right to remain silent," one is saying, pinning her arms behind her back with one hand, feeling for the handcuffs hanging from his belt with the other.

Momma has started a flood of words seems like she's been dying to say for years. She's slurring bad but I understand every word:

"Mountain girls are supposed to know how to keep a good clean house, keep their men happy, cook a square meal but Lord help me I never did know how to do all that right. And boy didn't my mama love to remind me. I never knew how to stop that squalling. You—look at you. You're doing it now. Like you always have. You stand there, staring at me, waiting for me to fail like I always do. Like you knew I'd fail—"

"No, Momma, please," I say, through hiccuping.

"You'd waltz on in there like you were schooled in child rearing, like *you* were the mother and I was the kid. Sure enough she'd quiet up the second you neared her—"

"Anything you say can be used against you in a court of law," the policeman says, clinking shut the second of the cuffs, then checking in a little notebook hid in his back pocket to be sure he got the words right.

"You'd get hold of her and rock her and look at me like *I* was the village idiot." Momma's talking to me like there's no one else in the room. Like she wasn't being arrested. "Well I've got a news flash for you: this is a *relief.* I've been knowing this day would come sooner or later."

Since I cain't stop Mr. Ford or the other policemen I run over to Mrs. Ford and the suit lady.

"Where're they taking my momma? Why're y'all taking her?"

The lady in the suit looks down at her clipboard and starts to answer, "Let's see now. Manslaughter. Child endangerment . . ."

Mr. Ford holds up a hand to hush her from going on and gives the other policemen a signal to hold up. He wants to hear what Momma has to say just as much as I do.

"It didn't matter I told him she was his." Momma keeps talking, as though they all understand who she's talking about. "We both knew different. You were his *precious baby* but *she* was *mine.* I knew he hated that I favored her but I never thought he'd *hurt* her. Shaking her so hard that night her head near to snapped off. I got her away from him, took her to your room. He and I fought pretty hard that night, sure we fought. But then we got tired of saying the same things over and over, threatening the same threats. I went to bed and when I woke up—he was gone and so was she. Well, I just lost it. The fury came on me. I got the gun from the shoe box he kept hidden in the garage—the gun he didn't think I knew about but oh, I knew about it all right. I was waiting on him to come back, training it on the door, and when I saw that smug face of his coming through the door I pulled the trigger and in a split second everything changed. I'll never know what he did with her body."

Mr. Ford says, "All right boys," and they walk Momma out.

I flatten up against the handrail so I can get around the knot of them, in front of them on the stairs. They move her slowly step . . . by . . . step. Her legs buckling don't matter—the policemen are holding her up.

"Stop staring at me!" Momma shouts down to me. "You see? Y'all see what she's doing? She's got the judge and jury in those eyes—look at her. Look at her and tell me you don't see what I been dealing with all these years."

"Momma, I don't know what you mean." I choke on my sobs and that makes me cough. "What about Selma Blake's husband, Momma? *He* killed Daddy. You were pinning clothes up out back when you heard someone banging on the front door . . ."

Momma shakes her head and as she gets closer I see a smile is lighting her face. "Y'all might want to look into extra help for this one—she's not exactly the sharpest tool in the shed," Momma says, passing in front of me.

"Watch yourself, ma'am." The policeman's hand is on the top of Momma's head, making sure she doesn't bump it getting into the squad car which I think is real nice of him. When he steps back I wriggle in close enough to hear my mother.

"Momma? I don't understand, Momma."

"You were small enough—with your daddy dead, I figured I could talk you into believing you made her up," Momma says, staring ahead even though the car ain't moving, looking at anything but me.

"I didn't know what else to do," she says. "You'd have called a telephone a banana if that's what I told you it was called."

"You mean . . ."

"Your daddy, well, he just plain never could get over the fact that she wasn't his. Not only that—if he hated Dan White before, he nearly boiled over when I came home from Mother's. When he saw that mark on her cheek, I'm telling you he nearly boiled over. You walked in when I was burning the family Bible with her birth date written in it—boy, that killed your daddy, when he saw I wrote that in there. I told him I'd get rid of it, if it bothered him that much I'd just get rid of it."

"All right, kid, you best step back now," the policeman says to me.

I guess it doesn't hit her that she's being arrested for real until the car door is shutting because that's when Momma's voice gets higher and she'd never admit to being scared but I can plainly see she is.

"Go on, now," she says through the glass, motioning at me with her chin toward Mr. and Mrs. Ford.

"Momma!" I manage to push out of whoever's arms are trying to hold me back so I can run alongside the car as it starts to pull away. I put the palm of my hand on the closed window.

Through the glass Momma says, "You got yourself a new life now."

"Step away from the car, young lady," the police officer driving says out his window.

I feel hands gently but firmly pulling me away.

"Momma!"

The police officer says something to Momma and the car moves forward.

"Carrie, honey," Mrs. Ford is saying. "Come on, Carrie," she's saying. "Shhhh, it's okay. Come on. Let's go home."

"Momma—Momma wait." I try hollering over the engine, through the glass, past Mrs. Ford calling my name.

The police car pulls away slow as it moves from the parking lot into the road letting out a whoop of siren. Words flutter to my ears when the quiet's restored: *let's go on home now.* And *oh, sweetheart, it's all going to be okay.* And *Caroline* . . . followed by . . . nothing. Because really, what can be said to soften the blow of the moment your momma's taken away by the police? What can anyone say to soften the blow of finally finding your sister only to learn she's long been dead? No pillow's *that* soft.

CHAPTER TWENTY-ONE

Three months later

Carrie

"Will somebody please pass the mashed potatoes before they get cold?"

"Wait, we forgot the cranberry sauce! Oh, I didn't see it over there."

"Caroline, honey, pass me that bowl, will you?"

I look from one to the other, trying to keep up, the talk reminding me of the alphabet songs on *Sesame Street* with the ball bouncing from letter to letter to help kids follow along.

"Yes, ma'am," I say to Mrs. Ford.

"What's the difference between white meat and dark meat?" Cricket asks.

"White meat's for girls, dark meat's for boys," Mr. Ford says.

"The turkey's just perfect, Honor," Miss Chaplin says, dabbing the corners of her mouth with her napkin. "Nice and tender."

"No way," Cricket says, scooping first stuffing then turkey onto her fork. "Mom? Is that true?"

"Is what true, honey?"

"Is white meat for girls and dark meat for boys?" Cricket asks. "That's not true, is it? Can you pass the salt?"

"Pass the salt . . ." Mrs. Ford raises her eyebrows and holds the saltshaker hostage until Cricket rolls her eyes and says: *"Please."*

"That's better," Mrs. Ford says. "And you know, girls, when you're asked for either the salt or the pepper you should always pass both, even if the person only wants one."

"Yes, ma'am," I say.

"That's just plain ridic," says Cricket.

"Excuse me?" her daddy says.

"I don't like that kind of language at the table, Cricket," Mrs. Ford says.

"Miss Ruth, you need me to carve up some more white meat?" Mr. Ford asks Miss Chaplin.

"Ridic isn't a bad word, Mom, jeez. It's short for *ridiculous.* Everybody says it."

"No, thank you, Edsil, I'm still working on what I've got here," Miss Chaplin says. She's starting to lose weight, and I think she's finally getting used to the way her house looks now, without all the Chaplin stuff crowding it up.

I think the overtalking might be my favorite thing about the Fords and the Chaplins. Their voices blending together, making pretty music.

The doorbell gives us all a start.

"Oh, heavens, they're early!" Miss Chaplin says. "Honor, help me up out of this chair please?"

"I'll get it!" Cricket, smiling wide, leaps from the table, but Mr. Ford's faster—he catches hold of her arm.

"Uh-uh-uh," he says to Cricket. "We went over this, girleen, remember?"

I have no earthly idea what's going on but that's nothing new. There's always stuff going on here that I don't know about so I'm used to it. These past months have been a whirligig. Helping pack up dolls, first in thin tissue then rolling them in the bubble wrap me and Cricket like to pinch and pop. Waking up to still more Charlies to send away, shelf by shelf emptying out. Tabletops clearing off. Trips to the post office. Loading up the car again. More trips to the post office.

Then, back-to-school shopping! And starting up at my new school. Cricket and me riding the bus there and back every day. New friends coming by, sometimes even sleeping over (but *not on school nights*).

Mr. Ford moving in with all of us, eating meals with us on nights he ain't—I mean, on nights he's *not* working. Surprise family outings. Picnics. The zoo.

I never saw the lady in the suit again but I did get to know her *colleague,* Arleen, who pops by for *unannounced visits* they make to all foster families.

Like I said, there's always something happening at this house so when the doorbell rings and Mrs. Ford rushes out from the dining room to answer it, I don't think much of it.

Until Mr. Ford tells Cricket to sit back down and then says he has something *real exciting* to tell me.

"Now, Caroline," he says. Mr. Ford's still the only one who calls me Caroline. "I thought we'd have a little more time to explain but this'll have to do for now. Honey, we haven't talked about it in a while but remember how we discussed the importance of family and roots and knowing where you came from so you can know where you're going?"

"Yes, sir," I say.

"We never finished working on it, but remember the family tree we started for you? Your grandmother—Gammy—she was a help with some of it. With her side of the family at least," he says.

Gammy's answered my letters, each and every one. She even

folded a five-dollar bill in the Halloween card she sent. I think she might feel bad about Momma being locked up, awaiting trial, leaving me all alone. I've told her a million times I'm happy here at Miss Chaplin's, though. It's the first real family I ever had but I don't tell her that part because I don't want to hurt her feelings. But soon, if the *paperwork goes through* like they're saying it will, we'll be a family for real!

I hear the low murmer of greetings and then footsteps approach us.

"Well, I did a little research of my own, wanting to solve a mystery," Mr. Ford's saying. He holds up a hand to someone behind me, wanting them to wait until he's finished, "but not really sure where it was going to lead. Well, lo and behold, I found out something really amazing. It took some doing but I did it. We have a big surprise for you, Caroline . . ."

But the minute I hear the word *surprise* I whip around before he can finish.

They say it was like I was in a trance. They tell me they hurried to explain how it all came together. They say I even nodded like I understood them, but I don't remember any of that.

I only remember staring at the two of them standing there in the doorway to the dining room, trying to figure out if my brain was again playing tricks on me. The red-haired lady wearing a sweater with fall leaves knitted on it, her arm around a little girl huddled so close to her mother's skirt she was almost hiding. The lady smiled at me and bent to whisper to the little girl, who then moved forward, one step closer to me. The colors of the girl's dress matched the leaf sweater the lady was wearing. She wore brown tights and polished dress-up shoes I knew probably weren't comfortable. She stood there with her shoulder-length blond hair combed nice, parted on the side, a barrette neatly holding her bangs out of her face, blinking back at me.

"Hi," she said, holding out her little hand to be shaken because that's what she'd been taught to do. She'd been taught good manners.

I didn't stare at the birthmark on her cheek. At least I tried not to. Because I was taught good manners too.

"I'm Carrie," I said, taking her hand, holding it instead of shaking it, not wanting to let it go even for a second.

"I'm Emma," she said.

They say we held hands the whole rest of the day. They tell me her adoptive mother was *just lovely* and *such good company* that Thanksgiving. They even say I insisted on sitting in the middle between Emma and Cricket—calling them *my two sisters.* But I don't remember that.

I only remember that it was the day Emma came back into my life. And I will never let her go again. Ever.

ACKNOWLEDGMENTS

It would have been impossible for me to write this novel without the support and encouragement of Random House and my extraordinary network of friends and family.

My deep gratitude to Caitlin Alexander, my brilliant, eagle-eyed editor. Thanks, too, to Larry Kirshbaum and Susanna Einstein.

Throughout the three years it took to bring this book to life, whether they realize it or not, the following people lifted me up when I needed it most: Jim Brawders, Bill Brancucci, Fauzia Burke, Laura Caldwell, Cathleen Carmody, Jodie Chase, Mary Jane Clark, Edouard Daunas, Junot Diaz, Catherine DiBenedetto, Liz Getter, Kathryn Gregorio, Markie Hancock, Eamon Hickey, Heidi Holst-Knudsen, Linda Lee, Gregg Lempp, Ellie Lipman, Rick Livingston, Erika Mansourian, Wayne Merchant, Kathryn Mosteller, Joan Drummond Olson, Dotty Sonnemaker, Rosario Varela, and Andy Weiner. For unwittingly keeping me from slipping down a rabbit hole into darkness, I am forever indebted to them all.

My extraordinary parents, Barbara and Reg Brack, are easily the most devoted, loving, and supportive people I know. Without them I would crumble and disintegrate into the abyss. To thank them for all they have done for me would be to say the least of it.

Jill Brack is more than my sister-in-law, she is one of my best friends. I am always grateful for her steadfast love. To my brothers and my girls . . . my love and appreciation.

Thematically, this is a book about identity: about who we are, who we pretend to be, and why the two rarely if ever coalesce. This is a book about that thread of self woven into the fabric of the relationships we forge and the suffering we endure only to become entangled beyond recognition. It's about family, the one we're born into and the one we choose. But, really, this is a book about mothers and daughters. Though I don't tell her this often enough, I hope my mother knows I love her most of all. I write because of her. I write for her.

And finally, my heartfelt thanks to the people of Hendersonville, North Carolina, for letting me take poetic license by turning their city into the tiny hill town that Carrie and her mother left behind when they turned the page.

Elizabeth Flock

What Happened to My Sister

A Reader's Guide

funeral of Princess Diana in London, with a myriad of other stories in between—I feel incredibly lucky to have reported such varied stories. Having said that, after a couple of years traveling the globe for CBS News I found the fast, frenetic pace to be too much for me. Toward the end of my time on television, when I was going through a particularly difficult time of my life, I was out in the field reporting on a plane crash. I was in a very dark place and I had less than one minute to pull myself together. By some miracle I did. But I remember I had about thirty seconds before going on live TV when I thought, *What would happen if that red light on the camera went on and I went mute?* It's a reporter's nightmare. I filed away that thought—that fear—and later used it as a launching point for my first novel (*But Inside I'm Screaming*). I had my main character freeze up on live national TV and the story was off and running.

As it turns out, the leap from journalism to writing fiction wasn't as difficult as you might imagine. Some subjects I write about are quite dark: child abuse, childhood trauma, neglect. Luckily I haven't had personal experience with any of those topics, so when I sat down to write *Me & Emma* [the precursor to *What Happened to My Sister*] I knew I had a lot of reading, researching, and interviewing to do, and those skills came right back to me. It was liberating to realize that I could exercise some latitude with the story, but I wanted to get the facts right about what would happen to a traumatized and neglected child. Since then I have made much use of the latitude. That poetic license. *What Happened to My Sister* is a good example—I set it in contemporary times even though I have told countless readers and book groups that I originally intended this book's predecessor, *Me & Emma*, which has some of the same characters, to be set in the 1960s.

CL: I had an editor once ask me, "How do you know what you know when you write?" I love this question so much I want to put it to you. How do you know what you know about these characters and their situation?

EF: Mental illness is a subject that I am deeply interested in—it has a stigma attached to it that is as infuriating as it is ingrained. So when I was initially kicking around ideas for my second novel, I kept thinking that I would love to tell a story where the main character's thoughts and actions are her own truths, absent of discrimination. I wanted to tell a story from the inside out. I wanted readers to become attached to the character before I upended everything.

Think about it photographically: The camera eye is tight on a face, and over time you come to know every crease, every curve, you attach a story to it, and perhaps you even come to love it. But then the camera slowly pulls back and the face is put in context. You see the environment it's in—maybe it belongs to an inmate on death row. Or a politician running for office. Or a patient in an insane asylum. Our world is so polarized right now—people make snap judgments based on very little information and I just hate that. Appearances are almost never what they seem. That certainly proved true in *Me & Emma* and, I hope, in *What Happened to My Sister*.

CL: As novelists, we fall in love with our characters, and it's often hard to say goodbye. We get so attached! What was it like to revisit the characters from *Me & Emma*? Did it take a while for them to come back alive, or were they fully formed on the page? Did anything surprise you?

EF: Only another writer would ask this question. Writers know exactly what it's like. Did you read *Charlotte's Web*? Remember at the end after Charlotte dies and all her babies are floating away on the breeze, calling out "Goodbye! Goodbye Wilbur!" in their little voices? Wilbur's heartbroken to see them go, but deep down he knows it's time for them to leave the web. That's usually what it's like for me when I come to the end of a novel I've written. I can practically *feel* my characters drifting away from me, going out into the world. It's hard to say goodbye, but it's necessary.

Well, Carrie Parker never left the web. I felt like I let go of her little hand too soon. So I decided to pick it back up, to reach for her again. If I hadn't, I would have felt that I was letting her down somehow, as corny as that sounds. I always wondered what happened when their car pulled away from the curb. When I began writing *What Happened to My Sister* I had lots in store for Carrie and her mother but, funnily enough, I look back at my original outline for the book and it's totally different from what came out in the writing. It always surprises me that a story I'm in the process of writing ends up having a mind of its own.

CL: Oh, I love that you said the outline changed! That happens for me, too. How did it change? And why do you think that happens to us?

EF: I don't know why it is. Maybe I was in a different place when I wrote *Me & Emma*, and I saw the story through the prism of my life then. Which is not to say I was unhappy when I was writing *Me & Emma* or *What Happened to My Sister*. Quite the contrary.

CL: Sometimes I feel that I'm the happiest when I'm writing the darkest . . .

EF: Me, too. I am incredibly lucky to have had as close to an idyllic childhood as it gets. Growing up, I had no concept of darkness or depravity, no experience with child abuse. Maybe that's why that proverbial dark side fascinates me so much. And believe me, the research I did for both *Me & Emma* and *What Happened to My Sister* was dark—and heartbreaking. But for *What Happened to My Sister,* for instance, I needed to understand child suggestibility. I wanted to convincingly write about a mother basically brainwashing her young daughter, and though I ended up with a lot of research material that I didn't use, all of it enabled me to know and understand my subject.

CL: I'm always really interested in process. How do you write? Do you have rituals? Are you an outliner or do you follow your characters wherever they take you?

EF: I'm fascinated by other writers' processes, too! Maybe because I have so many writing-related habits. They're more idiosyncrasies or peculiarities than actual habits, so I suppose I like to know that others are equally obsessive. Having to be at the proverbial writing table by a certain time, beverages at the ready, phones off. That sort of thing.

In terms of plotting, when I started out writing fiction, I never outlined. Now that I do, I frankly don't know how I ever did it any other way. I didn't study creative writing in school, and I've never been a part of a workshop, so in the beginning I flew by the seat of my pants. I didn't want to be married to an outline.

CL: For me, the outline is a lifesaver. It's like you're swimming in this huge, churning ocean and you fear you might drown, and then you look a few feet away and there is the outline—you can grab on to it for support. If you're overwhelmed, you can just pick a piece of it and write that one section, so you don't feel so intimidated by the scope of the novel. My outlines are really detailed, but I hate the perception that if you use an outline, you're not creative.

EF: Didn't John Irving say that he doesn't begin to write until he knows his last line? That makes complete sense to me. I've been held up by the book I'm working on now for almost a year because I haven't known how it is going to end. With *Me & Emma,* I knew what was going to happen. It was the best feeling because in getting from point A (the beginning) to point B (the end) that book practically wrote itself—the only time that's ever happened, by the way. With *What Happened to My Sister,* I simply wanted to do the characters justice. I couldn't let it end sloppily. By the time I was nearing the end it occurred to me that I will, perhaps, make this a trilogy. I really want to carry my characters over the finish line. I've made them suffer through an obstacle course of pain! I want to feel the satisfaction of seeing them flourish.

CL: Do you show your work to others or are you private?

EF: I'm a private writer, but I'm trying to come out of my shell a bit. It's a tricky process, though—knowing when and how to show one's work. For years I have stared at a Nietzsche quote I have on a Post-it beside my computer: "That for which we find words is already dead in our hearts." I feel that if I speak about what I'm doing, at least in the early stages, those ideas flutter away and I can't get them back. But I now recognize that my writing is better for having my agent or my editor weigh in early on, so I know I need to sprinkle in a few more "trusted readers."

Furthermore, writing is a solitary pursuit and sometimes you need a little encouragement. A bird chirping on your shoulder: "It's great! Keep going!"—the only way to get that is by sharing at least a few pages. Do you show your work?

CL: I was like you at first. I never did. Not until the last four books. I have four or five readers with wildly different views, and I've learned to listen to their comments, to take them in, and then see what resonates with me. Once a reader told me, "Every writer has a book they need to burn. This is yours," but the other four readers really liked it, so I didn't go back to that particular reader after that.

EF: I'm only half-joking when I say that, generally speaking, I think writers are insecure narcissists. We're riddled with insecurity, but our vanity, for lack of a better word, forces us onward. We keep putting ourselves "out there" because without words, without books, without stories, we would crumble. At least *I* would.

CL: Me, too! And speaking of *crumbling,* so much of this novel is about how we survive. Carrie has flashes of insight and at times her imagination seems to save her. As a writer, can you talk about how imagination saves you?

EF: I know you can speak to that, too. Imagination definitely saved me from some very dark times in my personal life, like illness and heartbreak. I can honestly say that in my whole life I have never been bored. I credit my mother for that. When we were kids, if one of us whined that we were bored, she'd say, "Boring people are bored. Read a book! Go find something to do. Use your imagination!"

CL: It makes me sad not to see kids just dreaming on a park bench or playing with dolls.

EF: When I was young, I loved the book *Harriet the Spy.* I would watch people closely and make up silly stories about their lives. Actually, I just loved reading, again, thanks to my parents, who are still voracious readers. I'll never forget my mother taking me to get my very own library card—oh, what a wonderful day that was.

I worry that we're losing a generation of creative types because we are all so programmed now. Every minute of our day is accounted for. We hurry from event to event, moving so fast, task to task, all these screens in front of us. Many kids don't have enough downtime to get lost in books read for pleasure, not homework. We need to get back to that unstructured time. So our imaginations can take flight.

CL: Agreed! So where is your imagination taking you these days?

EF: To the next story. [smiling] To the next story. I don't quite know what it is, but I imagine it will surprise me. It always surprises me.

QUESTIONS AND TOPICS FOR DISCUSSION

1. The mother-daughter relationship is an important theme in this novel. What lessons can be learned from Libby and Carrie, and from Honor and Cricket?

2. Why do you think Elizabeth Flock chose to narrate the story from Carrie's and Honor's points of view? How would the novel differ if it were told through the eyes of Cricket? Of Ruth?

3. Honor's relationship with Cricket is very different from Eddie's relationship with Cricket. Do you think that father-daughter relationships are inherently different from mother-daughter relationships? If yes, how so?

4. What are the characteristics of a strong mother-daughter relationship? Do you think that Honor and Cricket have a strong relationship? What in their relationship works? In what ways do you think Honor approaches motherhood differently than Ruth does?

5. Discuss Carrie's relationship with Cricket. How are the two girls alike? How are they different?

6. The death of a child has a devastating impact on parents, and the death of Caroline was one of the main reasons that Eddie and Honor separated. Do you think Eddie and Honor would have gotten back together if Carrie hadn't come into their lives?

7. Libby seems to put all of her needs before Carrie's. Do you think that she was always like this? Or was there a time when she was good to Carrie? Is Libby's act of confession at the end a sacrifice for her daughter, or is it a selfish act?

8. Carrie's flashbacks hint at what really happened to Emma. At any point before the ending, did you guess the truth? What surprised you most?

9. Ruth kept alive the dream that she was related to Charlie Chaplin for many years. Is her behavior in any way similar to Carrie keeping alive the dream that her mother cared about her? And that her "good" behavior could influence her mother's moods? Have you ever wanted something so much that you held out false hope? What are the benefits or consequences of fooling ourselves?

10. After losing her first child, Honor has a desperate need to keep control in her life. How does Carrie ease Honor's need for control?

11. Can you imagine living in a world like Carrie's? Do you think that you would be able to be as resourceful and optimistic as she?

12. In this book, Mr. Burdock is the only positive male figure in Carrie's life. Do you think that he should have called Child Protective Services when he saw that Libby wasn't really looking after

Carrie? How do you define the line between minding your own business and stepping in to help someone?

13. Do you feel differently about Mr. Burdock's inaction versus the Dressers' overreaction? If Honor and Eddie hadn't been wrongly accused of child abuse, do you think that they would have been quicker to intervene in Carrie's situation? Or do you think that Honor made the right decision by feeding and helping Carrie as much as she did?

14. Did Carrie's unfamiliarity with modern technology make you think about how much of the way we live our lives has changed over the past few years? How would this story be different if it was set in a time without the Internet? Do you think that Carrie would ever have learned the truth about her family?

15. Elizabeth Flock extensively researched child psychology and trauma in order to portray Carrie in a realistic way. Though Carrie is never officially diagnosed or labeled with a psychological condition, how did you interpret her character? Why do you think the author refrained from labeling her in the novel?

PHOTO: SARI GOODFRIEND

New York Times bestselling author ELIZABETH FLOCK is a former journalist who reported for *Time* and *People* magazines and worked as an on-air correspondent for CBS. She is the author of several acclaimed novels, including *Me & Emma*. Elizabeth lives in New York City.

Chat.
Comment.
Connect.

Visit our online book club community at
Facebook.com/RHReadersCircle

Chat
Meet fellow book lovers and discuss what you're reading.

Comment
Post reviews of books, ask—and answer—thought-provoking
questions, or give and receive book club ideas.

Connect
Find an author on tour, visit our author blog, or invite one of
our 150 available authors to chat with your group on the phone.

Explore
Also visit our site for discussion questions, excerpts, author
interviews, videos, free books, news on the latest releases,
and more.

Books are better with buddies.
Facebook.com/RHReadersCircle

THE RANDOM HOUSE PUBLISHING GROUP